PRAISE FOR *WELCOME TO NIGHT VALE: A NOVEL*

"This is a splendid, weird, moving novel. . . . It manages beautifully that trick of embracing the surreal in order to underscore and emphasize the real—not as allegory, but as affirmation of emotional truths that don't conform to the neat and tidy boxes in which we're encouraged to house them."
—NPR.org

"The book is charming and absurd—think *This American Life* meets *Alice in Wonderland*."
—Washington Post

"Longtime listeners and newcomers alike are likely to appreciate the ways in which *Night Vale*, as Fink puts it, 'treats the absurd as normal and treats the normal as absurd.' What they might not foresee is the emotional wallop the novel delivers in its climactic chapters."
—Austin Chronicle

"The charms of *Welcome to Night Vale* are nearly impossible to quantify. That applies to the podcast, structured as community radio dispatches from a particularly surreal desert town, as well as this novel."
—Minneapolis Star Tribune

"*Welcome to Night Vale: A Novel* masterfully brings the darkly hilarious, touching and creepy world of the podcast into the realm of ink and paper."
—Asbury Park Press

"*Welcome to Night Vale* lives up to the podcast hype in every way. It is a singularly inventive visit to an otherworldly town that's the stuff of nightmares and daydreams."
—BookPage

"All hail the glow cloud as the weird and wonderful town of Night Vale brings itself to fine literature. . . . The novel is definitely as addictive as its source material."
—*Kirkus Reviews* (starred review)

"Take Conan's Hyborea, teleport it to the American Southwest, dress all the warriors in business casual, and hide their swords under the floorboards—that's Night Vale: absurd, magical, wholly engrossing, and always harboring some hidden menace."

—John Darnielle, author of *Wolf in White Van*

"They've done the unthinkable: merged the high weirdness and intense drama of Night Vale to the pages of a novel that is even weirder, even more intense than the podcast."

—Cory Doctorow, author of *Little Brother* and coeditor of *Boing Boing*

"This is the novel of your dreams. . . . A friendly (but terrifying) and comic (but dark) and glittering (but bleak) story of misfit family life that unfolds along the side streets, back alleys, and spring-loaded trap doors of the small town home you'll realize you've always missed living in."

—Glen David Gold, author of *Carter Beats the Devil* and *Sunnyside*

"This small town full of hooded figures, glowing clouds, cryptically terrifying public policies, and flickering realities quickly feels more like home than home. . . . There is nothing like Night Vale, in the best possible way."

—Maureen Johnson, author of *13 Little Blue Envelopes* and *The Name of the Star*

"Brilliant, hilarious, and wondrously strange. I'm packing up and moving to Night Vale!"

—Ransom Riggs, author of the #1 *New York Times* bestselling *Miss Peregrine's Home for Peculiar Children*

"I've been a fan of *Welcome to Night Vale* for years, and in that time writers Jeffrey Cranor and Joseph Fink have delighted me with stories that are clever, twisted, beautiful, strange, wonderful, and sweet. This book does all of that and so much more. It's even better than I'd hoped. I think this might be the best book I've read in years."

—Patrick Rothfuss, author of *The Name of the Wind*

"Emotionally compelling and superbly realized. This seductive, hilarious book unfolds at the moment when certain quiet responsible people find they must risk everything on behalf of love, hope, and understanding. Not a single person who reads this book will be disappointed."

—Deb Olin Unferth, author of *Revolution* and *Vacation*

"*Welcome to Night Vale* brings its eponymous desert town to vivid life. Those of us who have gotten to know Night Vale through Cecil Palmer's biweekly radio broadcasts can finally see what it's like to actually live there. It is as weird and surreal as I hoped it would be, and a surprisingly existential meditation on the nature of time, reality, and the glow cloud that watches over us. ALL HAIL THE GLOW CLOUD."

—Wil Wheaton

MOSTLY VOID, PARTIALLY STARS

ALSO BY JOSEPH FINK & JEFFREY CRANOR

Welcome to Night Vale: A Novel

The Great Glowing Coils of the Universe:
Welcome to Night Vale Episodes, Volume 2

MOSTLY VOID, PARTIALLY STARS

Welcome to Night Vale Episodes, Volume 1

JOSEPH FINK AND
JEFFREY CRANOR

HARPER PERENNIAL

NEW YORK • LONDON • TORONTO • SYDNEY • NEW DELHI • AUCKLAND

HARPER PERENNIAL

Illustrations by Jessica Hayworth

FIRST EDITION

Library of Congress Cataloging-in-Publication Data has been applied for.

ISBN 978-0-06-246861-1
ISBN 978-0-06-265590-5 (B&N signed edition)
ISBN 978-0-06-265589-9 (BAM signed edition)
ISBN 978-0-06-265588-2 (Indigo signed edition)

16 17 18 19 20 DIX/RRD 10 9 8 7 6 5 4 3 2 1

To Kathy Fink and to Ellen Flood

CONTENTS

FOREWORD BY CORY DOCTOROW xiii

INTRODUCTION BY JOSEPH FINK xvii

EPISODE 1: "Pilot" 1

EPISODE 2: "Glow Cloud" 10

EPISODE 3: "Station Management" 19

EPISODE 4: "PTA Meeting" 28

EPISODE 5: "The Shape in Grove Park" 38

EPISODE 6: "The Drawbridge" 47

EPISODE 7: "History Week" 56

EPISODE 8: "The Lights in Radon Canyon" 65

EPISODE 9: "Pyramid" 74

EPISODE 10: "Feral Dogs" 84

EPISODE 11: "Wheat & Wheat By-Products" 93

EPISODE 12: "The Candidate" 200

EPISODE 13: "A Story About You" 120

EPISODE 14: "The Man in the Tan Jacket 121

EPISODE 15: "Street Cleaning Day" 131

EPISODE 16: "The Phone Call" 140

EPISODE 17: "Valentine" 150

EPISODE 18: "The Traveler" 160

EPISODE 19A: "The Sandstorm" 170

EPISODE 19B: "The Sandstorm" 181

EPISODE 20: "Poetry Week" 192

EPISODE 21: "A Memory of Europe" 206

EPISODE 22: "The Whispering Forest" 217

EPISODE 23: "Eternal Scouts" 227

EPISODE 24: "The Mayor" 236

EPISODE 25: "One Year Later" 246

DISPARITION MUSIC CORNER 256

LIVE SHOW: "Condos" 258

FOREWORD

THE RARE, GOOD KIND OF WEIRD

Being weird and funny is easy. Being weird and funny and *compelling* is hard.

We've all guffawed at some strange, surreal juxtaposition ("Two. One to take the bath and the other one to fill the tub with brightly colored machine parts."). You don't have to be stoned to crack up at a friend's fantastic, perfect non sequitur. Stories that inspire hilarity and mystification are good fun, but they're not great stories.

Stories become great by hacking your brain. Nothing that happens in fiction matters. The people in fiction are *fictional* so their triumphs and tragedies have literally no consequence. The death of the yogurt you doomed to a fiery death in your gut acid this morning is infinitely more tragic than the "deaths" of Romeo and Juliet. The yogurt was alive and then it died. Romeo and Juliet never lived in the first place.

Stories trick your naive, empathic mind into resonating in sympathy (literally) with the plights of their imaginary people. Usually they do this by scrupulously avoiding any reminder that these are imaginary people. That "willing suspension of disbelief" is a bargain between the creator and the audience: the creator tells the tale and hews to something that is plausible (or at least consistent) and the audience member doesn't pinch herself and say, "Cut it out with the quickened heart, the leaking tears, the smiles of triumph, you dope, this is all made up!"

This makes weird stories and great stories nearly incompatible. A story is a love affair on the last night of summer camp that depends on both parties not calling attention to the fact that the camp bus is coming in the morning, so they can pretend that the night could last forever.

Weird stuff happening to the characters is a reminder that this is all made up, the ending is coming, and when it's done, these invisible people will disappear into the nonspace whence they came, so stop cheering them on or crying for them.

Bringing me to Night Vale.

The remarkable thing about *Night Vale* isn't how delightfully weird it is. The remarkable thing is how *moving* it is. Cranor and Fink and cowriters and actors weave a world with haphazard internal consistency.

When things are weird, they make them weirder. It's a good, meaty sort of weird, steering clear of cliché and venturing into fresh, imaginative territory—but it's still undeniably weird.

It shouldn't work. We shouldn't root for Cecil, cheer on his love affair with Carlos. Tamika Flynn and Intern Dana and even that guy with the deerskin suitcase full of flies (whose story was so beautifully told in *Welcome to Night Vale,* a book that is, if anything, even *more* improbable than these podcast scripts)—they live through ridiculous events but they react to them with perfect aplomb. They manage to trip the empathic response that makes us care about their outcomes, despite their outlandish lives.

This shouldn't work. In theory, it shouldn't work. Like Wikipedia and many other marvels of the Internet age, *Welcome to Night Vale* only works in practice. In theory, it's a disaster.

I don't know how the writers pull this off. I suspect they might be witches. I got some clues from reading *Welcome to Night Vale,* in which I learned that in the writers' heads these characters have completely credible internal lives that treat their weird lives as real. Somehow, though, those internal lives usually stay internal in the podcast (the difference between drama and prose is that in drama you only get what people say and do; in prose you get what's going on inside their heads), they shine through the characters and their voices, ensnaring our empathy.

The creators' notes you're about to read give a hint at how this alchemy takes place. Usually reading how writers write (or even how actors act) is like listening to a stranger tell you about their boring dreams. Fink, Cranor, and their collaborators make the stories behind these stories fascinating, in part because of the light they shed on this most bizarre phenomenon.

In short, there are moving stories, there are weird stories, and then there's *Night Vale*. It's weirdly moving. Be prepared. Be mystified. Be delighted. Please don't burn the authors at the stake for their sorcery, no matter how tempting it may be.

—Cory Doctorow, Los Angeles, 2016

INTRODUCTION

WELCOME TO NIGHT VALE IS A HOBBY THAT GOT OUT OF HAND.

Maybe you know all about our show. Or maybe you have no idea who we are and just picked up this book because you're curious, or because the cover was cool.

Either way, welcome. This book is for you.

If you've never heard of us, well this book starts right from the very beginning of our story, so you can feel free to jump right in.

And if you're one of the people who have already listened to all these episodes many, many times, then there's a ton of behind-the-scenes stuff, plus weird illustrations by our favorite weird artist, Jessica Hayworth.

This is where I should talk about how *Welcome to Night Vale* went from a passing idea I had one day into a popular podcast, an international touring show, a novel, and then, finally, this collection of episodes for which I am currently writing an intro. That's a very long story, so I'll just tell the first part here; how it went from a group of friends with an idea to a podcast that a few people listened to.

Jeffrey Cranor (my cowriter) and I met soon after I moved to New York in 2008, when he was doing performance art with the theater group the New York Neo-Futurists. He did a piece in which he revealed he had burned a terrible book, and I approached him after the show to tell him that I thought his piece was immoral because there was no moral reason to ever burn a book. We've been friends ever since.

In 2010, Jeffrey approached me about writing a play about time travel. We spent the next year meeting occasionally to share pieces we had written and to talk about that writing. These meetings often started with lengthy discussions of the podcasts we were listening to. We both had a shared love of podcasts and after we performed the play (*What the Time Traveler Will Tell Us*, performed at Incubator Arts, the amazing and unfortunately short-lived venue for experimental theater in the East Village), I started thinking of a podcast we could make together.

The main thing I knew is that I didn't want to make a podcast that sounded like any other podcast anyone else was already making because, well, those people were already making those podcasts better than we could.

Eventually I came up with the idea of a town where every conspiracy theory is true and people just have to go on with their lives. I've always been fascinated by conspiracy theories, even though I believe almost none of them.

I don't know where the name "Night Vale" came from. I do remember it came at the exact same time as the rest of the idea, and was the only name I considered. It just fit.

The first script was written in short bursts between other projects I was working on. The very first *Night Vale* bit I wrote was the "lights above the Arby's" paragraph that would appear halfway through the first episode. I had this idea in my head about Night Vale and what it might be like as a show, but primarily I was trying to capture a mood, and that paragraph allowed me to define for myself what that mood was going to be.

For a long time, when I was trying to make something fit the world of Night Vale, I thought back to that first paragraph I wrote and tried to capture the same feeling I had when I wrote it.

After months of occasional writing, I had a huge text document of bits and pieces talking about this strange desert town, and I started trying to work them together into something whole. The result was the Pilot, which, as the name suggests, was a total test of concept, not for any outside force, but for myself. What did this show look like when written out in episode form, and was it still as interesting as it had seemed in my head?

Given its trial-and-error creation, it's amazing to me how much of the show is right there in the first script. Old Woman Josie and her angels. Beautiful Carlos. The Dog Park. I accidentally set up years of stories while just chasing a mood, a feeling in my stomach when I thought of small towns in vast deserts. I don't think I would have done it nearly as well if long-term storytelling had been my conscious goal at the time.

Cecil Baldwin (our lead actor, who shares a first name with our main character) is someone whom I also knew through the New York Neo-Futurists. He had once done a performance piece in which he talked about his deep, rich voice, so perfectly radio-ready, and that despite his voice he could not seem to get hired for any voiceover work. And so I thought: all right, let's do this. I e-mailed him asking if he wanted to try recording a weird thing I was working on, and then we met at a coffee shop so I could lend him my old USB mic.

I also knew I would need a score for the show. Jon Bernstein is someone I had worked with on the website SomethingAwful.com, and he had been making amazing music under the name Disparition for years. I sent him an e-mail asking him if I could use his music for this experimental project I was putting together, and he said sure.

Armed with Jon's back catalog, Cecil's recording of my pilot script, and my limited self-taught knowledge of the sound editing and recording program Audacity, I created a test episode. I genuinely had no idea how it would sound all put together. Once it was finished, I walked around my neighborhood in Brooklyn, listening to the episode over and over. I couldn't believe how alive and complete this ramshackle thing sounded. That test episode is the first episode of the podcast that we released, exactly as it was when I first listened to it.

I sent the file to Jeffrey with a note asking if he wanted to spend a good deal of his time working on a free project with me. He said he did. We started writing together, and soon had four or five episodes written. It honestly all felt pretty easy.

Our main goal for the show was that someone who wasn't a friend or family member would eventually hear it. That was also our only goal. We had no aspirations beyond that, because the idea of expecting anything else from a strange little hobby podcast had not even remotely occurred to us.

On our first anniversary, we held a party in a bar space that a fan got us for free. There were 115 people there (!). Many of them were people we didn't know at all (!!). We had had 150,000 downloads in our first year, more than our wildest expectations (!!!). It felt like we really had gone so much further than we ever thought we would.

And then, only one month after that party, the explosion came. We would get over ten million downloads that summer, and our lives would radically change. But that's a story for Volume 2.

Night Vale is still made as it has always been. Jeffrey and I alternate writing drafts of scripts, and then pass them back and forth, editing and talking about them. Continuity is tracked with our fallible memories and the help of Google Doc's search function. Cecil does his vocal magic at home, into a USB mic. I go through Jon's back catalog and select a track that seems to fit the moment I'm trying to create. I still only sort of know how to use Audacity. And then we put the episode out there and hope people enjoy it.

Here is the first year of our episodes. We hope you enjoy them.

—Joseph Fink, Creator and Cowriter of *Welcome to Night Vale*

EPISODE 1: "PILOT"

JUNE 15, 2012

I TALKED A BIT ABOUT HOW THIS EPISODE CAME TO BE IN THIS BOOK'S intro, so instead I wanted to take a moment here to talk about something else: the weather.

How is it where you are? Oh, okay.

Throughout these scripts, you'll see a reference to the weather section of the broadcast, followed by the name of a song and a musical artist. This is because in Night Vale the weather section is always a song.

One of the most common questions I get asked in interviews is why the weather is a song. And here's why: I don't know. Like a lot of my creative decisions (and important life decisions, come to think of it), I don't have any sort of rational account of my reasoning. It just felt right and I went with it.

Originally there was going to be a number of labeled sections that would each have the same type of content in every episode. For instance, there was going to be a traffic section that would be a monologue by a different guest writer/performer. By the time the episode took shape, the rest of those sections had been scrapped and only the weather remained. (Eventually, stuff like the traffic sections would return, but in forms that bore no resemblance at all to the original plan for them. We would also have a proverb at the end of every episode, modeled after the Torey Malatia jokes at the end of every *This American Life,* designed to give people a fun stinger at the end of every episode and also give them a reason to listen through the credits.)

Music has always been vitally important to me. I was raised in a house that had a room we called "the music room" that had everything from guitars to accordions to a grand piano. So being able to feature music by artists I enjoy is a huge draw for me.

The weather for this episode was a song I wrote and recorded myself. I also did the weather for episode 25. I like music as a hobby, and I had an idea that I could do one of the weather reports each year. And then I got really busy and it hasn't happened since. But who knows? Maybe I'll find time someday.

Feel free to pause reading at the appropriate time in each script and go listen to the listed song. Or don't. Some days the weather happens and we never look up or go outside and that's okay too.

—Joseph Fink

A friendly desert community, where the sun is hot, the moon is beautiful, and mysterious lights pass overhead while we all pretend to sleep.

WELCOME TO NIGHT VALE.

Hello listeners. To start things off, I've been asked to read this brief notice. The City Council announces the opening of a new Dog Park at the corner of Earl and Summerset, near the Ralphs. They would like to remind everyone that dogs are not allowed in the Dog Park. People are not allowed in the Dog Park. It is possible you will see hooded figures in the Dog Park. Do not approach them. Do not approach the Dog Park. The fence is electrified and highly dangerous. Try not to look at the Dog Park and especially do not look for any period of time at the hooded figures. The Dog Park will not harm you.

And now the news.

Old Woman Josie, out near the car lot, says the angels revealed themselves to her. Said they were ten feet tall, radiant, one of them was black. Said they helped her with various household chores. One of them changed a lightbulb for her, the porch light. She's offering to sell the old lightbulb, which has been touched by an angel (it was the black angel, if that sweetens the pot for anyone). If you're interested, contact Old Woman Josie. She's out near the car lot.

A new man came into town today. Who is he? What does he want from us? Why his perfect and beautiful haircut? Why his perfect and

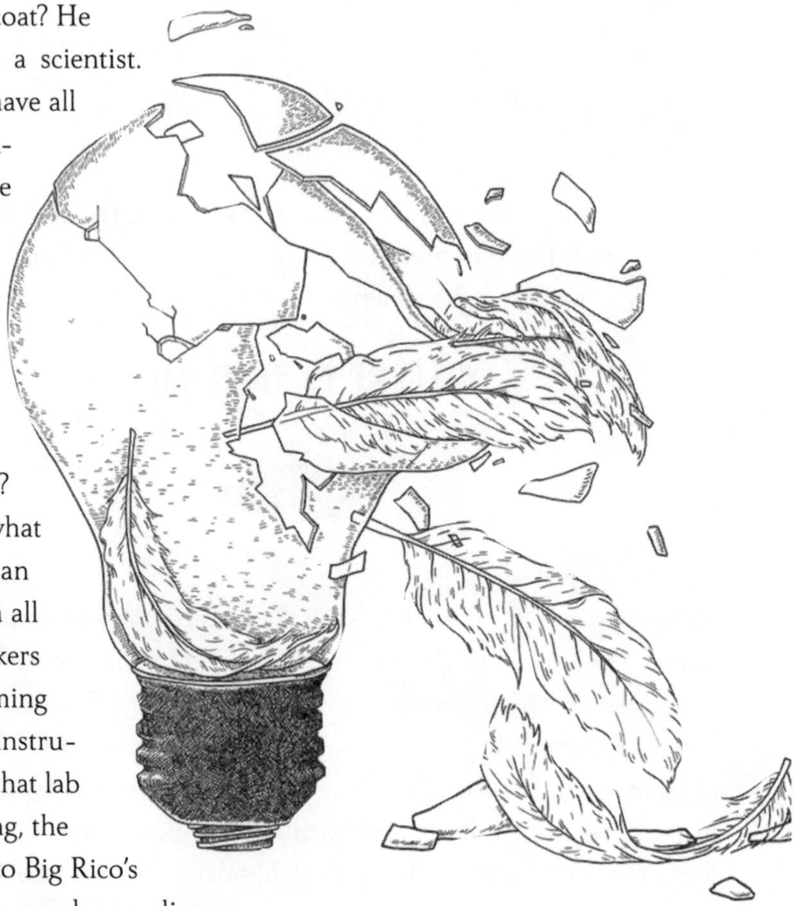

beautiful coat? He says he is a scientist. Well, we have all been scientists at one point or another in our lives. But why now? Why here? And just what does he plan to do with all those beakers and humming electrical instruments in that lab he's renting, the one next to Big Rico's Pizza. No one does a slice like Big Rico. No one.

Just a reminder to all the parents out there. Let's talk about safety when taking your children out to play in the scrublands and the sand wastes. You need to give them plenty of water, make sure there's a shade tree in the area, and keep an eye on the helicopter colors. Are the unmarked helicopters circling the area black? Probably World Government, not a good area for play that day. Are they blue? That's the Sheriff's Secret Police; they'll keep a good eye on your kids, and hardly ever take one. Are they painted with complex murals depicting birds of prey diving? No one knows what those helicopters are, or what they want. Do not play in the area. Return to your home and lock the doors until a Sheriff's Secret Policeman leaves a carnation on your porch to indicate that the danger has passed. Cover your ears to blot out the screams. Also, remember: Gatorade is basically soda, so give your kids plain old water and maybe some orange slices when they play.

A commercial airliner flying through local airspace disappeared today, only to reappear in the Night Vale Elementary gymnasium during basketball practice, disrupting practice quite badly. The jet roared through the small gym for only a fraction of a second, and before it could strike any players or structure, it vanished again, this time apparently for good. There is no word yet on if or how this will affect the Night Vale Mountain Lions' game schedule, and also if this could perhaps be the work of their bitter rivals, the Desert Bluffs Cacti. Desert Bluffs is always trying to show us up through fancier uniforms, better pregame snacks, and quite possibly by transporting a commercial jet into our gymnasium, delaying practice for several minutes at least. For shame, Desert Bluffs. For shame.

That new scientist, we now know he's named Carlos, called a town meeting. He has a square jaw, and teeth like a military cemetery. His hair is perfect, and we all hate and despair and love that perfect hair in equal measure. Old Woman Josie brought corn muffins, which were decent but lacked salt. She said the angels had taken her salt for a Godly Mission and she hadn't yet gotten around to buying more. Carlos told us that we are, by far, the most scientifically interesting community in the US, and he had come to study just what is going on around here. He grinned, and everything about him was perfect, and I fell in love instantly. Government agents from a vague yet menacing agency were in the back, watching. I fear for Carlos. I fear for Night Vale. I fear for anyone caught between what they know and what they don't yet know that they don't know.

We received a press release this morning. The Night Vale Business Association is proud to announce the opening of the brand-new Night Vale Harbor and Waterfront Recreation Area. I have been to these facilities myself recently on their invitation, and I can tell you that it is absolutely top of the line and beautiful. Sturdy docking areas made from eco-friendly post-consumer material. A boardwalk for pedestrians, and plenty of stands ready for local food vendors and merchants to turn into a bustling public marketplace. Now, there is some concern about the fact that, given we are in the middle of a desert, there is no actual water at the waterfront. And that is a definite drawback, I agree. For instance, the boardwalk is currently overlooking sagebrush and rocks. The business association did not provide any specific remedies for this problem, but they assured me that the new harbor would be a big boost to Night Vale nonetheless. Maybe wait until a flash flood and head down there for the full waterfront experience.

The local chapter of the NRA is selling bumper stickers as part of their fund-raising week. They sent the station one to get some publicity, and we're here to serve the community, so I'm happy to let you all know about it. The stickers are made from good, sturdy vinyl, and they read: "Guns don't kill people. It's impossible to be killed by a gun. We are all invincible to bullets and it's a miracle." Stand outside of your front door and shout "NRA" to order one.

Carlos and his team of scientists warn that one of the houses in the new development of Desert Creek, out back of the elementary school, doesn't actually exist. "It seems like it exists," explained Carlos and his perfect hair. "Like it's just right there when you look at it, and it's between two other identical houses so it would make more sense for it to be there than not." But, he says, they have done experiments and the house is definitely not there. At news time, the scientists are standing in a group on the sidewalk in front of the nonexistent house, daring each other to go knock on the door.

A great howling was heard from the Night Vale Post Office yesterday. Postal workers claim no knowledge, although passersby described the sound as being a little like "a human soul being destroyed through Black Magick." The Indian Tracker—now, I don't know if you've seen this guy around. He's the one that appears to be of, maybe, Slavic origin, yet wears an Indian headdress out of some racist cartoon, and claims to be able to read tracks on asphalt. He appeared at the scene, and swore that he would discover the truth. No one responded because it's really hard to take him seriously in that headdress of his.

Lights, seen in the sky above the Arby's. Not the glowing sign of Arby's. Something higher and beyond that. We know the difference. We've caught on to their game. We understand the lights above Arby's game. Invaders from another world. Ladies and gentlemen the future is here. And it's about a hundred feet above the Arby's.

Carlos and his scientists at the monitoring station near Route 800 say their seismic monitors have been indicating wild seismic shifts, meaning to say that the ground should be going up and down all over the place. I don't know about you, folks, but the ground has been as still as the crust of a tiny globe rocketing through an endless cold void could be. Carlos says that they've double-checked the monitors, and they are in perfect working order. To put it plainly, there appears to be catastrophic earthquakes happening right here in Night Vale that absolutely no one can feel. Well, submit an insurance claim anyway. See what you can get, right?

Traffic time, listeners. Now, police are issuing warnings about ghost cars out on the highways, those cars only visible in the distance, reaching unimaginable speeds, leaving destinations unknown for destinations more unknown. They would like to remind you that you should not set your speed by these apparitions, and doing so will not be considered following the flow of traffic. However, they do say that it's probably safe to match speed with the mysterious lights in the sky, as whatever entities or organizations responsible appear to be cautious and reasonable drivers.

And now, the weather.

WEATHER: "These and More Than These" by Joseph Fink

Welcome back, listeners.

The sun didn't set at the correct time today, Carlos and his team of scientists report. They are quite certain about it, they checked multiple clocks, and the sun definitely set ten minutes later than it was supposed to. I asked them if they had any explanations, but they did not offer anything concrete. Mostly, they sat in a circle around a desk clock, staring at it, murmuring and cooing. Still, we must be grateful to have the sun at all. It's easy to forget in this hot, hot, hot desert climate, but things would actually be slightly harder for us without the sun. The next time the sun rises, whatever time that turns out to be, take a moment to feel grateful for all the warmth and light and, even, yes, extreme heat that our desert community is gifted with.

The City Council would like to remind you about the tiered heavens and the hierarchy of angels. The reminder is that you should not know anything about this. The structure of heaven and the angelic organizational chart are privileged information, known only to City Council members on a need-to-know basis. Please do not speak to or acknowledge any angels that you may come across while shopping at the Ralphs or at the Desert Flower Bowling Alley and Arcade Fun Complex. They only tell lies, and do not exist. Report all angel sightings to the City Council for treatment.

And now a brief public service announcement. Alligators. Can they kill your children? Yes.

Along those lines, to get personal for a moment, I think the best way to die would be swallowed by a giant snake. Going feet first and whole into a slimy maw would give your life perfect symmetry.

Speaking of the Desert Flower Bowling Alley and Arcade Fun Complex, its owner, Teddy Williams, reports that he has found the entrance to a vast, underground city in the pin retrieval area of lane five. He said he has not yet ventured into it, merely peered down at its strange spires and broad avenues. He also reports voices of a distant crowd in the depths of that subterranean metropolis. Apparently the entrance was discovered when a bowling ball accidentally rolled into it, clattering down to the city below with sounds that echoed for miles across the impossibly huge cavern. So, you know, whatever population that city has, they know about us now and we might be hearing from them very soon.

Carlos, perfect and beautiful, came into our studios during the break earlier but declined to stay for an interview. He had some sort of blinking box in his hand covered with wires and tubes. Said he was testing the place for materials. I don't know what materials he meant, but that box sure whistled and beeped a lot. When he put it close to the microphone, it sounded like, well, like a bunch of baby birds had just woken up. Really went crazy. Carlos looked nervous. I've never seen that kind of look on someone with that strong of a jaw. He left in a hurry. Told us to evacuate the building, but then, who would be here to talk sweetly to all of you out there. Settling in to be another clear and pretty evening here in Night Vale. I hope all of you out there have someone to sleep through it with, or at least good memories of when you did. Goodnight, listeners. Goodnight.

PROVERB: Look to the north. Keep looking. There's nothing coming from the south.

EPISODE 2: "GLOW CLOUD"

JULY 1, 2012

THE FIRST THING I WROTE FOR *WELCOME TO NIGHT VALE* IS THE FIRST paragraph of this episode. I wasn't thinking about it at the time, but with a few years' perspective, it's interesting to note that my first take on Night Vale as an unformed concept was "let's visit this place."

Like any first-time listener—keep in mind, Joseph and I had only heard episode 1 at this point and had no roadmap for where it was going—I framed my experience of listening to Cecil as a newcomer to town. I needed a kiosk of bubble-fonted brochures and one of those hand-drawn town maps with ads for local car repair shops around the edges. Lacking this, I created the Night Vale Tourism Board in hopes they could lead my way into this strange town. (They could not.)

In our early days of writing *Welcome to Night Vale*, Joseph and I had shared a document called "rough material" where we could just write out full episode story ideas or shorter sidebar stories. The Glow Cloud was one Joseph already had written out, so I used it.

I'm always curious how Night Vale would have developed if we had waited until, say, episode 10 or 12 to use the Glow Cloud story line. Unlike the Tourism Board, the Glow Cloud really helped me (and I think a lot of listeners) wrap our heads around what Night Vale is.

"Oh, there's a giant glowing cloud that controls our minds and drops dead animals, and we don't know where it came from, and where it's going, and we're scared of its capabilities but not horrified by its very existence? Got it. Totally. Let's do this."

I knew the moment we posted the episode what the Glow Cloud truly wanted because I knew then what *Night Vale* was. The Glow Cloud wanted what any of us wanted: to settle down into a small town that intrigues and comforts us.

—Jeffrey Cranor, Cowriter of *Welcome to Night Vale*

The desert seems vast, even endless, and yet scientists tell us that somewhere, even now, there is snow.

WELCOME TO NIGHT VALE.

The Night Vale Tourism Board's "Visitable Night Vale" campaign has kicked off with posters encouraging folks to take their family on a scenery-filled jaunt through the trails of Radon Canyon. Their slogan: "The view is literally breathtaking." Posters will be placed at police stations and frozen yogurt shops in nearby towns, along with promotional giveaways of plastic sheeting and rebreathers.

And now, the news. Have any of our listeners seen the glowing cloud that has been moving in from the west? Well, John Peters, you know, the farmer? He saw it over the Western Ridge this morning, said he would have thought it was the setting sun if it wasn't for the time of day. Apparently the cloud glows in a variety of colors, perhaps changing from observer to observer, although all report a low whistling when it draws near. One death has already been attributed to the Glow Cloud.

But listen, it's probably nothing. If we had to shut down the town for every mysterious event that at least one death could be attributed to, we'd never have time to do anything, right? That's what the Sheriff's Secret Police are saying, and I agree, although I would not go so far as to endorse their suggestion to "run directly at the cloud, shrieking and waving your arms, just to see what it does."

The Apache Tracker, and I remind you that this is that white guy who wears the huge and cartoonishly inaccurate Indian headdress, has announced that he has found some disturbing evidence concerning the recent incident at the Night Vale Post Office, which has been sealed by the City Council since the great screaming that was heard from it a few weeks ago. He said that using ancient Indian magicks, he slipped through council security into the post office and observed that all the letters and packages had been thrown about as in a whirlwind, that there was the heavy stench of scorched flesh, and that words written in blood on the wall said "More to come . . . and soon." Can you believe this guy said he used "Indian magicks"? What an asshole.

Here's something odd: There is a cat hovering in the men's bathroom at the radio station here. Seems perfectly happy and healthy, but it's floating about four feet off the ground next to the sink. Doesn't seem to be able to move from its current hoverspot. If you pet him, he purrs, and he'll rub on your body like a normal cat if you get close enough. Fortunately, because he's right by the sink, it was pretty easy to leave some water and food where he could get it, and it's nice to have a station pet. Wish it wasn't trapped in a hovering prison in the men's bathroom, but listen, no pet is perfect. It becomes perfect when you learn to accept it for what it is.

And now, a message from our sponsors.

I took a walk on the cool sand dunes, brittle grass overgrown, and above me, in the night sky, above me, I saw. Bitter taste of unripe peaches and a smell I could not place, nor could I escape. I remembered other times that I could not escape. I remembered other smells. The moon slunk like a wounded animal. The world spun like it had lost control. Concentrate only on breathing and let go of ideas you had about nutrition and alarm clocks. I took a walk on the cool sand dunes, brittle grass overgrown, and above me, in the night sky, above me, I saw.

This message brought to you by Coca-Cola.

The City Council, in cooperation with government agents from a vague, yet menacing agency, is asking all citizens to stop by the Night Vale Elementary School gymnasium tonight at seven for a brief questionnaire about mysterious sights that definitely no one saw and strange thoughts that in no way occurred to anyone, because all of us are normal, and to be otherwise would make us outcasts from our own community. Remember: If you see something, say nothing, and drink to forget.

The Boy Scouts of Night Vale have announced some slight changes to their hierarchy, which will now be the following: Cub Scout, Boy Scout, Eagle Scout, Blood Pact Scout, Weird Scout, Dreadnought Scout, Dark Scout, Fear Scout, and, finally, Eternal Scout. As always, sign-up is automatic and random, so please keep an eye out for the scarlet envelope that will let you know your son has been chosen for the process.

This is probably nothing, listeners, but John Peters, you know, the farmer? He reports that the Glow Cloud is directly over Old Town Night Vale, and appears to be raining small creatures upon the earth. Armadillos, lizards, a few crows. That kind of thing. Fortunately, the animals appear to be dead already, so the Night Vale Animal Control department has said that it should be a snap to clean those up. They just have to be tossed onto the Eternal Animal Pyre in Mission Grove Park, so if that's the worst the Glow Cloud has for us, I'd say go ahead and do your daily errands, just bring along a good, strong umbrella, capable of handling falling animals of up to, let's say, ten pounds. More on the Glow Cloud as it continues to crawl across our sky. And hey, here's a tip: Take your kid out and use the cloud's constantly mutating hue to teach him or her the names of colors. It's fun, and it shows them the real-life applications of learning.

Alert: The Sheriff's Secret Police are searching for a fugitive named Hiram McDaniels, who escaped custody last night following a nine p.m. arrest. McDaniels is described as a five-headed dragon, approximately eighteen feet tall, with mostly green eyes, and weighing about thirty-six hundred pounds. He is suspected of insurance fraud.

McDaniels was pulled over for speeding last night, and the Secret Police became suspicious when he allegedly gave the officers a fake driver's license for a five-foot-eight man named Frank Chen.

After discerning that Frank Chen was actually a five-headed dragon from somewhere other than our little world, the Secret Police searched McDaniels's vehicle.

Representatives from local civil rights organizations have protested that officers had no legal grounds to search the vehicle, but they ceded the point when reminded by Secret Police officials that our backwards court system will uphold any old authoritarian rule made up on the fly by unsupervised gun-carrying thugs of a shadow government.

The Secret Police say McDaniels escaped custody by breathing fire from his *purple* head. He was last seen flying and shrieking over Red Mesa.

Secret Police are asking for tips leading to the arrest of Hiram McDaniels. They remind you that, if seen, he should not be approached, as he is literally a five-headed dragon.

Contact the Sheriff's Secret Police if you have any information. Ask for Officer Ben. Helpful tipsters will earn one stamp on their Alert Citizen Card. Collect five stamps and you get Stop Sign Immunity for one year!

And now, a look at the community calendar.

Saturday, the public library will be unknowable. Citizens will forget the existence of the library from six a.m. Saturday morning until eleven p.m. that night. The library will be under a sort of renovation. It is not important what kind of renovation.

Sunday is Dot Day. Remember: red dots on what you love. Blue dots on what you don't. Mixing those up can cause permanent consequences.

Monday, Louie Blasko is offering bluegrass lessons in the back of Louie's Music Shop. Of course, the shop burned down years ago, and Louie skipped town immediately after with his insurance money, but he sent word that you should bring your instrument to the crumbled, ashy shell of where his shop once was, and pretend that he is there in the darkness, teaching you. The price is $50 per lesson, payable in advance.

Tuesday afternoon, join the Night Vale PTA for a bake sale to support Citizens for a Blood Space War. Proceeds will go to support neutron bomb development and deployment to our outer solar system allies.

Wednesday has been canceled due to a scheduling error.

And on Thursday is a free concert. That's all it says here.

New call in from John Peters, you know, the farmer? Seems the Glow Cloud has doubled in size, enveloping all of Night Vale in its weird light and humming song. Little League administration has announced that they will be going ahead with the game, although there will be an awning built over the field due to the increase in size of the animal corpses being dropped. I've had multiple reports that a lion, like the kind you would see on the sun-baked plains of Africa, or a pee-stained enclosure at a local zoo, fell on top of the White Sand Ice Cream Shoppe. The shop is offering a free dipped cone to anyone who can figure out how to get the thing off. The Sheriff's Secret Police have apparently taken to shouting questions at

the Glow Cloud, trying to ascertain what exactly it wants. So far the Glow Cloud has not answered. The Glow Cloud does not need to converse with us. It does not feel as we tiny humans feel. It has no need for thoughts or feelings or love. The Glow Cloud simply is. All hail the mighty Glow Cloud. All hail.

And now, slaves of the Cloud, the weather.

WEATHER: "The Bus Is Late" by Satellite High

Sorry, listeners. Not sure what happened in that earlier section of the broadcast. As in, I actually don't remember what happened. Tried to play back the tapes but they all are blank and smell faintly of vanilla. The Glow Cloud, meanwhile, has moved on. It is now just a glowing spot in the distance, humming east to destinations unknown. We may never fully understand, or understand at all, what it was and why it dumped a lot of dead animals on our community. But, and I'm going to get a little personal here, that's the essence of life, isn't it? Sometimes you go through things that seem huge at the time, like a mysterious glowing cloud devouring your entire community. While they are happening, they feel like the only thing that matters, and you can hardly imagine that there's a world out there that might have anything else going on. And then the Glow Cloud moves on, and you move on, and the event is behind you. And you may find, as time passes, that you remember it less and less. Or absolutely not at all, in my case. And you are left with nothing but a powerful wonder at the fleeting nature of even the most important moments in life, and the faint but pretty smell of vanilla.

Finally dear listeners, here is a list of things:

- Emotions you don't understand upon viewing a sunset
- Lost pets, found
- Lost pets, unfound
- A secret lost pet city on the moon

- Trees that see
- Restaurants that hear
- A void that thinks
- A face, half-seen, just before falling asleep
- Trembling hands reaching for desperately needed items
- Sandwiches
- Silence when there should be noise
- Noise when there should be silence
- Nothing, when you want something
- Something, when you thought there was nothing
- Clear plastic binder sheets
- Scented dryer sheets
- Rain coming down in sheets
- Night
- Rest
- Sleep
- End

Goodnight, listeners. Goodnight.

PROVERB: Men are from Mars; women are from Venus; Earth is a hallucination; podcasts are dreams.

EPISODE 3: "STATION MANAGEMENT"

JULY 15, 2012

THE ACT OF RECORDING AUDIO NARRATION IS A RATHER LONELY PURSUIT. Locked in a soundproof booth with noise-canceling headphones amplifying everything including your own heartbeat, the narrator relies on a director or a sound engineer to help shape a performance. In the summer of 2012, we, the creative team behind *Welcome to Night Vale*, had none of these things.

Episodes were recorded in my cramped West Harlem apartment on free software in the occasional silences between door slams, police sirens, and giddy children called by the siren song of the neighborhood ice-cream truck. I recorded *Night Vale* (and still do) without direction or quality control by an outside ear, relying on my instincts as a theater performer and love of the horror genre to guide me. After each take, I would close my eyes and listen intently to what I had just recorded, hoping that my performance was interesting enough to hold the listeners' attention while capturing the underlying creepiness of this little desert town. If everything sounded good, the episode was sent off to Joseph to stitch together with music and special effects.

A few weeks after recording episode 3, I ran into Joseph in the lobby of the Kraine Theater on East Fourth Street and he told me that he had the completed, unreleased episode on his phone, and asked if I'd like to hear it. In that first listen, I became aware of why this episode was so special and marked a turning point in the series as a whole: it was the first time the main conflict involved the as-of-yet unnamed Cecil on air and in the present moment. The horror of confronting the Eldritch Abomination that is Station Management was happening live and was not being reported secondhand. Cecil was not safely tucked away in his booth, passively observing the horrors of life in Night Vale, he was facing them head-on. Supported by the ethereal music of Jon Bernstein, a.k.a. Disparition, and the sound effects Joseph had found through open-source sites (featuring "monster noises" made by digitally manipulating the sounds of drinking straws against plastic lids of all things), I realized that my lonely recording sessions were part of something larger, more terrifying, and more entertaining than I could have anticipated.

—Cecil Baldwin, Voice of Cecil Palmer

The Arctic is lit by the midnight sun. The surface of the moon is lit by the face of the earth. Our little town is lit too, by lights just above that we cannot explain.

WELCOME TO NIGHT VALE.

The *Night Vale Daily Journal* has announced that they will be cutting back their publication schedule to Monday through Thursday only, due to the economic downturn and a massive decline in the literate population. The Thursday *Daily Journal* will now be called the Weekend Edition, and on Sundays, newspaper kiosks usually filled with important newsprint will be filled with two-percent milk. When asked why milk, the *Journal*'s publishing editor, Leann Hart, said, "It is important that we maintain an unbiased approach to news reporting."

The Night Vale Business Association is proud to announce the new Night Vale Stadium, next to the Night Vale Harbor and Waterfront Recreation Area. This stadium will be able to seat fifty thousand, but will be closed all nights of the year except November 10 for the annual Parade of the Mysterious Hooded Figures, in which all of our favorite ominous hooded figures—the one that lurks under the slide in the Night Vale Elementary playground, the ones that meet regularly in the Dog Park, and the one that will occasionally openly steal babies and for reasons no one can understand, we all stand by and let him do it—all of them will be parading proudly through Night Vale Stadium. I tell you, with these new facilities, it promises to be quite a spectacle. And then it promises to be a vast, dark, and echoey space for the other meaningless 364 days of the year.

Here at the radio station, it's contract negotiation season with the Station Management again. That's always an interesting time. Now, obviously I'm not allowed to go into details, but negotiation is tricky when you're never allowed to glimpse what you're negotiating with. Station Management stays inside their office at all times, only communicating with us through sealed envelopes that are spat out from under the door like a sunflower shell through teeth. Then, in order to respond, you just kind of shout at the closed door and hope management hears. Sometimes you can see movement through the frosted glass, large shapes shifting around, strange tendrils whipping through the air. Architecturally speaking, the apparent size of management's office does not physically make sense given the size of the building, but it's hard to say, really, as no one has ever seen the actual office, only its translucence.

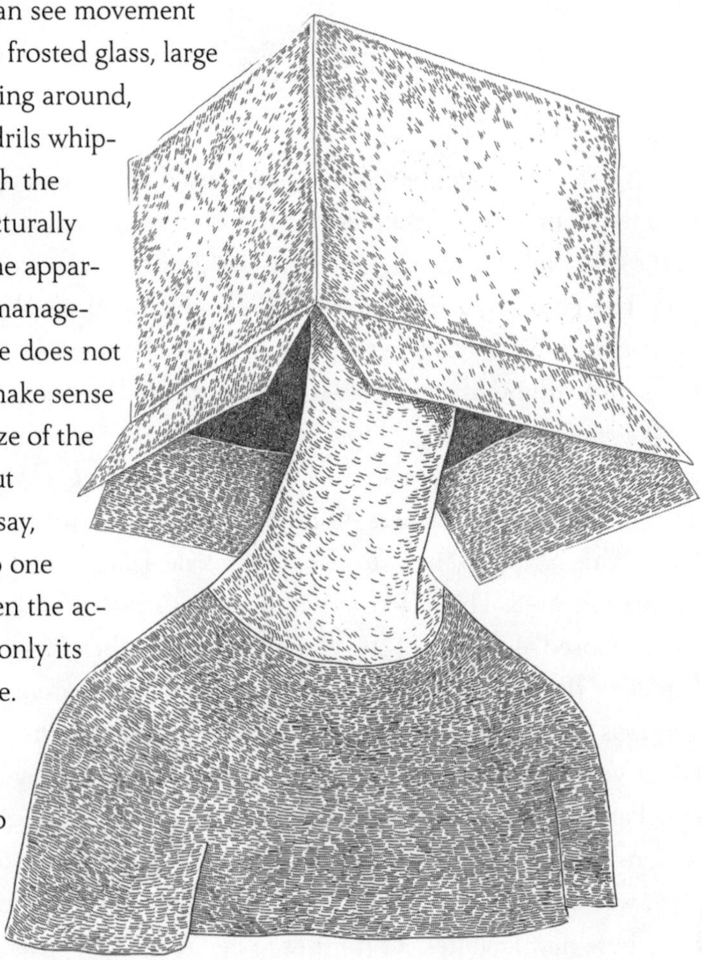

Look, I've probably said too much. I can see down the

hall that an envelope just came flying out. I pray it's not another HR retraining session in the Dark Box, ah, but what can I say? I'm a reporter at heart. I can't not report.

[*Sound of envelope tearing open and paper unfolding*]

Oh. My. Let's go to the seven-day outlook.

[*Sound of paper shuffling on desk, a bit frantic/hurried*]

Your daily shades of the sky forecast. Monday: turquoise. Tuesday: taupe. Wednesday: robin's egg. Thursday: turquoise-taupe. Friday: coal dust. Saturday: coal dust, with chances of indigo in the late afternoon. Sunday: void.

The City Council has asked me to remind everyone about the new drive to clean up litter. Night Vale is our home, and who wants to leave trash all over their home? Put it in the garbage can, listeners, and if you see any trash around, pick it up and throw it away! Do your part. Unless the trash is marked with a small red flag. The council has asked me to remind you that any litter marked with a red flag is not to be picked up or approached. Remember the slogan: "No flag=goes in the bag. Red flag=run."

Listeners, we are currently fielding numerous reports that books have stopped working. It seems that all over Night Vale, books have simply ceased functioning. The scientists are studying one of the broken books to see if they can understand just what is going on here. The exact problem is currently unclear, but some of the words being used include "sparks," "meat smell," "biting," and "lethal gas." For your own safety, please do not attempt to open a book until we have more information on the nature and cause of these problems. The City Council has released only a brief statement, indicating that their stance on books has not changed, and that, as always, they believe that books are dangerous and inadvisable, and should not be kept in private homes.

Another warning for Night Vale residents. Sources say that the used and discount sporting goods store on Flint Drive is a front for the World Government. This is based on extensive study of the location, and also because it has a helicopter pad on which black helicopters regularly depart and land, fairly unusual for a used and discount sporting goods store. We sent our intern, Chad, to try buying a tennis racket, and have not heard back from him for several weeks. This brings me to a related point. To the parents of Chad, the intern: We regret to inform you that your son was lost in the line of community radio duty, and that he will be missed, and never forgotten. May you all feel blessed to have the family that you have, and if you're looking for sporting goods, check out Play Ball! right over by our own Night Vale Community Radio Station. Play Ball! is only a front for the Sheriff's Secret Police, and so can be completely trusted.

Larry Leroy, out on the edge of town, reported that a creeping fear came into Night Vale today. He felt it first as a mild apprehension, then a growing worry, and finally a mortal panic. It passed from him to the employees at the car lot, who crouched behind their cars and cast fearful eyes at the empty sky. It did not affect Old Woman Josie, presumably because of her angelic protection, but it went from there to the rest of the town, until we all were shivering in anticipation for a terrible thing that we could not yet see.

I myself was frozen, sure that any movement would lead to death, that any word would be my last. Of course, that also could have been the contract negotiations with Station Management and the hideous envelope I just received. Also, I'm battling Lyme disease.

Meanwhile, the creeping fear passed, first leaving Larry Leroy, out on the edge of town, and then the car lot, where they went back to offering gently used cars at affordable prices, and finally the rest of us, who could go back to living with the knowledge that, at any given moment, we will either live or die, and it's no use guessing which. It is not currently known where the creeping fear will go next. Hopefully to Desert Bluffs. It would serve them right.

Two hawk-eyed listeners sent in reports that Carlos, our curious scientist visitor, was seen getting his beautiful, beautiful hair cut. He was having his gorgeous hair shorn. Cut! Cut short—so very short—from his perfectly shaped, brilliant head.

Listeners, I am not one to gossip (even if it IS a local celebrity), but please explain to me why Carlos would strip away, decimate, any part of his thick black hair (not to ignore the dignified, if premature, touch of gray in the temples)? What treacherous barber would agree to such depravity? Who takes mere money, or even soulless joy, in depriving our small community of such a simple but important act as luridly admiring Carlos's stunning coif?

Reports, from two intrepid sources, are that it was Telly the Barber. Telly, who likes sports and has posters of combs. Telly the Barber seems to be the one who betrayed our community. Telly the Barber.

It is Telly the Barber, at the corner of SW Fifth Street and Old Musk Road, with the red-and-white spinning pole and the sign that says "Telly's." Telly is about five foot nine with a small mustache and a thick potbelly. He talks with an accent and sneers. Telly the Barber cut Carlos's beautiful hair.

According to reports.

Telly.

Now, while I gather myself, let's have a look at traffic.

Oh, wow.

Well, that looks pretty good.

Yep . . . Yes . . . Okay, not too bad there, either, I see.

Oh, that gentleman needs to slow it down. It is not a race, my friend.

(Not a literal one, anyway.)

That has been traffic.

[*Worried*] And now for an editorial.

I don't ask favors much, dear listeners. That you know. But I'm asking all of you now to conduct a letter writing campaign to Station Management, which was not pleased with my discussion of their physical attributes and behavior, and is now threatening to shut down my show, or possibly my life, for good.

Their wording was kind of ambiguous.

Obviously we will not be able to deliver the letters directly to the Management, per se, as no one has ever opened their door, but we can shout the content of the letters outside their office, and we presume, given an anatomy that includes ears, they will be able to hear what you have to say. So if you like this show, and you want to hear more of it, then we need to hear from you. Make your voice heard to whatever it is that lies in wait behind that darkened office door.

[*Sound of a great rumbling*]

Oh, um . . . I'm sorry, dear listeners. We'll be back after this word from our sponsors.

This segment has been brought to us by Big Rico's Pizza. Listeners, we are proud to have Big Rico's as a sponsor of our show.

You will not find a better pizza joint in all of Night Vale than Big Rico's. Just the other night I stopped by Big Rico's. I was in the mood for a delicious pizza slice, and since Big Rico's is the only pizza place in Night Vale that has not burned to the ground in an unsolved arson case—and did I mention is also the best pizza in town!—I ordered a single Rico slice with two authentic toppings.

And boy was I satisfied. The flavor was scrumptious. The taste was also scrumptious. And it was warm, the pizza slice. I have been told that even the hooded figures eat there. The waitstaff looked like they avert their hollow gazes quite a bit.

Even the City Council offers its ringing endorsement of Big Rico's: All Night Vale citizens are mandated to eat at Big Rico's once a week. It is a misdemeanor not to!

Big Rico's Pizza: No one does a slice like Big Rico, folks. No one.

[*Whispered, afraid*] And now, sweet, sweet listeners, the weather.

WEATHER: "Bill & Annie" by Chuck Brodsky

[*Still afraid*] Hello, radio audience. I come to you live from under my desk, where I've dragged my microphone and am currently hiding in the fetal position. Did you write letters? Maybe you should not do this anymore. Station Management has opened its door for the first time in my memory and is now roaming the building. I don't know exactly what Management looks like, as that is when I took cover under my desk, and I can only hope that they are not listening to what's going on right now or else I may have sealed my fate. I can hear only a kind of clicking footstep and a faint hissing sound like releasing steam. An intern went to see what Management wanted and has not returned. If you are related to Jerry Hartman, afternoon board operator at Night Vale Community Radio, I'm sorry to inform you that he is probably dead or at least corporeally absorbed into Management permanently.

Jerry and Chad the interns will both be missed, but we will surely see them in the Thanksgiving Day Dead Citizens Impersonation Contest, which this year will be in the employee lounge under the Night Vale Mall from eleven a.m. to nine forty-five p.m. There will be a cash bar and two Twister boards.

[*Hissing sound*]

I am going to see if I can make a break for the door. If you don't hear from me again, it has truly been a pleasure. Goodnight, Night Vale. And good-bye.

PROVERB: There's a special place in hell. It's really hip. Very exclusive.

EPISODE 4: "PTA MEETING"

AUGUST 1, 2012

I AM TERRIFIED OF SPIDERS. I CAN'T EVEN LOOK AT A PICTURE OF A SPIDER. I mean, if it's kind of a wide shot, I might be okay. But I won't look long. When I see one of those 10 Photos That Prove Spiders Can Be Adorable links on Facebook and there's a giant photo of a spider's face, I shudder and sometimes even drop my phone.

A therapist once gave me a long description and it has to do with my father and the state of Idaho and latent stress, but I won't describe all that here. (Maybe in Volume 2.) Just know that I would trade having every film, TV show, and book spoiled for me for never having to see a spider ever again.

So as a true arachnophobe, it is my duty to litter Night Vale with spider/tarantula references. I feel safe in saying that at least ninety percent of the spider references in our episode scripts and novel are mine.

Here in episode 4, we have the first appearance of the worst physical ailment I could think of: "throat spiders." It's terrifying, but the absurdity makes me laugh (at my own joke—yes, I'm a humble man), and this is somewhat therapeutic.

In the next episode, we'll get a glimpse of Night Vale's "spider problem," and it is even more absurd and way less terrifying. And by the time we started writing *Welcome to Night Vale,* I already had a tertiary character of a possibly sentient tarantula.

I still can't bring myself to look at photos of spiders, but I can at least empathize with their struggles (illiteracy, lack of congressional representation) and contributions to society (both Franz Schubert and Charlotte Brontë were brown recluses).

—Jeffrey Cranor

The sun has grown so very, very old. How long cold, fading death? How long?

WELCOME TO NIGHT VALE.

Our top story: last night's Night Vale PTA meeting ended in bloodshed as a rift in space-time split open in the Main Street Recreation Center Auditorium, setting loose several confused and physically aggressive Pteranodons. The glowing portal remained open and shrieked incessantly, an unholy sound that witnesses say resembled noisy urchin children caught in a combine harvester and then slowed down and amped up through some kind of open-source, easy-to-use audio-editing software.

The Pteranodons mostly attacked women with glasses. Authorities are still unsure why Night Vale's only flying-dinosaur expert, Joel Eisenberg, still has not recovered from last year's bout with throat spiders. It took most of an hour to corral the panicked beasts back into the vortex and resume the meeting, which had mostly been about recent lunchroom price hikes and had devolved into name-calling because Susan Willman called Diane Crayton's son, Josh, a bit "tubby" and that he maybe "needs a financial incentive to eat a bit less."

In this reporter's opinion, Susan Willman is dangerously obsessed with the *New York Times* bestselling *Freakonomics* books. Dangerously so.

Fortunately no one was injured or killed in the incident, although experts from Timothy's Auditorium Repair Contractors, Inc., estimates close to $750,000 in damage has been done to the Rec Center Auditorium, and that cost includes free storm windows and a complimentary seasonal insulation consultation.

It's election season again, and you know what that means. Sheriff's Secret Police will be coming by to collect certain family members so that everyone votes for the correct council seats and there's no confusion. These family members will be held in a secure and undisclosed location, which everyone knows is the abandoned mine shaft outside of town.

But don't let the name fool you, listeners. It's been used for years for so many kidnappings and illegal detentions that the abandoned mine shaft outside of town is actually a pretty nice location these days, featuring king-size beds, free Wi-Fi, and HBO. Also, torture cubicles, but I don't think anyone's going to make the council use those. Remember, this is America. Vote correctly or never see your loved ones again. This message brought to you by the City Council.

The *Night Vale Daily Journal* today announced that due to the recent economic downturn they will start running ads on the front page. Any business interested in running one of these "Platinum Premium" ads should contact editor Leann Hart. Hart mentioned that they have also created a "write your own news story" program for interested citizens. Because every writer has been laid off, the *Daily Journal* now needs these community contributions to supply Night Vale with important news and features. The first Platinum Premium ad runs next Monday and features the terrified face of an infant primate with a superimposed spoon that has been stone sharpened to a rough point and the tagline "Better use Tide."

Hart also said that last year's explosion that decimated the *Daily Journal*'s distribution plant is still totally an accident and would like her insurance rep to call her back. Please call her back.

This just came across the wire. The Secret Police have issued a new statement shedding more light onto last night's PTA meeting incident. The noisy portal and subsequent dinosaur attack that brutally interrupted discussion of swing set repairs on the elementary school playground stayed open long after recreation center employees thought they had rounded up all of the ancestral avian beasts, and authorities warn there is still at least one more Pteranodon on the loose. Citizens should cover themselves with a low-SPF sunscreen and hide in a tiled bathroom.

Several curious handball players in the court next to the auditorium actually popped their heads into the portal just to see what was on the other side of the vortex and came back dramatically changed. The players aged several thousand years in what bystanders experienced as only a few seconds. Those handball players now straddle the unenviable border of millennially wizened and cripplingly insane. Since psychological and emotional damages are no longer considered valid claims by the greater medical insurance community, we are still reporting zero injuries. We'll update you as further details surface in our special ongoing and very special coverage of "Pteranodon Attack-Gate: Are We Safe From Dinosaurs? No Way."

City Council has asked me to read the following message: If you notice strange auras around any of the following objects in your house: blender, shower head, dog, husband, wife, table, chair, doorknob, baseboard, vacation souvenirs or photos, collectibles of any kind, especially those depicting or involving horses, DVDs, especially *Cliffhanger, There's Something About Mary,* and *The Wire* fourth season, and any bagged lettuce from California or Mexico, please report to the council for indefinite detention.

Speaking of the City Council, it voted this week to remove the large lead-plated door from the northeastern-most crook of Radon Canyon—you know, the area pulsing with green light and sotto voce basso humming? Proponents of the measure called the large yellow emblem and red lettering that spelled out DANGER! PLUTONIUM! DO NOT OPEN DOOR! RISK OF DEATH! were (at worst) an offensive eyesore and (at best) a hacky, sci-fi cliché.

Many Night Vale citizens attended the meeting—including, it was said, several angels—although, no angel has admitted to having been present for the City Council meeting or any other event ever, for that matter. Old Woman Josie agreed with the measure, adding that lead is a health hazard and that the old door was nothing but a ticking time bomb. According to the meeting minutes, Josie said: "That old door, ooh, that door. Someone's going to get some kind of lead poisoning."

Carlos, beautiful Carlos, tragically shorn of his locks, reportedly was the only dissenting voice, but it is not clear he actually opposed the measure as the minutes only report him stating: "There is no time! No more time!" into a black rectangle in his hand and then running, winded, from the community hall. According to Old Woman Josie, he was still absolutely perfect and smelled of lavender chewing gum.

More breaking news on the Pteranodons. We humbly offer the following retractions from our previous reports. Secret Police are now reporting that the offending beasts were not Pteranodons after all, but pterodactyls. Also, Pteranodons aren't even dinosaurs as this station previously stated, just winged reptiles that lived about seventy million years after pterodactyls. Finally, earlier we reported a death toll of zero when, in fact, the number is closer to thirty-eight. We regret these errors.

It's almost football season, and the Night Vale Scorpions are gearing up for a defense of their high school division title. But really, as long as we beat Desert Bluffs, fans and hooded figures alike will feel just fine. Coach Nazr al-Mujaheed told reporters that he's particularly excited for the progress junior quarterback Michael Sandero made during the off-season after that sentient lightning bolt struck him and gave him the strength of two jeeps and the intelligence of a heavily concussed René Descartes.

But if Night Vale is going to beat their bitter rivals this year and stave off the government-administered pestilence that follows a losing season record, Sandero will have to improve his accuracy. Last year, Sandero only completed two out of 130 pass attempts, most notably because he was in advanced stages of cerebral palsy and because his throwing hand had been removed due to several overdue library books. Apparently the off-season lightning strike has healed Sandero of his terminal ailments and court-ordered amputations, and he's ready to take on Desert Bluffs, which is probably the worst team ever. God, they're dreadful.

And now an editorial. Let's talk for a moment about apartment building etiquette. Now, I myself live in an apartment building, and there is a compassion and acceptance you have to have for a certain level of annoyance. It's people in close proximity to each other, and so there will be some things that you don't like and still have to let go. But, other things are absolutely unacceptable. For instance, a certain level of strange radiating light or heat on shared walls is expected, but any oozings or visible membranes are rude and thoughtless to all of your neighbors. Gibbering, howling, and chants in long-dead languages are the kind of thing that is fine at one p.m., but absolutely not fine at one a.m. We are all in this together. Put your trash in the cans, not in the hallway leading to the cans. Put on some clothes when standing in front of your windows. And keep any rituals or crazed experiments to hours in which no one is trying to sleep. It doesn't have to be hard.

We have a very unexpected treat today, dear listeners. Live, in the studio, we have one of the mysterious hooded figures often seen around town. We did not actually invite him here; he just was waiting for us when we unlocked the studio this morning. He has not moved nor spoken since then, and I'll be honest, I am only guessing that he is a he, because physical attributes are hard to determine under these robes and the face is entirely hidden in shadow as empty and as black as the void of space. But hey, we're doing radio, he's in a radio station. Let's see if we can get an interview.

Mr. Hooded Figure, how are you doing today?

[*Faint static*]

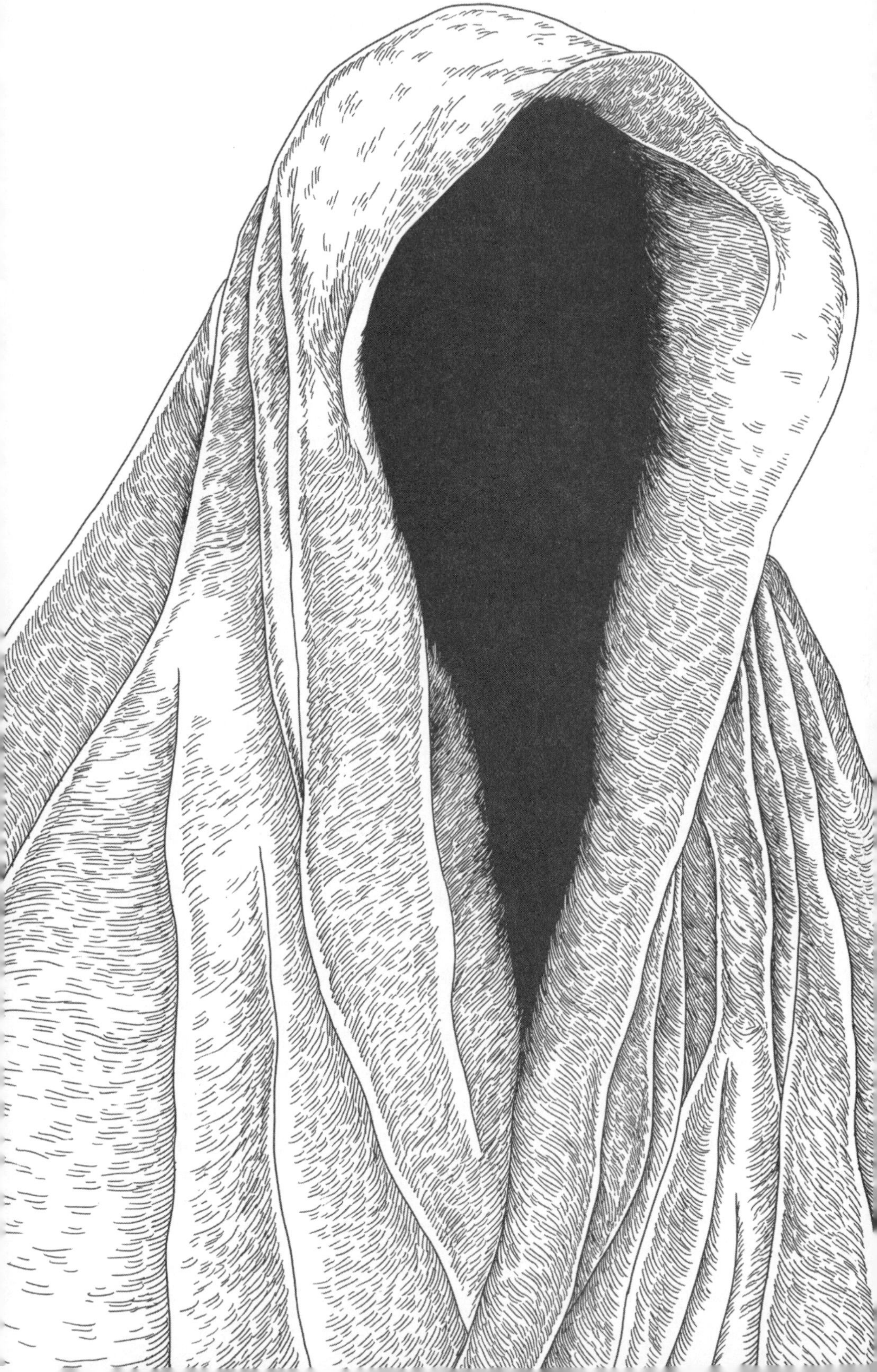

Ah, okay. Care to comment on the recent expansion of the forbidden Dog Park?

[*Louder static*]

Any comments at all? Anything you'd like to tell the ordinary folk of Night Vale about your organization?

[*Very loud static*]

Listeners, I'm sure you can hear this. It's not a problem with your radio or our transmitters; the hooded figure is making those noises in our studio. It's pretty deafening, actually.

All right, I don't think he's going to stop, and he's started to levitate, so let's go to weather.

WEATHER: "Closer" by The Tiny

Ladies and gentlemen, we have just received word from Secret Police that the rip in space-time that opened at last night's PTA meeting has been sealed at last. The final missing pterodactyl has been returned to its own timeline in either prehistoric or alternate universe Night Vale.

The creature's lifeless body was found a dozen yards outside of the Dog Park entrance, stripped of all flesh and with most of the organs inverted and strung around its exposed skull, like an old-fashioned soft-meats crown, as worn by the eighteenth-century religious leaders who settled our fair burg.

The dinosaur's body was returned to the vortex, the gateway closed, and the PTA meeting rescheduled for next Tuesday at six p.m. That meeting will continue to address the important issue of backpacks and whether or not they are causing autism. There will also be a memorial service for the thirty-eight parents and teachers who lost their lives in the attack, followed by a raffle. Remember: Winners must be present at the time of the drawing to claim their prizes.

City Council and Secret Police have issued a reminder that Night Vale citizens of all species and all geologic eras are not to enter, look at, or think too long about the Dog Park. This reminder, they say, is completely unrelated to anything that may or may not have happened today.

Coming up next: stay tuned for our one-hour special, *Morse Code for Trumpet Quintets.*

And listeners: Night Vale is an ancient place, full of history and secrets, as we were reminded today. But it is also a place of the present moment, full of life, and of us. If you can hear my voice, speaking live, then you know: We are not history yet. We are happening now. How miraculous is that?

Goodnight, listeners. Goodnight.

PROVERB: What has four legs in the morning, two legs at noon, and three legs in the evening? I don't know, but I trapped it in my bedroom. Send help.

EPISODE 5: "THE SHAPE IN GROVE PARK"

AUGUST 15, 2012

THIS EPISODE WAS AN EARLY FAVORITE OF MINE, ONE THAT FELT POLISHED and professional in a way that we hadn't quite hit yet. The main plot was a fun bit of throwback sci-fi that led into a fun bit of existential terror. The side bits include one of my favorite pieces of writing by Jeffrey, a paragraph about spiders that manages to take two very sharp turns in the course of one sentence. And the episode has the first hints of Cecil as a character, rather than a detached narrator. In short, it was us starting to figure out what we wanted this show to be.

Before and after this episode, Night Vale's park is referred to as "Mission Grove Park." Why did it lose the first word of its name for this episode? Mainly because I forgot what it was called. But also because "The Shape in Grove Park" had a pleasingly '50s pulp sci-fi sound to it. It may not surprise you to know that my mother was deeply into '50s and '60s sci-fi movies, and as a result I have seen both *It Came from Outer Space* and *It Conquered the World* not just once, but many times. (*It Came from Outer Space* is the vastly superior of the two, in case you were wondering.)

Speaking of names, this was the first episode in which we referred to the character Cecil by name. There was not a great deal of thought put into the decision. The show grew out of the aesthetic and techniques of the Neo-Futurists, where people perform under their own names, and so it seemed simple to just do the same here. Cecil, the actor, expressed some concern that this might confuse people and I assured him that I didn't see that ever being a problem.

Oops.

—Joseph Fink

Close your eyes. Let my words wash over you. You are safe now.

WELCOME TO NIGHT VALE.

Local historians are protesting the removal of the Shape in Grove Park that No One Acknowledges or Speaks About. While their protest has been hampered by the fact that none of them will acknowledge or speak about it, they did, through a system of gestures and grimaces, convey the message that, whatever the shape is, and whatever its effect on nearby neighborhoods, it is a Night Vale landmark that should be protected. The shape itself offered no comment, only a low moaning and a gelatinous quiver. The City Council would not provide any reason for the removal, but did say that any work in Grove Park was making way for a new swing set, picnic area, and bloodstone circle, which we all can agree are good contributions to our community.

The Night Vale Green Market Co-op announced today that after fifteen years they will begin selling fruits and vegetables. Green Market board president Tristan Cortez said that recent customer surveys indicated that shoppers have grown tired of empty pickup trucks and vacant tents lining the city hall parking lot every Saturday morning in the summer and fall. Cortez said that research indicates consumers are more likely to buy products if they are available and for sale, and that green market and grocery shoppers tend to purchase food items.

Cortez said the decision to sell food at the green market was a controversial one as many board members and co-op shareholders feel fruit and vegetable sales will interfere with their ongoing secretive domestic espionage operations. When reached for comment, our source within the Secret Police only breathed heavily into the phone while tapping an as yet-uncracked code into the receiver.

Michael Sandero, starting quarterback for the Night Vale Scorpions, has reportedly grown a second head. It is not currently known whether this is a result of the previously reported lightning strike, or just another odd coincidence in the kid's odd life. People in the know say that the new head is better looking and smarter than the first one, and even Michael's mother has issued a statement indicating that she likes it much better than her son, and that she will be changing the rankings on the public WHICH OF MY CHILDREN I LIKE BEST board outside her house. Sandero could not be reached for comment. Probably. We didn't try.

Friends, listeners, there's a real tarantula problem here in Night Vale. Many residents have called in to report that illiteracy, unwanted pregnancy, and violent crime are on the rise in the tarantula communities. Animal control is addressing these concerns through after-school programs called "Teach a Spider to Read: Stop the Madness." Those interested in volunteering should stand in their bathtubs and weep until it is all gone. Nothing left. You can let go now. Let go. Sssh. Let go.

And now for a message from our sponsor.

Tired of your home? Sick of comfort? Come to the hole in the vacant lot out back of the Ralphs and huddle with us. Who are we? Good question. Come to the hole in the vacant lot, out back of the Ralphs, and huddle with us. Why do we want you to come? Why did we spend money for this airtime? We understand you are confused. But: hole, vacant lot, Ralphs, huddle, us. For the low, low price. Act today. Or tomorrow. Not Wednesday. Wednesday is no good for us. Anyway, we're almost out of airtime, so just come on down to the hole in the vacant lot out back of the Ralphs and huddle with us or else.

Back to our regularly scheduled programming.

Ladies and gentlemen, the rumor mill is abuzz. We've had a celebrity

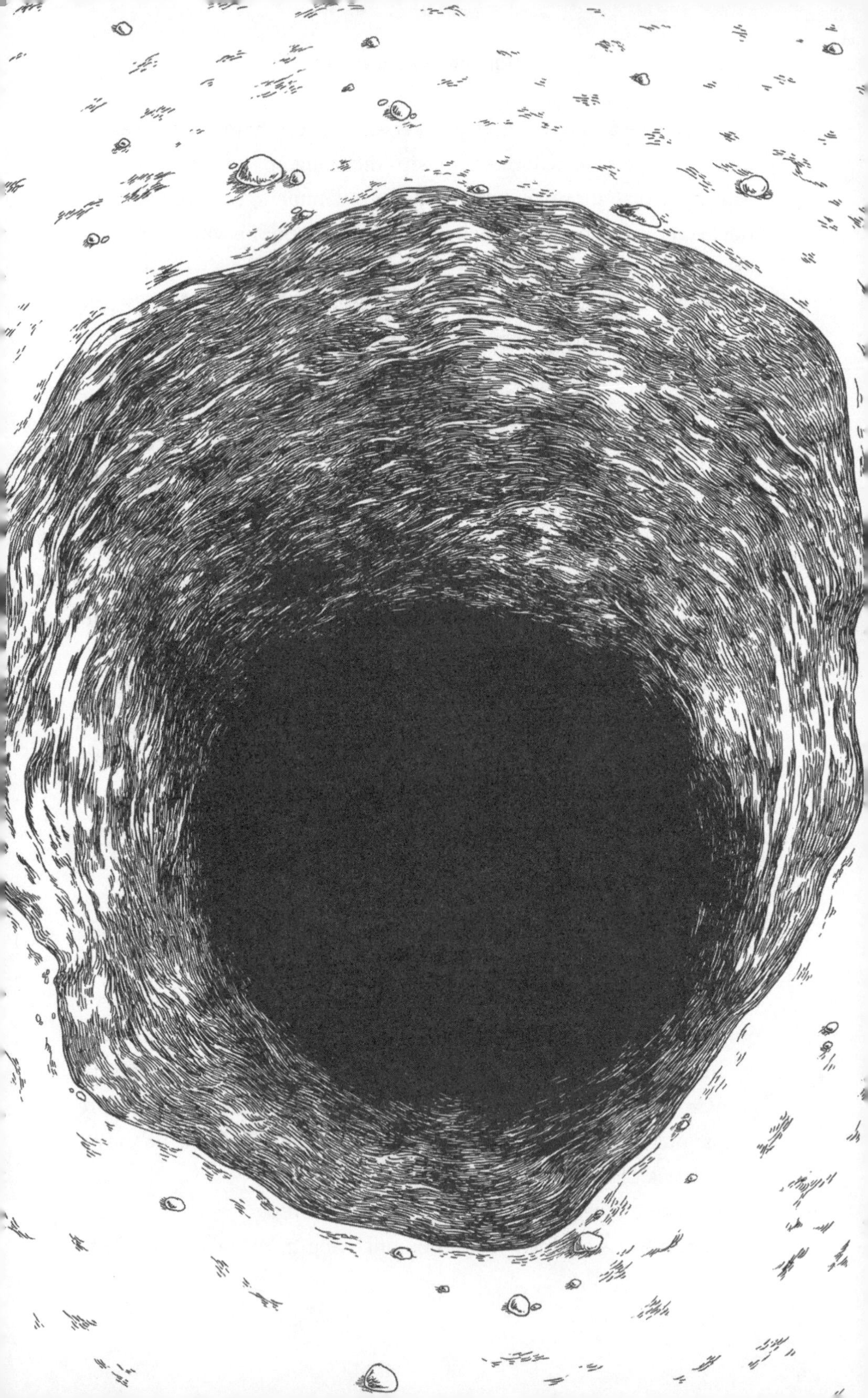

sighting in our little burg! Old Woman Josie and one of her angel friends reportedly saw Rita Hayworth getting gas at the Fuel and Go over by the bowling alley! Rita Hayworth, ladies and gentlemen, right here in Night Vale! Can you believe it? Old Woman Josie said Rita was looking a bit older, moderately obese, and considerably more Hispanic, but the angel assured her it was indeed Rita. He is an angel after all. He would know, right? Wow. Rita Hayworth. Here in Night Vale. Just imagine.

Update on the Shape Formerly in Grove Park that No One Acknowledges or Speaks About. It seems the City Council, in their superhuman mercy and all-seeing glory, have chosen to move the shape directly in front of our own radio station, where it is continuing to be what can only be described as indescribable. The shape was not available for comment, as I could find no one willing to speak to it, or even meet my eye when I mentioned it. It has occurred to me that I may be the only one able to see it. Now that I think of it, I have also never bothered to actually check whether this mic is attached to any sort of recording or broadcasting device, and it is possible that I am alone in an empty universe, speaking to no one, unaware that the world is held aloft merely by my delusions and my smooth, sonorous voice. More on this story as it develops, I say, possibly only to myself.

The Night Vale Community Theatre is holding auditions for its fall show, *Once on this Island*. Interested thespians should bring a headshot and résumé to the Recreation Center Auditorium on Thursday night. All auditionees must perform a one-minute monologue and sing one song. Bring sheet music if you would like piano accompaniment.

Auditionees will also be required to do a cold reading and give blood and stool samples along with mandatory radiation testing following the auditions. Do not sing anything from *South Pacific*. People of color are urged to audition, as Night Vale Community Theatre is an equal opportunity employer. Also, actors with long-range sniper training, Fortran computer programming, and top-notch wilderness survival skills are a plus. Final casting will be announced in secret, via dirigible. No one can ever know.

Update on the green market situation from earlier in our broadcast: Everything is exactly the same as when we last reported on it, and there is no new information.

Listeners, do you ever think about the moon? I was sitting outside last night, looking at the moon, and I thought: Does anyone actually know what that thing is? Have there been any studies on this? I went to ask Carlos, but he hasn't been seen much since that treacherous Telly's vile haircut. The moon's weird though, right? It's there and there, and then suddenly it's not. And it seems to be pretty far up. Is it watching us? If not, what is it watching instead? Is there something more interesting than us? Hey! Watch us moon! We may not always be the best show in the universe, but we try!

This has been today's Children's Fun Fact Science Corner.

Speaking of which, the Night Vale School District has announced some changes to the elementary school curriculum. They are as follows:

- In response to parent feedback, history class will focus more heavily on textbook readings and traditional exams, rather than live ammo drills.
- Geology is adding a new type of rock on the grounds that it's been a while since anyone has done that. The new type of rock is Vimby, and it is characterized by its pale blue color and the fact that it is completely edible. Points will be awarded to the first student to discover a real-world example of it.
- Math and English are switching names. Their curriculum will stay exactly the same.
- Astronomy will now be conducting stargazing sessions only with blindfolds on every participant, in order to protect them from the existential terror of the void. Also, Pluto has been declared imaginary.
- All classrooms will be equipped with at least one teacher physically present for the entire instruction period. Astral projection will no longer be used in any classroom situation.

- Finally, in addition to the current foreign-language offerings of Spanish, French, and Modified Sumerian, schools will now be offering Double Spanish, Weird Spanish, Coptic Spanish, Russian, and Unmodified Sumerian.

And now, a continuation of our previous investigation into whether I am literally the only person in the world, speaking to myself in a fit of madness caused by my inability to admit the tragedy of my own existence. Leland, our newest intern, recently brought me a cup of coffee. He is no longer in my field of vision, but I do still have the cup of coffee, which is well made and is giving me the needed pick-me-up to continue considering this terrifying possibility. Is it possible that I only imagined Leland, and forgot making myself this cup of coffee? But then, who would have grown this coffee? Where was this cup procured from? Oh, Leland's back in the room. He's waving at me. Hello Leland. He's saying . . . what was that, Leland?

I see, he's saying that the shape has turned a molten red and is causing small whirlwinds in front of our radio station doors. There is apparently a sound of a great many voices chanting, as though it were an army giving out a battle cry before raining down destruction on our arid little hamlet. He has stopped shouting and is now writing furiously on a piece of paper. I have to say, Leland's existence, as well as his finally speaking about the shape that no one else would speak about, has reassured me greatly about my lonely and solipsistic vigil here at this microphone. He is handing me a note. Thank you, Leland. Let me see here.

Ah, it says that the City Council believes the reason for the violent reaction of the Shape Formerly in Grove Park that No One Acknowledges or Speaks About is because I have been acknowledging and speaking about it, which has made it angry. They urge me to stop speaking of it, and never do it again, and in exchange they'll move it somewhere else so we can get our front loading zone back. After brief consideration, I have decided to accept the council's offer, because they are trustworthy leaders looking out for our better future, and also because Leland just got vaporized by a strange red light emanating from the station entrance. To the family of Leland, we thank you for his service to the cause of community radio, and join you in mourning his loss.

And, without further ado, nor ever again mentioning anything we shouldn't, let's go to the weather.

WEATHER: "Jerusalem" by Dan Bern

Hello listeners. In breaking news, the sky. The earth. Life. Existence as an unchanging plain with horizons of birth and death in the faint distance. We have nothing to speak about. There never was. Words are an unnecessary trouble. Expression is time wasting away. Any communication is just a yelp in the darkness. Ladies. Gentlemen. Listeners. You. I am speaking now but I am saying nothing. I am just making noises, and, as it happens, they are organized in words, but you should not draw meaning from this.

The service for Leland will be lovely. We will throw flowers and weep. He will be buried in the break room, as is the custom. His family will come and moon about the office, as though we have answers. We do not have answers. I am not certain that we even have questions. I have chosen to not be certain of anything at all.

This is Cecil, generally, speaking to you, metaphorically, for Night Vale Community Radio, and I would like to say, in the most nebulous terms possible, and with no real-world implications or insinuations of objective meaning, goodnight, listeners. Goodnight.

PROVERB: A million dollars isn't cool. You know what's cool? A basilisk.

EPISODE 6: "THE DRAWBRIDGE"

SEPTEMBER 1, 2012

My first new car purchase was a 1997 Nissan Altima, greenish-blue. It was a good car. I got about 150,000 miles out of it before the transmission fell completely apart. Fortunately, I had just moved to Queens, so it was easy to give up.

It was in bad shape: scratches on the paint, seats that reeked of smoke, only one working speaker, heat-torn dashboard, bald tires (which were not fun in Massachusetts winters), and ultimately zero hubcaps.

As an aside, not to kick Nissan or Toyota in the butt, but I cannot tell you how many Altimas and Corollas (Toyota's rival sedan) I saw with missing hubcaps. It is not a handsome look. I can only hope both manufacturers have addressed this issue.

Listen, we can blame the carmakers all we want, but replacement hubcaps aren't really that expensive. It's just that I was lazy when it came to car maintenance. I got it at age twenty-one and spent my twenties assuming that things just take care of themselves, because that's what happens when you grow up with a mom. Why wouldn't it just continue that way? Adulthood is just a number.

I look back on those times and deride my younger self and his smoking and sedentary physical lifestyle and lack of basic body/house/car care.

This episode is Steve Carlsberg's first appearance—or at least, Cecil's first mention of him. And Cecil *hates* him. I knew that as we wrote more and more episodes, we would learn that Steve was not as bad as Cecil thought he was. So I used the missing hubcaps thing to 1) suggest that Steve is either a slob or is generally inattentive to cleanliness or appearances, and 2) that Cecil is blowing up something relatively minor into a rage that might be difficult to come down from.

Remind me to tell you about the time I spent an entire year without a front bumper on my car, and then tell me you don't relate to Cecil's frustration with Steve.

—Jeffrey Cranor

Rabbits are not what they seem to be.

WELCOME TO NIGHT VALE.

We've had some power outages reported throughout Night Vale in the last couple hours. If you're experiencing one . . . well then you can't hear me, can you? The Night Vale Municipal Utility Department said that they are still working to determine the cause of the outages, which are roving back and forth across town in a continuous motion, like a great pacing beast. Those whose neighborhoods have been hit by the outages reported the shriek of hawks overhead, and that when the lights came back on, they felt that perhaps they were different people, their memories and identities the same as always, but suddenly felt like costumes that didn't fit exactly, as though it all were actually brand new to them, as though they had been switched out with someone who was exactly like them, as though all that was familiar would ever after be strange.

Keep some flashlights with spare batteries and a childhood photo album by you tonight, just in case.

The revitalization of the Old Town Drawbridge experienced another setback this week as engineers determined that the furniture upholstery used to construct the bridge towers soaks up water and creates an unstable foundation. This week's collapse was the third in as many months. Construction crews have tried building the bridge tower base

supports from corrugated cardboard, nondairy creamer, and ceramic bowls. Nothing has worked. Engineers are asking for help in determining how proper bridge towers are made. If you have any tips, please write them on notebook paper and mail them to Bridge Magic, LLC, PO Box 616. Do not use cursive or long words. Clearly labeled drawings are preferred.

Ladies and gentlemen, it's that time of year again. Time for our annual pledge drive. Sorry to have to do this, but, you know, Night Vale has a lot of community-supported radio, and the thing about community-supported radio—it's supported by listeners like you, as well as Guatemala and some teamsters who are sometimes too generous. Any amount you can give will help us continue our community programming. A dollar or two, or even plasma.

Take WZZZ, our local numbers station, broadcasting from that strange and tall antenna built out back of the abandoned gas station on Oxford Street. Did you know that it broadcasts a monotone female voice, reading out seemingly random numbers, interspersed with chimes twenty-four hours a day, seven days a week? As you can imagine, that kind of work doesn't bring in a lot of money, unless it does. To be honest, here at Night Vale Radio we don't know exactly what that station is for, or what master it is serving. But I do know that it is a vital part of this community and we should pitch in to help it. We welcome your support. Give us a call. We don't have a number. Just whisper "Forsaken Algonquinia" into your phone receiver, and angels (or Facebook or something) will deliver us an appropriate contribution from your bank account.

More on the drawbridge debacle: it was turmoil in city headquarters this morning. Following this latest in a long line of municipal failures, the City Council has come under fire from concerned citizens for wasting taxpayer money on inefficient services that go over budget and over schedule. One critic, who wished to remain anonymous, said, "We don't even have a river or bay in Night Vale. There would never be a boat to necessitate a drawbridge." He continued to . . .

You know what? Forget it. I can tell you right now that that was Steve Carlsberg who said that. And he is such a spoilsport, that Steve. Have you noticed how he never replaces his hubcaps? It's laziness. Pure and simple. Laziness. I just can't let him ruin our town by denying Night Vale a drawbridge when he can't even care for a tan Corolla.

The *Night Vale Daily Journal* has announced that, due to spiraling printing costs, they will be replacing the print edition of the paper with a special new Imagination Edition. Editor Leann Hart explains: "Instead of confining our customers to the outdated modes of ink on paper, we are allowing them to choose the news that interests them by imagining whatever news they want. This will not only save costs, but allow customers to experience the news as a full-color, full-motion experience, taking place in a mental world that is tailored to their needs." Subscription to this edition will be compulsory and automatic, and will cost a mere $60 a month.

This Friday at Night Vale High's Memorial Stadium, it's the annual softball showdown between the Night Vale Fire Department and the

Sheriff's Secret Police. Proceeds from the game will go to support development of nuclear weaponry for a strongly religious Indonesian militia that is looking to overthrow their heretical government, as well as to the Make-A-Wish Foundation. So even if you don't like softball, come on out and support a couple of great causes.

Last year's game ended in a rout, as the Secret Police hit three home runs in the eighth and ninth innings. The fire fighters claimed that there was some foul *play* involved (pun intended, dear listeners!), as their entire bullpen was assassinated in the middle innings with blow darts. Those murders remain unsolved and completely uninvestigated. Our hearts go out to the families of the deceased relief pitchers. Rest in peace.

Should be a fun one! Expect a real revenge-minded fire department to take the field on Friday! Tickets are only $10, or $5 if you bring enriched yellowcake uranium. Black helicopters will be mind-scanning the town on game day, hunting down those who do not attend. The first five hundred fans receive surgically applied working gills.

Notice: There is no digital, staticky hum coming from the Dog Park, Mayor Pamela Winchell announced today. The mayor stressed repeatedly in her ninety-second, impromptu press conference that there is no unbearable, soul-tearing sound that rips at the sinews of your very being coming from the Dog Park.

Mayor Winchell continued with a plea for all Night Vale residents to understand that there could not possibly be a deeply coded message emanating from a small, fenced-in patch of municipal grass and dirt. Citizens are not even supposed to be consciously aware of the Dog Park, so they could not possibly be receiving a menacing and unearthly voice instructing listeners to bring precious metals and toddlers to the Dog Park. Dog Park, she repeated. That could never, ever be real, the mayor shouted, pounding the podium with her bleeding fists. There were no follow-up questions.

And now a word from our sponsors: [*long, soft moan*]

And now, traffic.

There's a stalled car on the northbound on-ramp to the Eastern Expressway just south of Route 800. Commuters should have little delays as highway patrol is fiercely denying this report. In fact, police representatives have just issued a statement claiming that there are no cars anywhere and "what are you doing talking about them, talking silly lies, you silly people. There are no cars. What is this fiction? Oh, please. Do you seriously believe for a second. Wait. Wait! You thought that cars were real?" the highway patrol continued. "Oh, that is rich!"

All other roads seem clear. Expect delays, of course, at the drawbridge construction site, because it is years away from being competently finished.

Here are this week's horoscopes.

Virgo: Go see a movie today. It's a great escape, especially from all of this pollution and dangerous UV radiation. Say, is that mole new?

Libra: Your dreams will be filled with prophetic visions. Write them down. Hopefully there are some lottery numbers or sports scores in there.

Scorpio: Curse you. Curse your family. Curse your children. And your children's children. Vile, vile Scorpio.

Sagittarius: Eat well today. You've earned it. And by *it,* I mean massive food allergies. And by *earned,* I mean acquired. I should proof this stuff before I read it aloud. Let's try that again. You've acquired massive food allergies. Yes, much cleaner. Eat well.

Capricorn: Those were not contact lenses you put in this morning. Best not think about this again.

Aquarius: The white ball will be under the middle shell. Trust the stars. Invest all your money in this lucrative street game.

Pisces: You've won a brand-new car!

Aries: You will feel a haunting sadness about times gone by. Today's smell is wheatgrass and toast.

Taurus: Today is your annual Crime Day. All Tauruses are exempt from laws today.

Gemini: You will meet someone today who will have no effect on your life and who you will immediately forget. Retain hope for a possible future.

Cancer: I've gotta pay my phone bill and also get more milk. That wasn't me talking, that is what the stars say today. Interpret it as you will.

Leo: It's better that I don't read this aloud. Better that you not know. Tell your family you love them.

That has been this week's horoscopes.

Good news for radio-controlled airplane hobbyists! Those unidentifiable black metallic trees that appeared suddenly by the library back in June and caused all airborne objects above thirty feet to catch fire? Well, they've finally been cleared away as a new strip mall and parking lot are being developed. The Night Vale Airport, local bird watchers, and that nice epileptic couple who run the emergency services helicopter are just pleased as pleased can be about this news.

Several petitions, however, have cropped up from neighborhood improvement organizations. Juanita Jefferson, head of one such organization—Night Vale or Nothing—said, "Treeeeeeeeeees. They are us." Jefferson then paused for several minutes without blinking and whispered again, "Treeeeeeeeeees," before collapsing into tears and loud moaning.

Jefferson was then taken by helicopter to Night Vale General Hospital where she is reportedly in stable condition. This morning, Jefferson's lawyer issued a statement saying, "My client fully recognizes the irony of this helicopter trip, but she stands behind her earlier pronouncement: 'Treeeeeees. Treeeees. They are us.' "

Meanwhile, I hear from trustworthy informants that there will be a Pinkberry at the new strip mall. Delicious!

This just in on Drawbridgegate: The City Council said that in response to this week's collapse, they will increase the project budget by $20 million over the next fourteen years, the new timeline for the bridge. Money for these extra expenses will come from school lunch programs, a sixty-five percent hotel tax, and a $276 bridge toll, which will be discounted to $249 with E-ZPass.

And now for a station editorial. Large expensive projects are not uncommon in Night Vale. We are a patient but resilient little city. We have big dreams—sometimes scary, unforgettable dreams that repeat on the same date every year and are shared by every person in town—but we make those big dreams come true. Remember the clock tower? It took eight years and $23 million to build, and despite its invisibility and constant teleportation, it is a lovely structure that keeps impeccable time. It's a classy signature for Night Vale's growing skyline, unlike that hideous sports arena Desert Bluffs built last spring. Desert Bluffs can't do anything right. That's where Steve Carlsberg belongs. God, what a jerk.

And now the weather.

WEATHER: "Aye" by Dio

Apparently the Sheriff's Secret Police agree with me about old Steve Carlsberg, dear listeners. We just received a report from a reliable witness that two days ago Steve was whisked into the back of a windowless van only to reappear earlier this morning wearing thick head bandages and eating Styrofoam shaped like an ice-cream cone.

I want to take this moment to thank all of you out there for all of the generous donations you may or may not be aware that you just made. During this show, we have raised just a hair over $45,000, which includes a $45,000 donation from a certain anonymous world leader. I can't tell you who. Let's just say, *"Muchas gracias, el Presidente! Mano dura, cabeza y corazón."*

Thank you again for your involuntary support of community radio. We couldn't do it without the support of listeners like you, in conjunction with unethical contributions from nefarious organizations. And with that, I leave you alone with your thoughts, folks. Stay tuned next for *Zydeco: Note by Note,* a special two-hour verbal description of what zydeco music sounds like. *Buenas noches,* Night Vale. Goodnight.

PROVERB: Lost? Confused? Lacking direction? Need to find a purpose in your life?

EPISODE 7:
"HISTORY WEEK"

SEPTEMBER 15, 2012

How did Night Vale get to be the way it was? I wanted to explore that and hosting a special History Week broadcast seemed to be a good way to do it. I completely failed to establish any sort of understandable chain of historical events, but look: I dunno, art or something.

We've since expanded on much of the disjointed, alternate-universe chronology presented here, most notably in episode 67, "[Best Of?]," but there is no key that will suddenly make it function as a logical, real-world history. It is a history like Night Vale is a town: weird, desert bound, dreamlike, full of conspiracy and paradox.

Does the date of original settlement even make sense with the date of actual human settlement of America? I didn't look it up then and I'm not going to look it up now.

This episode features the first reference to immortal screen legend Lee Marvin, who would end up having his own rich mythology in the *Night Vale* world.

We also get some glimpses of Night Vale's terrible future. If we're still doing this show in 2021 (which would be around episode 201), we will need to remember that according to episode 7, there will be no Night Vale mayor anymore. Someone please remind us when we get to that point, okay? And if we're still doing this show in 2052, then good for us. We'll be enjoying our old age and please don't come bothering us about a paragraph we wrote forty years earlier.

The episode ends with a reminder that history is not just made up of the things we remember a hundred years later, but all the little things we forget a week after they happen. History is us squinting into the past, mistaking millions of tiny vibrations in all directions for unified, unidirectional movements by entire civilizations.

—Joseph Fink

It is almost complete. It is almost complete. At last.

WELCOME TO NIGHT VALE.

Hello there. As you well know, faithful listeners, it is Night Vale history week, in which we all learn a bit about what made our bustling little town what it is. Or, as the official motto released by the City Council goes: "Poke about in the black recesses of the past until it devours our fragile present."

In the interest of civic participation, Night Vale Community Radio will be pitching in with short lessons about some points of interest from our town's history. Starting with:

4000 BC: Archaeologists believe this is the earliest date of human settlement in Night Vale. Little remains of these ancient inhabitants, except a few cave paintings of their towns and their hunting practices, and of the dark shapes that would watch them in the distance. Inhuman, shimmering shapes that never came closer or farther away, but whose presence could be felt even with eyes shut tight, huddled in fur and the company of another human's naked skin. Or so I'm extrapolating from the evidence. The cave paintings mainly resemble smudges now, after their original discoverer attempted to power-wash them off the wall because he, on religious grounds, did not believe in the past.

And now, the news.

The Night Vale Tourism Board asks that whoever is telepathically assaulting the tourists please stop.

According to the NVTB executive director Madeline LaFleur, there were two separate incidents in one week of entire tour buses suddenly shrieking in unbridled terror and trying to blind themselves using rolled up Visitable Night Vale brochures, all to the utter confusion of the bus drivers. LaFleur added: "We just had those brochures printed."

LaFleur claims that tourism accounts for tens of thousands of dollars annually for Night Vale, and the town prides itself on hospitality. She said if good-hearted families travel to Night Vale only to find their subconsciouses besieged with unforgettable revelations, horrors buried so deep as to be completely indescribable, revealing wholly unbearable new truths, then we certainly can't expect these people to return, let alone leave good Yelp ratings for local businesses.

The city is asking residents for help in determining who, or what, is causing these psychological infractions. The tourism board is offering puppies as a reward for information on this case. Or even if you don't have information, the city asks that you come get a puppy or two anyway. Seriously, downtown municipal offices are overrun with them. In the trees, walls, carpetry. The exterminators are completely stymied by this infestation. Please help.

It has been several weeks since anyone in Night Vale has seen the Apache Tracker, that white guy who wears the inaccurate and horribly offensive Indian headdress everywhere. He has not been seen since he began investigating the great screaming heard at the post office, and the words written in blood inside. Also, the entire structure of his house has vanished, and the lot where it had stood is now a bucolic meadow that neighborhood kids will not ever enter for reasons even they are unable to explain. I think I speak for everyone in the community when I say good riddance to that local embarrassment. He made the whole town look ignorant and racist.

And now, let us continue with our Night Vale history week special feature.

The year 1745: The first white men arrive in Night Vale, which was not Night Vale then but was rather just another part of a large and featureless desert. I think we all can agree though, that even as large and featureless as the desert was, the part that would eventually become Desert Bluffs was still probably awful and drab in comparison to our part. In any case, the story goes that a party of explorers came to the area that would be Night Vale, looked around, and immediately left to go find somewhere with more water and maybe some trees. Then another three parties of explorers did the same thing. Then finally one party of explorers all looked at each other, shrugged, and plopped down their stuff. And thus was a proud city born.

And now, traffic.

Crews from the Department of Public Safety will be repainting highway lane markers this week. The common white dashes and double yellow lane dividers will be replaced with colorful ceramic mosaics depicting disgruntled South American workers rising en masse against an abusive capitalist hegemony. The protective steel barriers along curves in the road will be taken down to make room for some really lovely and provocative butcher-paper silhouettes of slavery-era self-mutilation, reflective of centuries of slow genocide and dehumanization by Western imperialists, designed by contemporary art darling Kara Walker.

Also, Exits 15 to 17 along Route 800 will be closed for the next two Saturdays because of the biennial Lee Marvin Film Retrospective.

So, please watch for working crews this weekend. Lower your speed and don't forget to tip the DPS shift leaders. Twenty percent of your current mileage is standard. Lack of tipping is the leading cause of sinkholes in the US.

The year 1824: The first meeting of the Town Elder Council, predecessor to the City Council. Picture them, crimson robes and soft-meat crowns, as was traditional at the time, setting the groundwork for the splendor of today's Night Vale. A number of elements of our modern civic process were invented in that single three-hour meeting, including the City Council membership (since unchanged), the lovably byzantine tax system (as well as the system of brutal penalties for mistakes), and the official town song, chant, and moan. All records of this

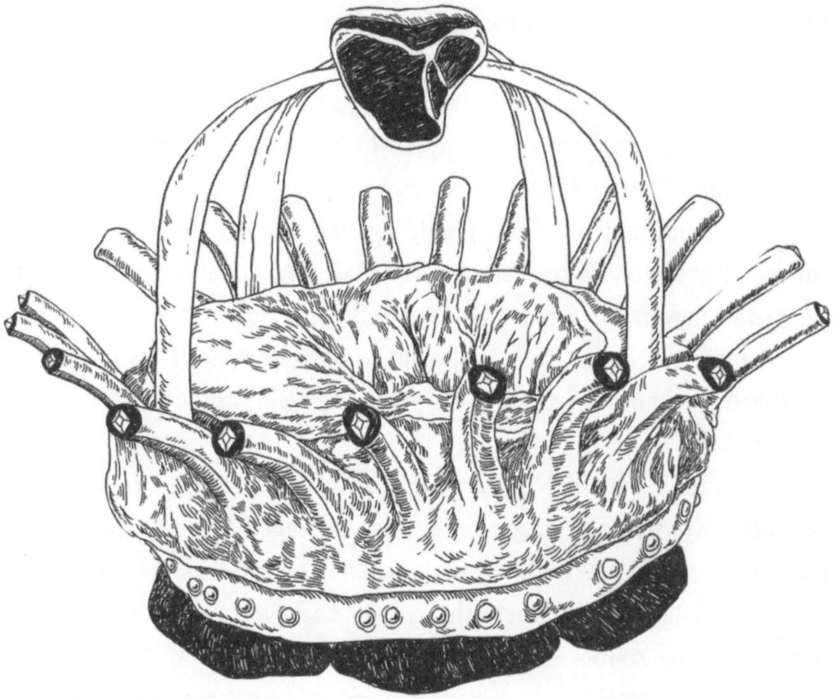

meeting were destroyed, and, according to a note being passed to me just now, I am to report to city hall for reeducation effective tomorrow morning. Oh dear.

The results of a recent survey of Night Vale residents came to light this week. The study found widespread dissatisfaction with our town's public library, and, when considering the facts, it's easy to see why. The public computers for Internet use are outdated and slow. The lending period of fourteen days is not nearly long enough to read lengthier books, given the busy schedules of all our lives. The fatality rate is also well above the national average for public libraries. The library bloodstone circle does not appear to have seen any maintenance or cleaning in some time. There are reports of a faceless specter moving about the biographies section, picking off lone browsers one by one. And that biographies section, by the way, is far too small and has been oddly curated, containing thirty-three copies of the official biography of Helen Hunt and no other books. From top to bottom, the public library is a disgrace to our fair city, and I can only hope our City Council does something about that soon, or I may find myself hoping that the faceless specter puts the library to the same mysterious, violent end as its many victims.

Night Vale High won the grudge match against the Desert Bluffs Vultures last night. Two-headed quarterback Michael Sandero credits the win to help from angels. The angels have made an adamant denial of any involvement whatsoever in the game. The school district ethics committee has announced that they will look into any possible angelic interference.

Speaking of which, Night Vale High School is adding metal detectors, and parents and students alike are outraged. Several parents we talked to said that NVHS students have long been recipients of shadow government–issued Uzis and rifles, as well as Tasers and armor-piercing munitions. The school board's decision to put up metal detectors, according to parents, impinges on the clandestine operation's rights as a vast underground conspiracy of giant mega corporations and corrupt world leaders to bear arms via teenage paramilitary proxies.

The school board countered that studies indicate that weapons distract from educators' ability to educate, and that students who bring firearms to classrooms are more likely to use firearms than students without firearms. The school board says that school shootings can only get in the way of a quality education.

Well, at risk of becoming too much a part of this story, dear listeners, might I say that the Night Vale School District is overstepping its bounds by telling us whether or not our children can be armed by undercover militants? Should it be a school's job to say, "No, child, you cannot have grenades or assault rifles in the classroom?" I think not.

Beginning November 1, all students at NVHS will enter through metal detectors. Any firearms or weaponry found will be confiscated and held in the counselor's office until after school, when the students can pick them up again.

Seriously, listeners, what's next? Removing the line "Praise the beams; Praise o ye knowing beams that guide our lives, our hearts, our souls. Praise o highest to ye all-powerful beams!" from the Pledge of Allegiance?

Let's return to another key moment in Night Vale history.

The year 1943: As part of the war effort, Night Vale citizens dedicated themselves to chanting. The young, the old, men and women alike, gathered around their bloodstones and chanted for the victory of the United States. While some credit must be given to the strategic planning of US Command, and to the brave fighting of American soldiers, most reputable scholars believe that Night Vale's chanting was the deciding factor in America's eventual victory over the Axis powers. The City Council erected a seven-story monument in Grove Park saying so in large neon letters, until a federal lawsuit forced them to take it down.

And now for a word from our sponsors. That word is *carp*.

This next installment in our exploration of Night Vale's storied past takes place in the future.

The year 2052: The Scion of the Dark Order will descend, realize he mistimed the prophecy, and re-ascend. The seventh siege of the Great Night Vale Temple will rage on. The plague of buzzing boils will kill thousands, and annoy thousands more with its buzzing. The City Council will reveal its true form and eat half of Night Vale's population. Approval ratings for the mayor will hover in the low forties, which will be surprising, as there will have been no mayor for over thirty years.

And now, the weather.

WEATHER: "Despite What You've Been Told" by Two Gallants

The Night Vale Business Association announced today that the Night Vale Harbor and Waterfront Recreation Area was not actually something that ever existed in reality but was instead a shared hallucination of the entire town's population. As such, they are proud to declare that they have never suffered any sort of disastrous business failure, and the reportedly massive amounts of money lost on building waterfront facilities in a desert are fabrications of our collective consciousness. They recommend consulting your dream interpretation manuals to determine exactly what this Night Vale Harbor vision could mean. They also said that if you happen to stumble on the waterfront buildings out in the desert exactly where you remembered them, and they seem completely real, standing as vacant and useless as the day they were built, that's because you are still hallucinating and should seek medical treatment immediately or have a member of the City Council howl at you if you are of the olden faith and do not believe in modern medicine.

For our final story in this week's featured look into the history of Night Vale, let's look at the very recent past.

Yesterday: I had cereal for breakfast, a sandwich for lunch, steak for dinner. Cars were driven. Cars were not driven. The sun gave a great shout of light and then, after several hours of thought, quietly retracted the statement. Old Woman Josie dug up a box in a shady corner of her yard, and carried it, cradled in her arms like a baby or a delicate explosive, to another part of her yard where she buried it again. An unknown person did something that no one else saw, the nature and extent of which is impossible to determine, and the result of which will be lost in the chaotic chain of causation and consequence that is history.

But most importantly: all of us, all of us here in Night Vale, in America, in the world, in the secret orbital bases, all of us got through another day. We passed the time, from one end of twelve to the other, without stopping once. Well done, us. Good job, people who experience time. Time experiencers, good job.

And, from this moment in history, the one that's happening right now, goodnight.

PROVERB: It must be 3:23 p.m. somewhere. Maybe space?

EPISODE 8: "THE LIGHTS IN RADON CANYON"

OCTOBER 1, 2012

SCATTERSHOOTING HERE:

1. Shirley Jackson "Lottery" shout-out in paragraph 1.
2. The idea for the Glow Cloud joining the school board came from Twitter. Back then, we had fewer than five hundred listeners, so we interacted with anyone who had anything to say at all about what we were doing. So thumbs-up to you, people making weird short jokes online!
3. Before Night Vale Fan Art became an enormous thing, and mostly dominated by three-eyed Cecil and handsome lab coat–wearing Carlos, we would get drawings of much weirder aspects of our show. This episode kicked off a tiny onslaught of photos of sandwiches with HARLOT printed across them.
4. Somehow Coach al-Mujaheed wanders off into the "woods." This is the desert. I definitely wrote this because: 1) I don't know what a desert is and 2) I write most of the sports things.
5. Originally I wrote this entire Subway ad in German, but it was too difficult to get the grammar/syntax/tone right given that I only took four semesters of the language twelve years ago, and it's just not funny at all if you are of the not-

knowing-German demographic, which seems to be the majority of our listenership.

6. *The Wire* is a pretty good show. Have you seen *The Wire*?
7. I grew up listening to a lot of rock and country from the 1970s. My stepsister Marsha was obsessed with *The Wall*, and while I'm not much of a Pink Floyd listener myself, I certainly respect their contributions to music. As a town out of time but filled with so many strange rules and residents, the idea that they would be obsessed with Floyd shows and lasers and all that seemed fitting. Syd Barrett's ghost is here, and this short era of modern rock will never fully leave them.
8. Danny Schmidt's song "This Too Shall Pass" is my favorite weather we've had on the show. This being a book, you can't hear it, but it's the song Joseph picked for the weather segment, and it's lovely. Later I would use his song "Esmee by the River" (from the same album, *Parables & Primes*) in a short performance-art piece that involved me eating vegetable shortening and having people spit milk and flour into my mouth, mama-bird style. I'm still not sure I ever explained this last part to Danny very well.

—Jeffrey Cranor

Silence is golden. Words are vibrations.
Thoughts are magic.

WELCOME TO NIGHT VALE.

Next Saturday is the big lottery drawing, listeners, right out in front of city hall, and your community radio station has put together a few helpful tips for winning.

The lottery is, of course, mandatory, but how can *you* get the best odds for drawing a blank white paper and not one of the purple pieces that means you'll be ceremoniously disemboweled and eaten by the wolves at the Night Vale Petting Zoo and Makeshift Carnival? I know to some of you young people this lottery seems like a barbarous, outdated tradition, but, if not for municipally planned citizen sacrifice each quarter, how else would we find satisfactory meats to feed those sad, scrawny animals?

So, here now are the three *I*s of playing the lottery:

"I" 1: Identify. Learn to sense colors. Purple has a grittier emotional aura than white.

"I" 2: Ignite. Set fire to your home. While it's not true that wolves refuse to eat arsonists, it's a scientific fact that they're unable to detect the presence of one.

"I" 3: Imitate. If you happen to draw a purple piece, impersonate someone who drew a white piece. You might be mistaken for a person who is colorblind. This, of course, will lead to months of painful color reeducation at city hall, but in most cultures that's better than being eaten by wolves.

Also, make sure to visit the Food Truck Festival, which will be downtown as part of the lottery festivities. Popular truck treats include Korean BBQ, vegetarian chili, and veal ice cream.

Carlos, this station's favorite scientist (no offense to Dr. Dubinsky in the Night Vale Community College Chemistry Department), dropped by our broadcast location earlier this morning for a little chat. Sadly, dinner or weekend plans were not among the topics. However, Carlos did request that we ask listeners for anyone who saw a series of bright, colorful flickers coming from Radon Canyon this past weekend. These flickers would have also been accompanied by unintelligible noises, possibly some form of coded communication or signal jamming technique. Carlos suggested that there could be some very sinister forces at work here. He declined to be interviewed live, claiming only that he was scared for us. Scared for all of us in our strange town. Then he drove away quickly in his economical but attractively sporty hybrid coupé.

If anyone out there knows anything about these otherworldly lights and sounds, please contact us immediately.

Night Vale school superintendent Nick Ford announced today that the Glow Cloud has joined the school board.

The Glow Cloud passed over the entirety of Night Vale several weeks ago, dropping small and large animal carcasses, controlling our thoughts and tertiary muscle groups, and erasing every last recording device. We're still unsure the Glow Cloud even existed, as no one remembers it or has any digital record of it. If not for a few intrepid citizens who used old-fashioned pens and pencils to record the event in their diaries, we would have no remaining knowledge of that day.

I, of course, can only thank those journal writers anonymously here on the air, as the Night Vale City Council long ago banned writing utensils, along with margarita glasses and barcode scanners, and I don't want to get my fellow reporters in any trouble with the Sheriff's Secret Police.

According to Superintendent Ford, the Glow Cloud's visit on that nearly forgotten day was simply an effort to find a nice neighborhood with good schools to raise a child.

Now, what kind of progeny a powerful, formless cloud of noxious nightmares and spiritual destruction might produce, I dare not even speculate. But I do know one thing: that little cloud is going to get one heck of an education in the Night Vale School District.

And isn't it heartening to hear that the little puff of despair's father (or . . . mother?) will serve on the school board?

I mean, no matter how good the school, a student can only get out as much as the parents put in. We should *all* take such an impactful role in our children's scholastic lives. Especially you, Steve Carlsberg, you don't do anything except bring unacceptably dry scones to PTA meetings and take grammatically disastrous minutes on your shifts as meeting secretary. Get it together, Steve.

Superintendent Ford offered the following statement of support for the newest school board member: "All Hail! All kneel for the Glow Cloud! Sacrifice! Pestilence! Sores! All Hail the Glow Cloud!"

And now, traffic.

This morning I saw a running man. He passed by my home, panting, limping, running desperate. I tried to stop him but he would not meet my eye. This noontime I saw a running man. He was coming down from the mountain holding a bag, his knees were bloody, and face covered in tears. This evening I saw a running man. He was leaving town, legs pumping like a terrified heart. I think he was missing a hand. Is it that he wouldn't meet my eye, or that he had no eyes? Now I wish I could remember. There are many things I wish I could remember. This has been traffic.

New billboards have appeared all over town, bearing the image of a turkey sandwich and the single word HARLOT in large block letters. These billboards have caused some confusion, both due to their ambiguous message, and to the fact that the entire structure of the billboards materialized overnight in places billboards are not usually

constructed, such as the living rooms of local homes, the middle of busy thoroughfares (causing multiple car accidents), and, in one case, directly through a living dog, who has not appeared harmed by the addition to his body and has carried the entire billboard around town while going about his usual canine business. The Department of Health and Human Services recently claimed responsibility for the billboards, saying that they were part of a campaign to promote nutrition and healthy living among children. The original draft of the release also mentioned something about an offering to a long-dead god, but this was altered to "Fun, active lifestyles are important for kids of all ages" in a subsequent addendum.

We're receiving several phone calls from listeners and from the Parks Department that those flickering lights and unintelligible noises we reported on earlier were coming from the Pink Floyd Multimedia Laser Spectacular.

I contacted Carlos about this, and he said that the situation is even worse than he imagined. He, again, did not mention weekend plans.

A sports scandal has shook our quiet little town. The Night Vale Scorpions have faced multiple allegations of possible game tampering this football season. Representatives for the Desert Bluffs School District, speaking in unpleasant and high-pitched voices indicative of weakness of will and character, complained to the Regional Football and Traffic Code Authority that Night Vale quarterback Michael Sandero's recently grown second head counts as a twelfth man on the field, thus invalidating the wins brought on by his also recently acquired superhuman agility and strength. The RFTCA said that they would look into these allegations with the utmost seriousness, along with their concurrent investigation into whether Night Vale's "Invisible Crosswalk" policy is actually a desperate bid to save town funds at the cost of pedestrian lives.

Meanwhile, the school board is due to announce its decision in their ongoing hearings as to whether appealing to angels for a win constitutes illegal game tampering. Several angels agreed to testify at the hearings; however, their testimonials were cut short when it became apparent that the hearings were actually elaborate traps set up by the City Council to finally capture the angels, whom the council does not recognize as actually existing. Fortunately, the angels easily escaped from their cages in a blaze of heavenly light, presumably returning to Old Woman Josie's house, out near the car lot, which has become something of an informal shelter for local angels.

When asked about the controversy over his team's winning record, Coach Nazr al-Mujaheed said, "Our boys are good boys. They're good boys at football. We win 'em, with the boys, the football." He then smiled vacantly, waved at no one, and wandered off in the direction of the woods. More on this story as it develops.

And now a word from our sponsor.

Step in to your nearest Subway restaurant today and try their new six-inch mashed potato sub. Top it with a delicious assortment of fresh vegetables, like French fries and Nutella. They'll even toast or poach it for you.

There are several Subway locations in Night Vale, all easily accessible through witchcraft and chanting.

And between now and November 30, buy nine reverse colonics and get a free forty-ounce soda or freshly baked tobacco cookie.

Subway: Devour your own empty heart.

Exciting news about the abandoned mine shaft outside of town where people who vote incorrectly are taken by the Secret Police: HBO On-Demand will be made available to prisoners during their indefinite detention. All your favorite shows, such as *The Wire, Sex and the City,* and even new hits like *Game of Thrones* will be available in every cell. Additionally, the Secret Police announced they will be randomly executing one prisoner a day until all incorrect votes are corrected.

This just in: We're receiving word from the City Council that there was absolutely *not* a Pink Floyd Multimedia Laser Spectacular this weekend at Radon Canyon. That there never was a Pink Floyd Multimedia Laser Spectacular, ever, near Night Vale. Pink Floyd is not even a thing, said the council in a very stern, but quiet statement just received by me, here, via phone. The council, and this is strange, the entire council—not just a representative of the council—the entire council issued this statement, all speaking in unison, just now, over the phone, that Night Vale citizens are prohibited from discussing any lights or sounds coming from Radon Canyon this past weekend and that they should just stop remembering Pink Floyd shows all together.

The council reiterated that there is no way that they are *huge* Floyd fans privately using public funds on a laser-powered séance to talk hard-rockin' classic jams with the ghost of original front man Syd Barrett, and that Syd wouldn't even say anything juicy anyway, because he is such a gentleman and an artist. This did not happen at all.

So, listeners, we urge you to look away from Radon Canyon. Avert your eyes, ears, and memories from that which is no longer allowed you. Comfort and distract yourselves with dense food and television programming. As the old adage goes: *"A life of pain is the pain of life and you can never escape it... only hope it hides, unknown, in a drawer like a poisonous spider and never comes out again even though it probably will in unexpected and horrific fashion, scarring you from being able to comfortably conduct even the most mundane, quotidian tasks."* Or, at least, that's how my grandparents always phrased it.

And now the weather.

WEATHER: "This Too Shall Pass" by Danny Schmidt

Teddy Williams, over at the Desert Flower Bowling Alley and Arcade Fun Complex, has an update on the doorway into that vast underground city he found in the pin retrieval area of lane five. He says that every window of the city is now glowing both day and night, and he heard the shouts and footsteps of what sounded like an army marching upwards toward the world above. He also said that, given that nothing really matters now, bowling is half off and each game comes with a free basket of wings. Mmm. Nothing like those Desert Flower wings.

Let me leave you with this, dear listeners. We lead frantic lives, filled with needs and responsibilities but completely devoid of any actual purpose. I say, let's try to enjoy the simple things. Life should be like a basket of chicken wings: salty, full of fat and vinegar, and surrounded by celery you'll never actually eat, even when you're greedily sopping up the last viscous streaks of buffalo sauce from the wax paper with your spit-stained index finger. Yes, that is as life should be, Night Vale.

Stay tuned next for a special live broadcast of the Night Vale Symphony Orchestra performing Eugene O'Neill's classic play *The Iceman Cometh*. It is a good night, listeners. Goodnight.

PROVERB: We are living in an immaterial world, a ghost world, and I am an immaterial girl—a ghost.

EPISODE 9: "PYRAMID"

OCTOBER 15, 2012

CONTRIBUTOR: REGIS LACHER

THIS EPISODE MARKS THE FIRST COLLABORATION WITH AN OUTSIDE WRITER. Unlike later episodes, where guest writers would cowrite the main story line and eventually entire scripts, this was a blind collaboration experiment, where our guest writer wrote based on a vague prompt and then I built a story around what he had written.

The messages from the pyramid were written by our Twitter friend Regis Lacher. I've known Regis for years on the Internet on various sites and under various usernames. He, at the time, had a Twitter avatar of a pyramid and specialized in making cryptic all-cap pronouncements. Essentially, we asked him to imagine that his Twitter pyramid had landed in Night Vale and began doing its thing there. We edited his messages a bit for length, but for the most part kept exactly what he sent us.

The beauty of having a completely independent podcast with only two people overseeing the writing is that we can do things like invite a friend to write weird messages and then put those messages in a loose framework of a story primarily based on the fact that I personally like to eat cereal at night.

This isn't quite a TED Talk yet, but I'm getting it there.

—Joseph Fink

Weird at last. Weird at last. God Almighty, weird at last.

WELCOME TO NIGHT VALE.

The Sheriff's Secret Police are asking the public's help in catching a dangerous fugitive on the loose in the greater Night Vale area. They say he is armed and should be approached with extreme caution. For everyone's protection, they are keeping the name and description of the fugitive secret, but indicate that all strangers should be mistrusted and avoided, as well as friends and loved ones because how well do you know those people anyway? Are you aware of their location every second of every day? Who among us does not have secrets? The fugitive is wanted dead or alive, and vigilante justice is, as always, highly encouraged.

Our top story today: a large pyramid has appeared in the center of the Beatrix Lohman Memorial Meditation Zone, destroying over half of the zone's state-of-the-art meditation equipment and paraphernalia. Experts have been contacted as to what could cause sudden pyramid existence; however, as it turns out, there are no experts in pyramid materialization, and the town's other experts offered up merely shrugs, followed by panicked conjectures, and, finally, screams and moans, all of which fell uselessly upon the City Council's merciless ears.

The pyramid has been described as a kind of triangle shape, only three-dimensional. It has made no movement despite repeated Taserings by the Sheriff's Secret Police.

Many suspect that this may be a publicity stunt pulled by our own local cereal company Flakey O's, who are launching their new line of nighttime-only cereals next month. An angry mob has formed outside of the cereal factory just in case.

Telly. You remember, the deceitful barber with a shriveled soul who, just a few weeks ago cut perfect scientist Carlos's perfect beautiful hair very short, so very, very short, thus depriving our community of our only remaining pleasure. Well, Telly was seen recently wandering the sand wastes, howling at the sky, and holding up Carlos's shorn locks, as though begging God to reverse the crime he has done. Reports indicate that his skin was blistering, that his eyes were bleary, and that he was recently seen trying to give a cactus a haircut, whispering and cooing into what he seemed to think was its ear. Listeners, I am not one to stand aside harshly and say that a man deserves the punishment that comes to him, but I also am not sorry to see Telly in this state, given his crime. In any case, if your cactus is in need of a haircut, try Telly, out wandering the sand wastes.

Ladies and gentlemen, I must say that I am not a cat person, but I have really grown to love Khoshekh, the stray cat that has made his home here at the radio station. I discovered Khoshekh several weeks ago hovering in a fixed location in the men's bathroom, and he's remained there since. The men at the station, of course, have taken to keeping the sink at a light trickle so he can get water, and we even take turns buying Science Diet Low Calorie Cat Food (turns out little Khoshekh is getting a bit chubby since he can't actually exercise in his unmovable, levitating state).

And thanks to our new intern, Brad, we've finally solved the litter problem. Brad is very excellent at both carpentry and dark magic, so he rigged us up a fine-looking litter box that our floating feline friend can reach. Oh he's just adorable, that cat. As a lifelong dog lover, I've really turned the corner. Khoshekh is wonderful. I know several others here at the station that feel the same way. After meeting Khoshekh, McKayla, who works in sales, put her three-year-old Weimaraner to sleep and then adopted six tabby kittens. She's that much of a convert! Make sure to take some cute videos, McKayla!

And for others of you interested in getting a new cat, the Night Vale SPCA strongly recommends that you have your cat spayed or neutered, bring them in for their shots, and, once the cat reaches eighteen months, begin using the little beast to harvest human organs for those "just in case" moments. The SPCA has several one sheets on preventing heartworms and using pets to grow small "replacement" organs.

To get your copy, go online or simply make up your own informative facts!

An update on the pyramid reported on earlier: Word is in that the pyramid has spoken. It is broadcasting on low-wave frequencies a repeated message. The message is the following:

> I WILL PLACE WITHIN SOME OF YOU QUESTIONS. WITHIN OTHERS, I WILL PLACE ANSWERS.
>
> THESE QUESTIONS AND THESE ANSWERS WILL NOT ALWAYS ALIGN. THE QUESTIONS I PROVIDE MAY HAVE NO ANSWERS, AND THE ANSWERS I PROVIDE MAY HAVE NO QUESTIONS.
>
> I WILL STUDY THE EFFECTS OF THESE QUESTIONS AND THESE ANSWERS.
>
> SOME OF YOU WILL HURT OTHERS AND OTHERS WILL HEAL.
>
> GROW MY SEEDS INSIDE YOU AND LET THEM FLOWER.

The Flakey O's marketing department must be complimented for the best use of viral marketing in Night Vale since Stan's Pawnshop released a virulent strain of Ebola back in '98, and, as a communicator by trade, I applaud their ingenuity.

The Sheriff's Secret Police has responded with surface-to-surface missiles, which they say will "silence the dark heart of the beast." So far, they have not so much as created a smudge on the pyramid's broad, shiny surface.

Home handymen. Fix-it vixens. Ladies and gentlemen who love to get their hands dirty. Let's talk about home repair. Certain jobs are fine for the amateur, and certain others should be left to the professionals. Leaky sinks, sticky windows, minor exorcisms, and bleeding doors . . . all these are the kind of quick fixes that a toolbox and a quick search on the Internet should allow you to take care of. On the other hand, structural damage, major remodeling, seeping darkness, major exorcisms, roof boils, and lawn care . . . these are all the kind of work that should not be attempted by anyone without years of expertise and a valid Hammer License from the City Council. Finding the right professional for the job is easy. Just look in the yellow pages, or head down to the squatter shacks by the edge of the sand wastes and ask around among the homeless.

And now a public service announcement from the Night Vale medical community.

Being in the desert, we get a lot of sun, and doctors are encouraging Night Vale citizens to do regular skin checks. You may think that freckle or mole is harmless, but you never know when it will grow into something much worse.

Surgeons at Night Vale General Hospital are noting an uptick in dermatological growths related to sun exposure. Doctors describe these growths as fifteen-inch spiraled horns. The horns mostly protrude from the lower back or knees. Unchecked, these horns can develop a glistening shine, small leather saddles, and bright red lips on the very tip.

So check your skin at least once a week in the mirror. Dermatologists recommend a three-step process:

1. Search meticulously for fifteen-inch horns protruding from your body. Don't overlook anything.
2. If you find any suspicious growths, mark them with a chalk pentagon.

3. Gently remove the affected skin area with a sterilized razor blade (or similarly clean crafting blade). If you are not one of the fifty-three percent of our community that was born without pain-sensing nerves, you should first consult your primary care electrolysist for tips on how to numb yourself to the nigh unbearable pain of existence.

The Department of Public Safety announced that all street signs in Night Vale will be replaced with traffic cops wielding semaphore flags. Drivers will be required to learn this physically expressive maritime alphabet.

This decision is not without its controversy, as the existing street signs are entirely in Braille. One critic, Paul Birmingham, says removing these signs will deflate the earth. As a member of the Air-filled Earth Society, Paul believes the earth is a precariously inflated orb that could pop or sag at any moment. "We've got to stop teaching all this religious propaganda in our schools and start teaching real science," Paul shouted from his lean-to behind the library.

I have to admit, listeners, he makes a valid point.

And now, a word from our sponsor. Today's program is brought to you by Audible.com, your online source for recorded books.

There are thousands of great titles at Audible.com that you can download to your computer or portable device and listen to on the go. I use Audible to catch up on bestselling titles like *The Help* and *VangoNotes for Technical Communication, 11/e.*

I'm on their website right now, and I'm typing in a search for "Dog Park," because I was thinking about this town's beautiful new fixture and how I will never, ever take my dog there. Let's see what Audible comes up with. Ah, it's a flashing black and red screen that says "Thought Crime" in all caps. And below that a little animation of two digging workers: "Under construction." That's adorable!

So check out Audible.com. New Audible members can get one free audiobook just by smudging their computer monitors with baby's blood and humming the Spanish translation of "The Battle Hymn of the Republic." Audible.com: You can't burn what you can't even touch.

Update on the pyramid situation: Flakey O's board of directors are vigorously denying, some of them at gun point, that they have any part in the pyramid that is stubbornly continuing to exist in our town.

They are sneaky ones. I hope the new line of cereal turns out to be worth the hype.

Meanwhile the pyramid itself has altered its broadcast, sending out a second message, which is as follows:

> EVERYTHING YOU DO MATTERS EXCEPT YOUR LIFE. DEATH WILL BE THE LAST ACTION YOU UNDERTAKE.
>
> I DO NOT LIVE BUT I EXIST. WHAT IS MY PURPOSE? I WILL NOT TELL YOU.
>
> ONE DAY, YOU WILL DISCOVER YOUR PURPOSE, AND THEN YOU WILL TELL NO ONE.
>
> AND THEN YOU WILL DIE.

I'm not too good at this viral marketing thing, so I can't see all the codes and hidden web addresses that I'm sure are all through that message. I'll leave that to all the dedicated amateurs out in the listening world.

Sheriff's Secret Police are now attempting to charge the pyramid with resisting arrest, on the grounds that they couldn't figure out how to arrest it. More as the story develops. In the meantime, let's go to the weather.

WEATHER: "Last Song" by Jason Webley

Well, listeners, it seems the pyramid has disappeared as mysteriously and suddenly as it arrived. Too late, I'm afraid, for the Flakey O's board of directors, who have all been taken to the abandoned mine shaft outside of town for processing by the City Council.

The Sheriff's Secret Police are declaring victory in their standoff against the pyramid, because, they say, it's about time they won something.

Meanwhile, the pyramid has left behind a much tinier pyramid, a mere souvenir of its looming, inscrutable mass. This tiny pyramid is broadcasting one final message, a farewell from the geometric shape that stole our hearts. So, let us wrap up our show today with its words:

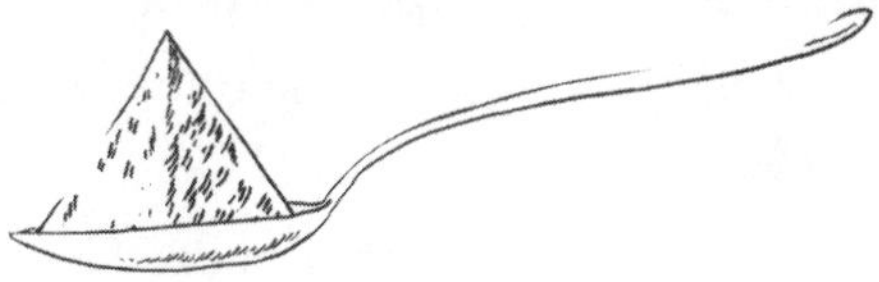

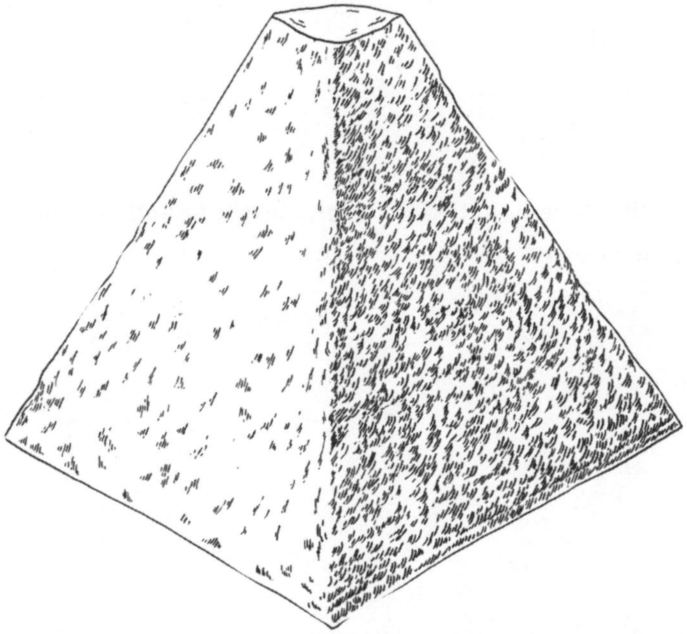

SOMEWHERE THERE IS A MAP. AND ON THAT MAP IS EARTH. AND ATTACHED TO EARTH IS AN ARROW THAT SAYS YOUR NAME AND LISTS YOUR LIFE SPAN.

SOME OF YOU DIE STANDING, OTHERS SITTING. MANY OF YOU DIE IN CARS.

I CAN NEVER DIE. IT IS DIFFICULT FOR ME TO UNDERSTAND THE CONCEPT THAT I AM ATTEMPTING TO CONVEY.

I CANNOT SHOW YOU THIS VISION BUT YOU MAY IMAGINE IT. STEP FORWARD AND TELL SOMEONE OF IT, PLEASE.

You heard it here, folks. Tell people. Tell people about Flakey O's new line of cereals for nighttime only. Do it in memory of its board of directors.

Stay tuned now for an hour of dead air with the occasional hiss and crackle.

Speaking of the nighttime, I truly hope you have a good one, Night Vale. Goodnight.

PROVERB: "Nice bolo tie" is the greatest compliment a person can ever receive.

EPISODE 10:
"FERAL DOGS"
NOVEMBER 1, 2012

I DELIBERATELY COMBINED ONE OF MY FAVORITE MOVIE MOMENTS WITH one of my least favorite.

First off, I think I have seen *Clash of the Titans* (1981) more than any other film. I haven't seen it in more than twenty-five years, so do with that as you will. But I love the two-headed dog, Cerberus.

I love *all* of Ray Harryhausen's Dynamation creatures, but *Clash of the Titans* was on cable constantly in the early and mid-'80s, so it is my one true cinematic love.

So Cerberus: pretty cool. Two-headed killer dog. For this episode of *Night Vale,* I made the leader of the feral dogs a three-headed dog, so like, one better than Cerberus?

Now for one of my least favorite movie moments: that plastic bag from *American Beauty.* I don't particularly enjoy this film. I'm not telling you not to like it. It's simply not for me. But there's that whole fluttering bag video and accompanying monologue on the nature of art and beauty, and I thought I'd use that image here.

When Mayor Winchell reveals the dogs were merely plastic bags caught in the wind, it seemed the perfect idiotic cover for a city in careful public denial.

Other notes about this episode:

- Our friends Eevin and Carl own a dog named Fanny Brice, so in my mind, while "Fanny Brice Approximation syndrome" is a good joke, it's even better if you've met their dog.
- Joseph wrote the spider bit in this episode and it made me drop the script and concentrate on calm breathing.
- Dark Owl Records was named after Night Owl Records in Easthampton, Massachusetts. It was owned by my friends Jen and Mark. The store is no longer in business, but it was a great store. One time I bought a Dar Williams album there (among other things), and Mark teasingly called me a "folkie." This comment probably contributed to the creation of Dark Owl owner and music snob Michelle Nguyen (whose first appearance isn't until episode 37).
- Try ending all your conversations with "This has been Health Tips." It really does keep people on their toes.
- I would totally listen to Dr. Brandon's show.

—Jeffrey Cranor

Regret nothing, until it is too late. Then regret everything.

WELCOME TO NIGHT VALE.

Our top story today: a roving pack of feral dogs has been terrorizing Night Vale for the past several hours. The dogs have been described as mostly mutts, possibly pit bull mixes. Witnesses say their apparent leader is the three-headed one wearing dozens of decorative service medals and chevrons.

Sheriff's Secret Police confirm that the dog pack has already attacked a group of elementary school children this morning around eight, as they were getting on the bus. Injuries were minor, as the children protected themselves ably with their school-issued nerve gas canisters and automatic pistols.

The dogs' motives are not yet known, although authorities believe it could be meth- and/or gang-related. More on this story as it develops.

This Friday afternoon the Parks Department will be spraying pesticide in all public park areas and in neighborhoods with dense foliage and predominantly Irish heritage.

Night Vale is making a strong effort to reduce the mosquito population and the dangerous diseases they carry. Last year, mosquitos were responsible for outbreaks of West Nile, influenza, panache, elephantiasis, and Fanny Brice Approximation syndrome.

Please stay indoors from one p.m. Friday to ten p.m. Saturday to avoid dermal contact with the pesticide, which has been known to cause skin abrasions, epilepsy, super-epilepsy, and organ inversion. The Parks Department also notes that the pesticide has a half-life of 2,100 years, which means we'll be safe from those annoying mosquitoes for a long time.

We just received word from Wayne Tyler, assistant shift manager at the new Pinkberry, that the pack of feral dogs was seen this morning rooting around in the Dumpsters behind the library. They made off with some discarded Chinese takeout containers, a rusty futon frame, and two homeless men (likely to become henchpeople to the wild dogs). If you are near the library, be warned that these dogs are dangerous. Also be warned that penalties for overdue books has skyrocketed to fifty cents per day and, after thirty days, jaw mutilation.

The Night Vale Medical Board has issued a new study indicating that you have a spider somewhere on your body at all times but especially now. The study said that further research would be needed to determine exactly where on your body this spider is and what its intentions are, only that it is definitely there and is statistically likely to be one of the really ugly ones.

Let's go now to Community Health Tips. Listeners, are you suffering from carpal tunnel syndrome? Are you enjoying carpal tunnel syndrome? Are you surprised by carpal tunnel syndrome? Are you enraged by carpal tunnel syndrome? Do you feel a throbbing sadness that you almost cannot stand from carpal tunnel syndrome? Do you feel a bounty of love and appreciation for your fellow human beings traveling through this confusing and finite lifetime with you from carpal tunnel syndrome? Do you get sexually aroused by carpal tunnel syndrome? That would be weird. Not to be judgmental but... it would be weird. This has been Community Health Tips.

Listeners, we've just learned that the drawbridge construction site has been hit by graffiti vandals. The Sheriff's Secret Police suspect the feral dog pack to be responsible for the giant spray-painted lettering along the bridge scaffolding that reads GOLD STANDARD IS OUR STANDARD and READ YOUR CONSTITUTION. There was also a very elaborately painted portrait of Alexander Hamilton wearing Groucho Marx nose

glasses and a caption that reads FEDERALIST PAPERS but where "Federalist" is crossed out and "Toilet" has been written in red. Actually you should see this. It's truly stunning. All that with spray paint. I'm impressed. These guys are really good artists.

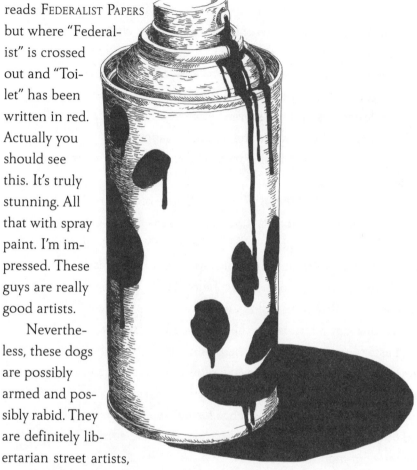

Nevertheless, these dogs are possibly armed and possibly rabid. They are definitely libertarian street artists, and that has police and city officials working double time to solve this problem. If you have any tips that could lead to the capture of this roving band of dogs, please keep them to yourself. We've also received word that they have tapped your phone and computers, so best not leave the house or talk loudly.

Let's have a look at the community calendar.

This Sunday afternoon the Night Vale Fire Department will be holding its biweekly Fireperson Appreciation Parade. All of the town's firefighters will be riding through Main Street on their bright red engines, which will be turned into floats depicting some of the greatest fires in Night Vale's history. One of my personal favorites is the 1983 Earthquake Dust Fire, when tremor-initiated fires became so intense that the airborne sand burst into deadly flames. Nearly the entire city population was lost, and the FDNV does a fantastic job capturing the drama with streamers and papier-mâché. The fire department would like to remind Night Vale citizens that the parade is free, and to check your coffeemakers and gas stoves before you leave home, because they will not fight any fires while the parade is happening.

On Monday the staff of Dark Owl Records will be wearing sweater vests.

Tuesday night is the Boy Scouts Court of Honor. The BSA will name its first ever Blood Pact Scouts, the rank just above Eagle Scout. So far, no scout has attained the coveted position of Eternal Scout, but we have heard that two local boys—Franklin Wilson and Barton Donovan—have earned the Invisibility Badge, which is a prerequisite for the rank. Well done, Frank and Barty.

Wednesday afternoon is the Citywide Fitness Fair at the Rec Center. Last year's event was canceled, as it was held on the same day and time as the Fried Chicken and Cigarette Fair. This year's event, however, promises to be a huge success, as they have secured a large corporate sponsorship from The Intelligence Group International, who will provide free prostate screenings, mammograms, and surgically embedded government monitoring devices.

Thursday morning the National Weather Service and National Security Agency have scheduled a giant sandstorm.

Friday is an oasis, only a metaphor for something unattainable, a haunting dream of meaning for our lives. But don't look. Turn your head. Your life is here. Stay here. You are alone. You are so peacefully alone. That's it. Yes. Good.

We've contacted the Night Vale Zoo hoping to find out more information on how dogs behave in packs. Perhaps these skilled animal experts could give us some insight into how to catch these dogs, or at least understand them.

Night Vale Zoo director Emily Munton told us that all animals prefer tiny cages and scheduled food pellet consumption, and that it didn't make sense that any animals would want to wander freely about town. She added a high-pitched roar, followed by a watery gurgling sound, and then our conversation was ended by repeated cloudless thunderclaps.

A reminder to anyone looking for fun on a budget today in Night Vale, it's free admission day at the Night Vale Museum of Forbidden Technologies. As always, the museum features many fascinating permanent exhibits, including the cheap, pollution-free source of energy created by Nikola Tesla, multiple time machines (some of them not even yet invented!), and pocket calculators, which were outlawed by the City Council twenty-two years ago for undisclosed reasons. Along with that, there is a temporary exhibit displaying many different exciting and extremely dangerous uses for lasers. Be sure to splurge on the guidebook at the museum store, as the exhibits themselves are entirely shrouded with thick burlap at all times, and all explanatory plaques have been blacked out with permanent marker. The Museum of Forbidden Technologies: If you don't know about it, we may or may not have it.

And now a word from our sponsor.

You come home. The lights are off. You get an uneasy feeling. Suddenly, the phone rings. You remember that you do not have a phone. It rings some more. You do not know what to do. Then, you remember that, yes, you do own a phone. Why wouldn't you own a phone? Everyone owns a phone. The phone is still ringing. Ha ha ha ha. How silly to think you didn't own a phone. It rings again. You smile and shrug and answer the ringing phone. It is still dark. "Hello," you say. "They are waiting for you," a whispery, gender-indeterminate voice tells you. "It is your time," it says. You turn on the light. You laugh again, wondering why it took you so long to turn on the light. "Gosh, it was dark," you think. "Hello?" the voice asks. You hang up, glad you remembered to buy Tropicana orange juice at least.

Tropicana Pure Premium Orange Juice is made from the freshest oranges with no added flavors or preservatives. Also, you should get caller ID. It's the twenty-first century. How do you not have caller ID? Really? Tropicana.

This just in: Two more school children were attacked by the wild dogs this morning near the playground at Night Vale Elementary School. One of the boys was taken to Night Vale General with treatable leg injuries. The other boy, we understand, was unharmed because he was a better boy, and more loved by the angels. We've also received confirmation that a handful of mangy curs broke into the senior center, stole their televisions, and made the Internet stop working.

This has gotten out of hand, ladies and gentlemen. We simply cannot live in fear for our safety because of wild dogs. Allow me a brief editorial here, if you would. First off, please have your pets fixed. It's an inexpensive and quick process. You can take your dog or cat to the Night Vale SPCA, to your local veterinarian, or to Big Rico's Pizza. Rico studies taxidermy as a hobby, so he's happy to help out in whatever way he can. Second, many of these dog packs are formed by dogs that are not raised to be loved but bred to fight. Trainers are teaching these dogs everything from jujitsu to kickboxing to knife work. This is simply unacceptable. Dog fighting is illegal, cruel to animals, and a danger to society when these dogs are untethered. But, we are a strong, united community here in Night Vale. We must stand up to violence.

Our town was founded by peace-loving, imperialist conquerors who, to escape taxation, overwhelmed a potentially violent race of indigenous people and founded this beautiful city on principles of family, fortitude, fence building, and friendly propaganda. Let's not forget our long-standing town motto: "We have nothing to fear except ourselves. We are unholy, awful people. Fear ourselves with silence. Look down, Night Vale. Look down, and forget what you've done." That is the motto of a determined, unified community!

And now the weather.

WEATHER: "I Know This" by Rachel Kann

Ladies and gentlemen, good news. Mayor Pamela Winchell called a press conference moments ago declaring an end to our dog-pack terror. The mayor announced that the dogs were not actually dogs . . . just some plastic bags caught in the breeze that people mistook for wild dogs. There are no wild dogs in Night Vale, she said. And if there were, they'd be sweet little dogs with big, meaningless eyes and tongues like flypaper. The plastic bags, meanwhile, have been safely returned to the Dog Park, from whence they came, and which is to remain unknowable and unremembered.

Journalists asked about the injuries and aftermath of this morning's dog pack–related crimes. The mayor responded with a hollow stare. She promptly shook the podium off its base and whispered through gritted teeth: "Plastic bags. Plastic. Bags." The Sheriff's Secret Police then ethically kettled the pool of reporters, gently coercing them with pepper spray. Most were taken away peacefully in handcuffs and black hoods.

Thank goodness it was all a misunderstanding. Dear listeners, I don't want to say I told you so, but wasn't I right when I said we were a determined, resilient little town? In the face of wild beasts, we did not crumble. We did not back down. We stood eye to eye with violence and it blinked first. Stand proud, Night Vale. Be afraid on the inside, of course. You are, after all, your own downfall. But stand proud against those predators that would harm your family.

And that is our show. Thank you for listening, listeners. Stay tuned next for the popular advice program *Dr. Brandon*. This week, Dr. Brandon offers a step-by-step on how to remove your own appendix without surgery.

The sky tonight is a soft, quivering green. The wind is calm, but prepared. Get your sleep, Night Vale. And don't forget to dream. Goodnight.

PROVERB: Eating meat is a difficult moral decision, because it's stolen, that meat. You should apologize.

EPISODE 11: "WHEAT & WHEAT BY-PRODUCTS"

NOVEMBER 15, 2012

MANY EPISODES OF *NIGHT VALE* START WITH A SINGLE PHRASE OR IMAGE that gets stuck in my head and stays there until I write a podcast script to get it out. This episode is one of those.

The phrase "wheat & wheat by-products" occurred to me one day and would not let my mind go. I loved the sound of it, and what it implied about the food system that would advertise "wheat by-products." I had no real plot arc in mind when I started the script, and the chaos caused by the wheat as well as the solution (remember writers, if you're stuck, just have something mysteriously vanish) all were improvised as an excuse to keep using the phrase over and over.

For some reason, in my head, the phrase "wheat & wheat by-products" had to be written with an ampersand. When I asked Jeffrey to change it to that in the title on the feed, the addition of the ampersand somehow caused a bug in the code and crashed our whole feed. Which is when I learned that my own private insistence on writing stuff out a certain way maybe wasn't worth sharing with the world.

Bread is deeply important to me. I make it from scratch and by hand regularly. Nothing is as calming as kneading dough and then putting it in to rise. If I had to live in a world without wheat & wheat by-products, I would be very, very sad.

—Joseph Fink

Today's air quality is mauve and speckled.

WELCOME TO NIGHT VALE.

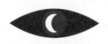

Representatives from the greater medical insurance community announced this week that major insurance providers would no longer cover government-disseminated illnesses. These ailments were created to control undesirable populations and include AIDS, most cancers, irritable bowel syndrome, telekinesis, tingling, and any kind of food allergy.

Doctors advise that the best way to avoid acquiring any of these conditions is to limit questionable public activities. Try not to be in a lower economic class, and give regularly to an approved religious organization. Take these precautions and you should live a healthy (or at least medically insured) life.

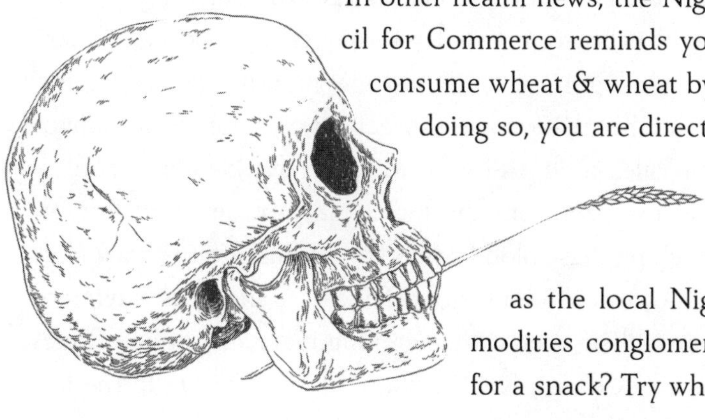

In other health news, the Night Vale Council for Commerce reminds you to regularly consume wheat & wheat byproducts. By doing so, you are directly supporting the local Night Vale farmer, as well as the local Night Vale commodities conglomerates. Looking for a snack? Try wheat or a wheat by-product. Dinner? Wheat &/or its by-product. Trying to patch a leaky roof? We have just the thing for you, and we also have its by-products. Wheat & wheat by-products. By Americans, for Americans, in Americans, watching Americans.

New information on the Apache Tracker, who you might remember as that white guy who wears the cartoonishly inaccurate and offensive Indian headdress, and who disappeared some weeks ago after investigating the strange occurrences at the Night Vale Post Office. Well, word is in that he has reappeared, except it now seems he is actually Native American. Witnesses say his features are still recognizable, but during the disappearance he has transformed into that which he always absurdly claimed to be. More explanation of course is needed, but the Apache Tracker is also now only able to speak Russian, and I did not bother to get his statement translated. Apparently he has taken to leaning on the hood of an old Honda Accord in the parking lot of the Desert Flower Bowling Alley and Arcade Fun Complex, shaking his head slowly and checking his watch. Does his complete racial transformation make his previous actions less offensive, listeners? Write us a letter telling us what *you* think, and then put it away in a drawer for ten years. Reading it again, you'll get a little pang of nostalgia for the person you used to be, once upon a time.

The City Council today issued a strong warning against the manufacture and sale of discount bloodstones. They say that these bloodstones of inferior design and construction have the potential to cause major accidents in even common, day-to-day chanting rituals. These accidents have included, in just the past few months, locust swarms, pus tornadoes, and the creation and subsequent obliteration of a mirror version of Night Vale, forcing all of us to watch our identical counterparts perish and thus confront the inevitability of our own futures. Anyone caught selling these bloodstones will be put into the Dark Box, pending erasure from recorded history. The lesser charge of buying or possessing them will be met with mere summary execution. Critics charge that the City Council is lying about all of this, due to the fact that the council owns the only certified bloodstone factory in town, but the council has vehemently denied this charge, by gibbering, howling, and knocking over microphones.

Oh dear. I apologize listeners. We at Night Vale Community Radio are experiencing the following technical problems: the need for air, eye movement, and gooey stuff inside. Please stand by.

[*Pause*]

Thank you. These problems have been corrected.

An update on our previous message about wheat & wheat by-products. You should not eat wheat or wheat by-products, say several frantic scientists waving clipboards in our studio. As it turns out, all wheat & wheat by-products, for unknown reasons, have turned into venomous snakes, which are crawling all over our small city, causing even more chaos than is normal. These snakes have been described as terrifying, loathsome, and probably from the bowels of hell itself. Also, green and three feet long. If you have any wheat or wheat by-products in your home, you are almost certainly already dead. Sorry about that.

Property taxes are going up again, Night Vale. Several citizens are justifiably upset over this latest increase, but municipal services do, after all, cost money. Schools, public transportation, parks and recreation facilities, and of course the multibillion-dollar pulsar-development facility. Speaking of which, scientists say they are on the verge of developing the first-ever human-made neutron star. Usually the aftermath of a supernova, this pulsar would be roughly four miles in diameter but with a nearly incomprehensible density that makes it about half the mass of our own sun. And to think, this rapidly rotating sphere of radioactive matter will be right here under the sands of Night Vale, producing enough energy to power the earth for billions of years. The city of Night Vale plans to use the pulsar to light the high school football stadium, which still uses whale oil lamps.

John Peters, you know, the farmer, is particularly upset not only about the pulsar development but also about the higher taxes. As owner of more than 150 acres, John will certainly have to pay a large share. And given that John is a peach farmer in a desert, he hasn't actually raised a successful crop in ever. His only income is his half-a-million-dollar annual subsidy for imaginary corn, which has been one of Night Vale's greatest exports. People come from all over (even Desert Bluffs, unfortunately) to buy his imaginary corn.

I like to butter up a piece of bread and then rub the imaginary corn along it and then sprinkle it with a little bit of salt and cayenne. Boy is that a delicious, and low-carcinogen, summer treat!

But even our town heroes, like John Peters, you know, the farmer, have to pay their fair share. No citizen is above paying taxes. Well, except Marcus Vanston, but that's understandable because he's so wealthy. When you're worth as much as Marcus Vanston, you have proved your value to society through hard work and determination and are no longer required to show anyone any further proof that you care about anything or anybody else, because you obviously do. Look at all your money. According to some, Marcus is worth over five billion dollars. And that's five billion reasons Marcus is our town's greatest citizen.

Further updates on wheat & wheat by-products. The good news is that they are no longer poisonous serpents. The bad news is that they have transformed into a particularly evil and destructive form of spirit. Please be aware that wheat & wheat by-products are now malevolent and violent supernatural forces, capable of physically moving objects up to two hundred pounds and entering human souls of up to soul-strength 4. The frantic scientists, who are now hopping up and down just outside my recording booth, indicating various charts and figures, recommend creating a simple lean-to out of animal bones and mud, such as you might have made and played in as a child, and hiding there until the spiritual forces of wheat & wheat by-products have passed.

A reminder to all Night Vale citizens that the annual SorrowSongs Sing-Along is this Thursday. There will be a potluck lunch and the softball team will be selling refreshments to fund things that each of them individually want to buy for themselves. Anyone who has their own SorrowSong they'd like to add to our communal vocal malaise should submit it to city hall by Tuesday at the latest. Remember that low moans and minor key chants do not count. The composer of the best Sorrow-Song, as indicated by our audience participatory Weep-A-Meter, will be ritualistically drowned in a pool of our townspeople's tears. Good luck!

Listeners, the City Council, for national security reasons, has replaced the following report with the sound of a burbling brook, followed by the sound of a running blender.

[*The sounds happen as described*]

City Comptroller Waynetta Barnett received a $1.5 billion check from the federal government this week. The check was to support rebuilding efforts from this past week's massive earthquake, reaching 9.7 on the Richter scale, the epicenter of which was directly below Night Vale. Of course, we experienced absolutely no damage to the town, and nobody reported feeling any effects at all from this enormous seismological event.

Comptroller Barnett said that she suspects that FEMA just saw the meter reading, declared this a disaster area, and sent a check. She doesn't think they have any interest in visiting Night Vale, so we can probably just spend the money however we want. Barnett added that those new MINI Cooper sedans are really cute and wanted us all to look at their website.

We asked Carlos about our inability to experience tectonic shifts. Carlos, lovely Carlos, had previously recorded other massive tremor activity underneath our city. His response was a few seconds of stammering, followed by a sigh and slow head shake. His eyes were distant, distracted, yet beautiful. I asked him where he got his shirt. It fit him so well. He said he would look at his notes and computer models and see if he could figure out what was going on. I don't know if he listens to me sometimes.

Ladies and gentlemen, I take you from an unreal disaster, to an un-unreal one. It is my sad duty now to announce that the City Council is officially putting Night Vale under an emergency state, due to the ongoing and life-threatening wheat & wheat by-products situation. The council states that anyone who has come into contact with wheat & wheat by-products and has by some happy miracle survived, should consider themselves infected and proceed to the usual quarantine area, just behind the playground in Mission Grove Park, there to spend the rest of their days in quiet contemplation and weaving. Everyone else should head immediately to the wheat & wheat by-product shelter that has been sitting unused for decades under the public library. When asked why a wheat & wheat by-product shelter already existed, the City Council answered, simply, "prophecy." May you all be safe. May you all be well. May you be strong, and flexible, with ruddy cheeks and legs like tree trunks. And now, the weather.

WEATHER: "Cigarette Burns Forever" by Adam Green

News from Old Woman Josie, out near the car lot. She reports that the angels have gathered in a circle in her living room, blocking her view of the television. They are shoulder to shoulder, facing each other, radiant with holy light. "The bowling alley," they are chanting. "The bowling alley." She says that a repeat of *The West Wing* she had really hoped to watch is on, and she is quite annoyed by her usually considerate angelic houseguests. More on this story, maybe, if there ever is more.

And finally, some good news. All wheat & wheat by-products have mysteriously vanished from Night Vale, and the City Council promises that they will be gone forever. This scourge, this siege upon us, this salvo of food-based warfare, is finally over. Never more will we be threatened in our homes by this enemy, or its by-products. We also will never eat bread again, and that's a pretty big bummer. But this is the balance that must be made, between what we desire and what we fear. Between pain and pleasure. Between wheat, dear listeners, and its by-products.

Many of you are huddled now (and forever) in the quarantine behind the playground in Mission Grove Park. For this community-minded sacrifice, we thank you. I know you were forced there by martial law, but still, you should be commended for your brave action. Terminal quarantine might seem scary now, but I understand they have a well-stocked supply of canned lentils and the Silver Screen edition of Trivial Pursuit. And of course, you have the radio. I hope you will let my dulcet voice and our humble community station into your ears and hearts until your final wheat-loving breath.

Dear listeners, stay tuned next for a live broadcast of a man locked in a recording booth, silently staring at the microphone with intense suspicion.

And, as always, since always, and for always: Goodnight, Night Vale. Goodnight.

PROVERB: Today is the last day of your life up to this point.

EPISODE 12: "THE CANDIDATE"

DECEMBER 1, 2012

WHEN I WAS A KID, MY MOTHER WOULD NOT LET ME PLAY DUNGEONS & Dragons. It was a fact, according to television news in the 1980s, that if you played D&D you would become so obsessed with your character that you would either kill other people in real life or yourself.

I wasn't really clamoring to play D&D, but it looked fun, and I had friends that were into it. Horror movies had taught me that if you are a kid and you break any kind of rule, you will be chased down and chopped up.

Then the Saturday morning cartoon of D&D came on and I saw Tiamat, a five-headed dragon. I wasn't able to watch the show at home with my mom around, because of the whole TV news murder and suicide story. So I watched it at my friend Nick's house, and I wanted to play this game and to battle Tiamat.

I didn't actually play D&D until high school, but by then I felt like the people I knew who played it were way better than I could be so I just started watching sports and collecting football cards instead.

Tiamat stuck with me, though. He was the coolest and the obvious visual basis for Hiram McDaniels, a literal five-headed dragon in Night Vale, and in this episode hopeful Night Vale mayor.

Hiram's heads are different colors from Tiamat's, and he's quite a bit more charming and social than Tiamat. And having Jackson Publick voice his five different heads has really led to Hiram having five different personalities in one body. As a writer, I couldn't want for a better character.

Other notes about this episode:

- Walton Kinkade: last name spelled like Thomas Kinkade because I love only the finest of art. Also Kinkade (the fictional one) has an arachnid-like eight eyes because I hate myself.
- Upon rereading this episode I wondered, "Whatever happened to Intern Stacey?" Then I found her next mention in episode 17. Oh, poor Stacey. How depressing.
- You remember when Oprah would have one of those shows where everyone in the audience would get a gift and Oprah would shout "A VOLKSWAGEN BEEEEEEE-TLLLLLE!" or "UGG BOOOOOTS!" Cut to the audience who were all jumping and screaming. I always imagined Oprah saying "IM-MOR-TAL-I-TYYYYYYY!" and then cut to the audience who would all be jumping and screaming, but the camera would zoom closer and we would see that there were tears and that they were screaming in terror.

—Jeffrey Cranor

The policeman in that intersection is not directing traffic, he's coding an urgent message to all of us.

WELCOME TO NIGHT VALE.

First, the news. Old Town Night Vale residents are complaining about extremely noisy sunsets. Several agitated citizens are pushing for the City Council to do something about the solar shrieking every evening for the past few weeks. One homeowner described the sound as "the parched cries of sad buzzards, or perhaps even the unholy voice of Old Scratch himself."

The City Council, speaking in unison at a televised press conference, said that the noise is just the windmill farms that litter the unfortunate wastelands of Desert Bluffs, and that the noises do not fall under Night Vale jurisdiction.

Walton Kinkade, president of the community group Soundproof Old Town!, said that the windmills can't possibly be the source of the noise, as they are nonexistent and also don't work because of Desert Bluff's staggering incompetence.

The City Council called a second press conference wherein they all wordlessly stared down Kinkade for fourteen uninterrupted minutes. Their dark eyes tore holes straight through the community spokesman, metaphorically speaking, until his soul was compacted into what looked like a partially chewed black-eyed pea, literally.

To date, only Old Town residents have reported hearing these inconceivable noises every evening as the sun crosses the indifferent horizon. And the noises seem to be taking their toll. There have been two heart attacks, twelve cases of significant muscular atrophy, and at least two dozen claims of folks growing third eyes (including Kinkade himself, who had an arachnid-like eight eyes when he spoke before City Council yesterday morning).

No other neighborhood can hear the sounds. I spoke to Simone Rigadeau in the Earth Sciences building at Night Vale Community College about this scientifically fascinating story and she called it a simple case of celestial "just deserts." Full disclosure listeners, Rigadeau does not work in Earth Sciences. She is a transient living in the recycling closet of the Earth Sciences building, and she collects cans as pets.

There is another hearing scheduled at four a.m. tomorrow on the highest ledge overlooking Skeleton Gorge, which can only be accessed by government helicopters. (All previous endeavors to scale the cliffside by rock-climbing enthusiasts have failed in extravagantly gory fashion.)

The council issued a statement wishing Kinkade luck in attending this mandatory hearing.

Breaking news: We've received confirmation from the Sheriff's Secret Police that fugitive Hiram McDaniels was finally apprehended. McDaniels has been on the lam since August. He was wanted on several counts of insurance fraud, falsifying identification papers, evading arrest, and assaulting a police vehicle with fire. McDaniels was spotted near his Earl Road apartment early Saturday morning by several alert neighbors.

The neighbors said they were able to identify McDaniels because he matched police sketches of an eighteen-foot-tall, five-headed dragon that had been posted across Night Vale. Fingerprints later confirmed that McDaniels was definitely a dragon.

Secret Police are still unsure of McDaniels's motive for returning home, and . . . well, listeners, our station intern, Stacey, just handed me a photo of Hiram McDaniels. He is a very dynamic-looking dragon. The raw power. The intensity in those five faces, those many sets of piercing blue and red and black and green and yellow eyes.

I can certainly see how he charmed his way out of an arrest. He must never get tickets! What a guy.

An unsigned press release I found under my pillow this morning announces the following: There is a free party this Friday at the abandoned missile silo outside of town. The purpose of this party is to celebrate. There will be no sign or music, but the party is inside the silo. This party takes place at three a.m. and will be over at 3:05. It will be dark, both inside and outside the silo. Grope blindly toward happiness. Keep your mouth open and your teeth together, to indicate you are at a party. You will hear noises and later you will not. This party will feature special guest Bon Jovi, although he does not yet know it. See you there!

An interesting note on Hiram McDaniels: Intern Stacey tells me that she's been googling the roguish dragon. Did you know he had a blog? He's a very smart fellow—some really groundbreaking ideas! Here's one post from last week: "If I were mayor of Night Vale, I would give incentives for small business development and focus on youth physical fitness programs. Human youth are the human future, after all."

Well, it seems a certain multi-headed fugitive wants to become mayor of Night Vale. You have my vote, Hiram!

Thursday night, the City Council is voting on a new measure that would prohibit breathing as an involuntary muscular action. Historically, the human body has been able to control breathing without the brain needing to consciously activate the diaphragm. Under the new rule, all residents of Night Vale would be required to make the physical choice of whether or not (and when) to breathe.

The City Council said that we have too long taken the receipt of oxygen for granted and that this sense of entitlement must cease. If the vote passes, residents will have until March 1 of next year to learn to control these involuntary muscle groups during lucid sleep.

Detractors say that it is our constitutional right to breathe how we want, and that it is not the government's job to legislate breathing. The council responded by waving a brick in the air at reporters and shouting, "We learned to beat our own hearts! We taught ourselves to wet our own corneas! We have pulled ourselves up from nothing! It is the American dream!" They then took a deep breath all together, lowered the brick, broke it into pieces, and devoured it.

And now a word from our sponsor.

We all want to live forever, right? Wrong! Think about watching your family die as you selfishly carry on. Your children aging and passing, your grandchildren, and so on. Think of all of the friends you'll make but eventually lose. You don't want that! No! You know the earth is eventually going to be swallowed by the sun, right? And one day you would be present for this greatest of all apocalypses. As fascinating as this event would be, scientifically speaking, this excitement would fade as the pain of thousand-degree flames engulfed your tender body and your aged mind would be so alone in this interminable torture. Does this sound like something you want? We didn't think so.

Immortality is stupid. Think before you wish.

This message brought to you by DIRECTV.

Dear listeners, right after we reported on Hiram McDaniels's interest in becoming Night Vale mayor, the dirty campaign tactics came into play, stirring up bad feelings and slinging the old municipal mud. Incumbent mayor Pamela Winchell issued a statement citing township bylaws that prohibit prisoners from running for public office.

Now, isn't it just like a career politician, such as Mayor Winchell, to make such unethical, ad hominem attacks on a great reptilian beast, simply because he's in jail? It sounds to me like the mayor is feeling McDaniels breathing down her neck. Breathing dragon fire that is! Give 'em hell, Hiram!

The following is a test of the Emergency Dream Broadcast System. In the event of an actual emergency, you would just now be experiencing a dream in which you were in the neighborhood where you grew up,

only all the houses are now black, featureless cylinders. Just row after row of these blank, dark cylinders stretching out around you. You are home, but you are also somewhere from whence you will never find home again. There is someone waiting for you, at the end of the longest street. You know that, although you do not know who. You try to run down the street and it grows longer and longer. You pass by one cylinder in particular and know that it's your house. You stop running. You approach the blank face of the cylinder, its surface seeming to devour light and sound. You reach out, and you are inches from touching it. Just then you hear a ding. You look above you to see words in the sky. POSSIBLE FLASH FLOODS, they say, ALERT VALID UNTIL 3:00 P.M. Once again, this has been a test of the Emergency Dream Broadcast System.

The Night Vale Mall is having to deal with angry calls from parents after the Santa they hired for Christmas photos was once again a no-show. Mall public relations officials said that the missing Santa is actually a performance-art piece meant to show people how our capitalist idols are truly nonexistent; ghosts of materialistic ideals that we have embraced as replacements for true spiritual meaning.

A long line of upset parents and crying children stretched from Santa's empty chair to just past the Hollister. The mall PR officials added that they have a really cool idea for Valentine's Day. They're thinking, like, moving pictures of actual beating hearts projected onto a large teddy bear, which has been stretched open like a vivisected frog from seventh-grade life science. Officials added: "It's going to be monstrous and beautiful. You don't even know what art really is. You don't even know yourself."

They concluded by chanting and pumping their arms in unison, like a Lower Paleolithic version of the "YMCA" dance.

And now, the weather.

WEATHER: "Of a Friday Night" by Anais Mitchell

During the break, I received a message from Mayor Winchell's office responding to our previous reports. According to the mayor, mayoral elections aren't for another three years, and Hiram McDaniels is ineligible to run not only because of his jail stay, but also because he is neither a Night Vale resident nor a human being. There is, she says, no precedent for a five-headed dragon as elected official.

Mayor Winchell also pointed out that writing the throwaway phrase "if I were mayor of Night Vale" on a blog is not an official declaration of candidacy. "There is paperwork!" Mayor Winchell shouted into my voice mail. "You can't just . . . Aaaaggghh," she continued, trailing off slightly at the end. What followed was about ninety-five seconds of loud stomping and what sounded like wood chopping in the distance before the message finally ended.

Allow me a retort, dear listeners, with this brief editorial.

With all due respect, Madam Mayor, have we not had enough dragon bashing? Our great country once held to some terrible old customs, but we grew up. We learned. We abolished slavery. Women won the right to vote. Ghosts can now marry (but of course, not have children. I mean, that would be a real slippery slope!). And our own little burg is on the verge of becoming the first city in this great nation to legalize time travel.

So let's loosen our collars. Let's march into the reptilian future, not cling to the narrow past. Just because a dragon is a dragon and has five heads doesn't mean he can't lead our community.

Sure, critics will say, "Oh, but Cecil, what if his five heads don't agree on something. What if one's like 'Yeah, let's build this school,' but another's like 'No more schools,' and the others are drunk or sleepy or something? How can we agree to elect five heads that can't agree with themselves?"

To this I say, shame on you for your negative stereotypes of multi-headed beings. Free your mind. The rest, as our official town song says, will follow. The song also says "Lap deeply of the scarlet mud after the bloodrains of the apocalypse," but I don't think that quite applies here.

So with this, I am proud to offer my endorsement of Hiram McDaniels for mayor of Night Vale.

Sure the election isn't for three years, but it's never too early to effect change!

And in that time, we will rally, we will petition to get what we want. And soon a great leader will rise. Lead us to that future, Hiram.

Ah, but that is later. Now? It is dark. It is quiet. Just you and me, dear listener. Just my voice, traveling from this microphone, traveling silent and immediate across sleepy homes and lost souls to your ears. You curl under a blanket, protecting your body from the world (excepting a few clever spiders), and you are listening, hearing me. Sleep heavily and know that I am here with you now. The past is gone and cannot harm you anymore. And while the future is fast coming for you, it always flinches first and settles in as the gentle present. This now? This us? We can cope with that. We can do this together, you and I. Drowsily but comfortably.

Stay tuned now for our two-hour special: *Car Alarms and Their Variations*, brought to you, commercial-free, by Canada Dry.

Goodnight, Night Vale. Goodnight.

PROVERB: Does the carpet match the drapes? No, it doesn't. You're the worst interior decorator. Please leave my home.

EPISODE 13: "A STORY ABOUT YOU"

DECEMBER 15, 2012

THIS EPISODE STARTED AS A DOCUMENT IN OUR SHARED GOOGLE DOCS folder that I titled "A Story About You (an experiment in *Night Vale* storytelling)." I had this idea of doing an episode with a completely different format from all the previous ones, but I didn't know if it would work. I stuck it in that separate document so there was no pressure for it to turn into a producible episode.

What ended up saving it was a disastrous beach vacation. My wife and I were staying in a beach house for a week, and both got sick on the first day, so that we spent the week on the couch not doing much and feeling bad. Also it rained the whole week. It was during this enforced week of having nothing to do but sit indoors in a beach house and be sick that I finally got this episode into shape.

Who are you in this story about you? Several episodes later it occurred to me that I really wish we had implied that you were Larry Leroy, out on the edge of town. But by then we had already done other things with Larry that contradicted that idea, so instead you are just some nameless Night Vale resident, now never to be seen again.

Originally the "dark planet of awesome size, lit by no sun" only appeared once in the story. It was an image I loved but didn't know how it related to the story. On a second run, I restructured the story to center around the image. Once I figured out that the dead planet was the heart of the story, the rewriting into its final form was quick and easy. That planet has appeared occasionally in later episodes and in the *Night Vale* novel. The dark planet has a very specific meaning and logic for me within the Night Vale world that I won't spell out here or anywhere else.

A word about the music in this episode. I wanted the episode to center around a single musical theme, since it centered on a single story, and I found a Disparition track that for whatever reason I hadn't used before called "Vortex Shedding" that was both distinctive and gorgeous. It's a track I love and still try to use only for very special moments.

—Joseph Fink

This is a story about you, said the man on the radio, and you were pleased, because you always wanted to hear about yourself on the radio.

WELCOME TO NIGHT VALE

This is a story about you. You live in a trailer, out near the car lot, next to Old Woman Josie's house. Occasionally she'll wave to you, on her way out to get the mail, or more snacks for the angels. Occasionally, you'll wave back. You're not a terrible neighbor, as far as it goes. At night you can see the red light blinking on and off on top of the radio tower, a tiny flurry of human activity against the implacable backdrop of stars and void. You'll sit out on the steps of your trailer, with your back to the brightness of the car lot, watching the radio tower for hours. But only sometimes. Mostly you do other things. This is a story about you.

You didn't always live in Night Vale. You lived somewhere else, where there were more trees, more water. You wrote direct-mail campaigns for companies, selling their products. *Dear resident,* you wrote often, *Finally some good news in this dreary world. At last, a reason not to kill yourself.* Then you would delete that and write something else, and it would be sent out and it would not be read by anyone.

You had a friend, and then a girlfriend, and then a fiancée. The same person. She cooked dinner sometimes, but sometimes you cooked. You often touched.

One day you were walking from the glass box of your office to your old Ford Probe and a vision came to you. You saw above you a planet of awesome size, lit by no sun. An invisible titan, all thick black forests and jagged mountains and deep, turbulent oceans. It was so far away, so desolate, and so impossibly, terrifyingly dark, and that day you did not go home. You drove instead. You drove a long time, and eventually you ended up in Night Vale and you stopped driving.

You have been haunted, ever since, by how easy it was to walk away from your life, how few the repercussions were. You never heard from your fiancée or your job again. They never looked for you, which doesn't seem likely, or maybe it's that in Night Vale you cannot be found. The complete freedom, the lack of consequence, it terrifies you.

You have a new job now. Every day except Sunday you drive out into the sand wastes, and there you find two trucks. You move wooden crates from one truck to the other while a man in a suit silently watches. It is a different man each time. Sometimes the crates tick. Mostly they do not. When you are done, the man in the suit hands you an amount of cash, also different each time, and you go home. It is the best job you've ever had.

Except today it was different. You moved the crates. The man in the suit, a stranger, watched. But then, as had never happened before, the man in the suit received a phone call. He walked off at some distance to take it. "Yes sir," he said. And "No sir." Also he made hawk-shrieking sounds. It wasn't terribly interesting. You moved crates. But then an impulse, an awful impulse, came over you. And for no other reason than that you are trapped by the freedom to do anything in this life, you took one of the crates and put it in your trunk. By the time the man came back from his phone call, you were done with your job. He gave you the money. It was nearly $500 today, the second highest it had ever been. And you drove home, with the crate in your trunk.

When you got home, you took the crate into your trailer and left it in the kitchen. The crate did not make a ticking sound. It made no sound at all. Nothing made a sound, except you, breathing in and breathing out. You cooked dinner. You always cook dinner. The red light on the radio tower blinked on and off in your peripheral vision, a message that was there and then wasn't, and that you could never quite read. You wondered how long it would take them to miss the crate. You did not wonder who "they" were. Some mysteries aren't questions to be answered but just a kind of opaque fact, a thing which exists to be not known.

Which brings us to now, to this story. This story about you. You are listening to the radio. The announcer is talking about you. And then you hear something else, a guttural howl out of the desert distance, and you know that the crate's absence has been discovered.

The crate, well it sits, that's all, on the kitchen floor, that's all. It's warm, warmer than the air around it. It smells sharp and earthy, like freshly ground cinnamon. And when you put your ear against the rough, warm wood, you hear a soft humming, an indistinct melody. It does not appear to be difficult to open. All you would need to do is remove a few nails. You do not open it. You decide, instead, to go to the Moonlite All-Nite Diner and have a slice of pie.

The wind is hot, like always, and smells like honey and mud. Night is your favorite time. Daylight brings only a chain of visual sensations, none of which cohere into meaning for you anymore. Life has become out of focus, free of consequence. As you drive, you turn off the headlights for a moment. In that moment, you feel again above you, not even far away now, that planet of awesome size, lit by no sun. An invisible titan, all thick black forests and jagged mountains and deep, turbulent oceans. You see nothing but the faint moonlight on your dashboard, but you know the planet is out there, yawning in the unseen spaces. The moment passes. You turn your headlights back on and all you see is a road, just asphalt, just that, and you pass a man waving semaphore flags, indicating that the speed limit for this stretch is forty-five.

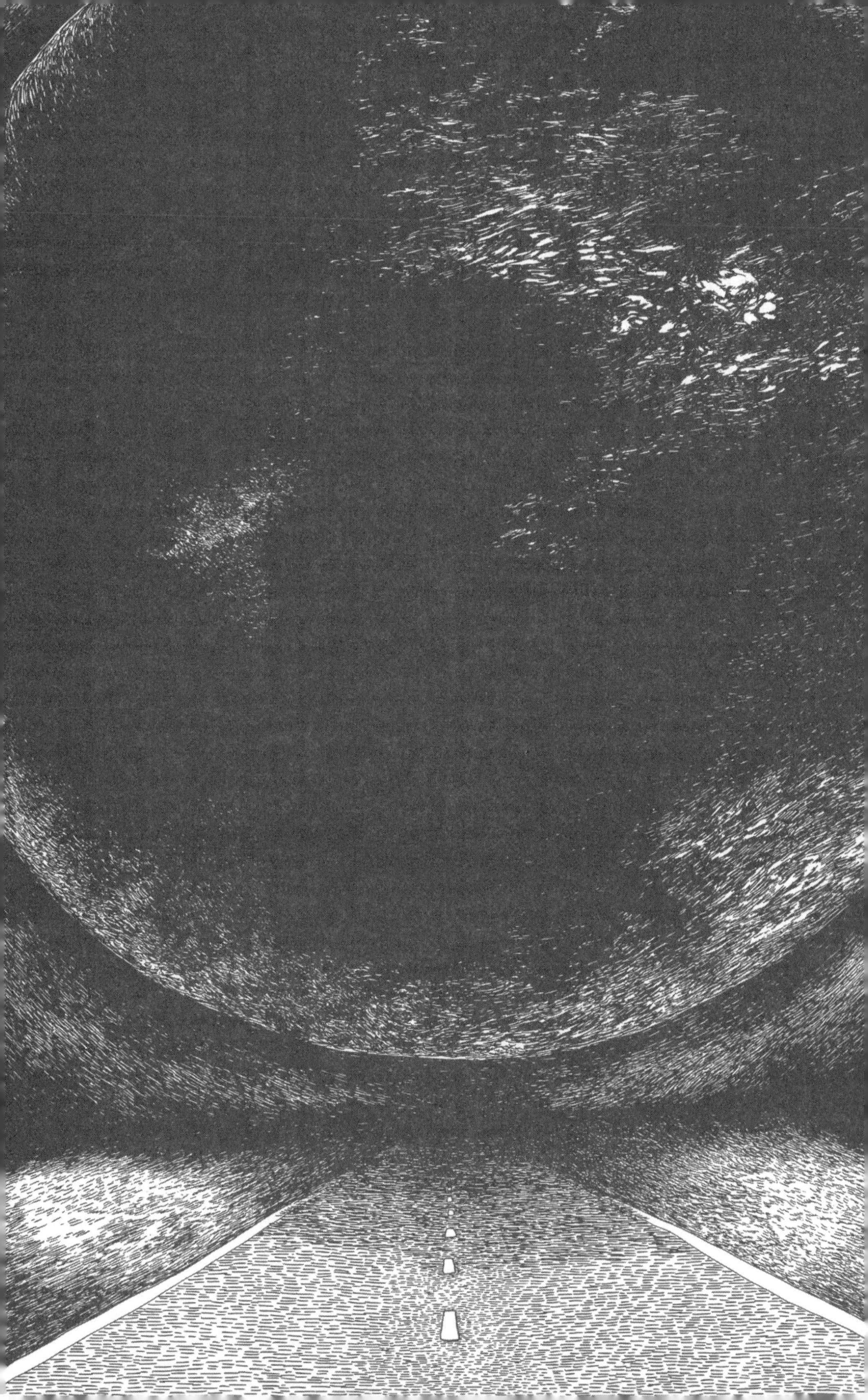

The Moonlite All-Nite is radiant green, a slab of mint light in the warm darkness. You squint when you see it, like it hurts your eyes, but it does not hurt your eyes. You park near the front door. A man rolls by on the ground, his eyes bleary and sightless, whispering the word "MudWomb" over and over, but you don't have the money to tip him, so you go inside. You order a slice of strawberry pie, and the waitress indicates, through words and movements, that it will be brought to you presently. The radio speaks soothingly to you from staticky speakers set into a foam tile ceiling. It is telling a story about you, your story, at last.

A man slides into the booth across from you. You recognize him vaguely, although he looks considerably different now. It is that man who appeared to be of Slavic origin but who dressed in an absurd caricature of an Indian chief and called himself the Apache Tracker. Except now, it's difficult for you to miss, he has actually transformed into a Native American. You wonder if the pie will get there soon. The Apache Tracker smells of potting soil and sweat. He leans across the table and touches your hand lightly. You do not pull the hand away, because you know that there will be no consequence for any of this.

"Вы находитесь в опасности," he says. "Они идут."

You nod. He taps the table, then, bringing his thick eyebrows together and pursing his lips, he leans down and taps the ground. You nod again.

"I think my pie is here now," you say, unnecessarily, as the pie is quite visibly placed in front of you. You did not order invisible pie. You hate invisible pie.

He looks at the pie for a long time then lets his breath hiss out slowly through his nose.

"Они придут снизу. Пирог не поможет." He leaves. What an asshole that guy is.

You finish the pie and ask for the check.

"Check, please," you say, whispering it into your drinking glass as is custom, and then lifting the tray of sugar packets to find it, filled out and ready to be paid. You drop a few dollars onto the check, place it back under the sugars, wait for the sound of swallowing, and leave the diner. The waitress nods as you leave, but not at you. She nods slowly and rhythmically to music only she can hear, her eyes riding the curved line of neon lights above the menu.

As you start the car, the man on the radio says something about the weather.

WEATHER: "You Don't Know" by Mount Moon

The crate is in your kitchen, where you left it, and you get down on your knees to embrace it more fully. It has grown warmer, even hot. It still is not ticking.

It had taken you no time to get back home. Now that you think about it, were there any other cars on the road? Where did all the cars go? The man with the semaphore flags, explaining the speed limit, he wasn't there either. Your heart pounds.

Without allowing another stray thought to wander through your mind and delay you, you grab the crate and throw it in your trunk. You turn the ignition, and your car radio comes alive with a pop just as the announcer says that your car radio comes alive with a pop.

Where to now? You don't know, but you go there anyway, a pair of headlights, a pair of eyes, and two shaky hands speeding through the silent town. Behind you, you see helicopter searchlights sweeping down onto your trailer. There are sirens. A purplish cloud hangs over the town, glittering occasionally as it rotates. The whole works.

You drive past the Moonlite All-Nite, still aglow and full of people slowly eating what sounds good only late at night, and Teddy Williams's Desert Flower Bowling Alley and Arcade Fun Complex, which has taken to not only locking, but barricading its doors at closing time. You pass by city hall, which, as always, is completely shrouded after dark in black velvet. Moving farther out, following the pull of the distant, uncertain moon, you pass by the car lot, where the salesmen have been put away for the night, and Old Woman Josie's house, where the only sign that the unassuming little home could be a place of residence for angels is the bright halo of heavenly light surrounding it, and the sign out front that says ANGELS' RESIDENCE. Then the town is behind you, and you are out in the scrublands and the sand wastes. By the road you see a man holding a cactus in one hand and a pair of scissors in the other. He shakes both at you as you pass and howls.

And then you are alone. Just you and the desert. You stop the car and get out. Pebbles crunch in the sand in response to your movement. The radio murmurs behind the closed door of the car. The headlights illuminate only a few stray plants and the wide dumb eyes of some nocturnal animal. Looking back, you see the bulge of light that is your Night Vale.

The purple cloud, now floating over the heart of the city, reaches its tendrils in and out of buildings. You hear screams and gunfire. You open the trunk and lay one hand on the crate. It pulses with some kind of life. Still no ticking, though. You look back. Several buildings are on fire. Crowds of people are floating in the air, held aloft by beams of light, and struggling feebly against power they cannot begin to understand. The ground shifts, like it was startled.

It's so quiet when it finally comes. You see the black car long before it arrives. It comes to a halt nearby, and two men step out. You don't run. Neither do they.

"How did you find me?" you ask.

"Everything you do is being broadcast on the radio for some reason. That made it pretty easy," says one of the men, the one that isn't tall.

"Yeah," you say, "I see that now."

"You have the item?" the man who is not tall asks. You say nothing. The man who is not tall signals the man who is not short, and he walks past you, looks into the trunk, and nods.

"Even easier," says the man who is not tall.

There is an unexpected click. One of the rear doors of the black car has opened, and your fiancée has stepped out. Her eyes are wet like they were the night you left. She does not appear to have aged, but then you can't actually remember how long it has been. Could it have been last week? Or was it ten years ago?

"Why?" she says. "Why? Why?"

You don't know what to say.

The man who is not short steps up to you, puts a knife against your throat. Nobody says anything. Your fiancée shakes her head. Her eyes are empty, broken, gushing. The radio is saying all of this as it happens. You hear it dimly through the car door. You can't stop smiling.

All at once, the consequences. All at once, you are no longer free. It's all coming back around, all at once. Life, bleary, washed out, snaps back into focus. The red light on the radio tower still blinks in the distance and every message in this world has a meaning. It all makes sense and you are finally being punished. You can't think of a time you have ever been happier.

Your fiancée abruptly gets back into the car. Neither of the men seems to notice her. One opens the crate with a couple of quick taps and pulls out of it an intricate miniature house. The hours that must have been spent building it, every detail is accounted for. Inside the house, you think you see for a moment lights and movement.

"Undamaged," says the man who is not tall.

You beam at him. The knife presses harder against your throat, but it doesn't hurt. Your eyes wander up, and you see above you the dark planet of awesome size, perched in its sunless void. An invisible titan, all thick black forests and jagged mountains and deep, turbulent oceans. A monster spinning soundless, forgotten. It's so close now. You see it just above you. Maybe, even, if you tried very hard, you could touch it. You reach up.

This has been your story. The radio moves on to other things. News. Traffic. Political opinions, and corrections to political opinions. But there was time, one day, one single day, in which it was only one story, a story about you. And you were pleased, because you always wanted to hear about yourself on the radio.

Goodnight, Night Vale. Goodnight.

PROVERB: I'd never join a PEN15 club that would allow a person like me to become a member.

EPISODE 14: "THE MAN IN THE TAN JACKET"

JANUARY 1, 2013

In 2004 I was at a teacher's conference in New Orleans and I drove up one night to Jackson, Mississippi, to have dinner with an old friend of mine. I drove back to my New Orleans hotel late that night.

The highways around the Gulf Coast in Louisiana and Mississippi are mostly elevated above swampland. Low concrete bridges contained by guardrails and green marsh. At night you can feel how isolated you are on those miles-long passages without exits or direct access to real land.

Around one or two in the morning as I had crossed into Louisiana, the only car on the road, I could see an orange light up ahead, more powerful than the dull street lamps arching over my path. It was bright, shimmering. I could see it was on the road itself.

It became clear as I approached, slowing down to less than thirty mph trying to understand what was happening and see if anyone was in danger. On the narrow shoulder was a sedan (in my memory it was an early '80s Chevy Malibu, but who knows?) completely engulfed in flames. I took my flip phone out and dialed 911.

As I passed the fiery vehicle, about one hundred feet up the road, leaning against the guardrail, was a man half-shadowed by the blaze. He was smoking a cigarette and appeared completely relaxed.

I told the operator my mile marker and what I saw and then hung up and carried on with the rest of my weekend and teacher's conference.

Nearly a decade later, that image still haunted me. Like, did he set the fire? What level of sinister was that man? Or perhaps it was an engine fire on an old car, and he just happened to have great auto coverage and a fresh pack of 100s.

It only took fourteen episodes to put this mystery into *Night Vale.* I gave him a tan jacket and a forgettable name and face. Also a refrigerator for some reason. I mean listen, not everything needs to make sense all the time.

—Jeffrey Cranor

Look to the obelisk. We don't know where it came from, but it's attracting a lot of cats.

WELCOME TO NIGHT VALE.

Happy New Year Night Vale! Last night's fireworks extravaganza at the Night Vale Harbor and Waterfront Recreation Area was beautiful. This is despite the fact that the Night Vale Harbor and Waterfront Recreation Area never really existed, and was in no way a multimillion-dollar failure of municipal planning. And just because the only things remaining on the premises are several large piles of rubble and a red sign reading NOTHING IS HERE. NOTHING WAS EVER HERE does not mean that they failed to correctly use tax dollars to build a harbor, a waterfront, or a recreation area.

Anyway, the fireworks over the city-made sign were lovely. Happy 2013.

Ladies and gentlemen, surely you have noticed: there's a man in a tan jacket. Countless residents have seen him, but no one can seem to remember exactly what he looks like. Just that he has a tan jacket and a deerskin suitcase. And he has been spotted all over town. But no one can quite recall specifically where they saw him or what time of day it was, just that they saw him.

Frances Donaldson, the tall woman with the green eyes who manages the antiques mall, thinks maybe the man in the tan jacket is simply a shared dream, but I know I saw him, Night Vale. I know what

I saw. This man couldn't possibly be a dream, he was so vivid. His eyes were . . . Well, his nose and chin . . . Oh, I can just see. I just can't remember. The man was clear as day. He had a tan jacket and a deerskin suitcase. He can't be a dream, can he? Please call in, listeners, and let us know if you can remember anything else.

This Monday through Friday is the annual Night Vale Career Fair at the downtown convention center. There will be dozens of booths representing phony local businesses that will take your résumés and photos (via hidden surveillance cameras) and conduct sample interviews designed to badger you into implicating yourself in nefarious activities.

First-generation Night Vale residents (particularly those whose parents were originally born in Maine, Massachusetts, Canada, Micronesia, and Suriname) are strongly encouraged to attend.

This year's keynote speaker is an audio tape of droning moans laden with subliminal tips about achieving personal prosperity and how to come clean about the terrible things you have done, you cretin.

Last year's fair featured several very high-profile arrests and exciting door prizes. Tickets are twenty-five dollars, or fifteen if you still have working retinas to scan.

Over the weekend, Teddy Williams, owner of the Desert Flower Bowling Alley and Arcade Fun Complex, sent us some security camera footage of what he believes to be the first ever glimpse of citizens of the underground city deep below lane five.

Early Saturday morning, Fun Complex cameras picked up blurry motion near the soda machine. The footage is quite fuzzy and difficult to discern. Perhaps it is merely rats or raccoons digging through an uncovered supply of junk food, but it is, of course, much more likely that a lost nation of people living in the bowels of a small-town bowling alley are finally revealing themselves, taking our food supplies, and preparing for war.

Teddy told us that he believes this city to be thousands strong and ready to move into Night Vale, ready to take arms against the "Upper World," as they probably call us, ready to conquer this heaven and become the righteous owners of our sun-soaked precious land, we assume! It takes very little extrapolation to believe that they worship a god named Huntokar who demands sacrifice to keep their underground city thriving in the absence of nourishing sunlight, and a fair assumption is that they are ruled by a child king, recently coronated, who is too weak to rein back the generals intent on marching upon us in war.

Ladies and gentlemen, if you care for your community, your town, your Night Vale—like I do—you will arm yourselves. You will rally your neighbors to militia. You will point fingers at those who do not wish to fight and have them rounded up into pens. This is no time for the weak. We are at a presumptive war with a projected enemy whom we cannot yet see or even be certain of, but who are probably bloodthirsty giants.

If you would like to learn more about starting a militia, simply learn to be a true American. That's how you'll know.

And remember, Night Vale is at war. Your careless talk costs lives. They know we are here, and it seems somebody talked. Who was it, Night Vale? Was it Steve Carlsberg? Did Steve Carlsberg talk? Maybe a group of good citizens should go have a chat with Steve and find out what he's been saying . . . and to whom.

Stay by your radios, listeners. We will report further, as events warrant.

More now on the man in the tan jacket.

Old Woman Josie called to tell us that her angel friends are saying that the deerskin suitcase is full of flies.

The angels would not tell her more, explaining that knowing more would jeopardize her eternal soul, as well as their own statuses as angels. They did *not* want to mess with that.

Old Woman Josie added that she thinks the man in the tan jacket is just a salesman of some sort. A fly salesman, she bets, wandering from town to town with polished shoes and a suitcase full of flies. "Oh I just can't stand those fly salesmen," she said, "ringing my doorbell at three a.m. wanting to show me samples and asking for glasses of orange milk."

The *Night Vale Daily Journal* has announced that, despite recent cost-cutting measures and mandatory subscription laws, it is facing a huge budget shortfall this year. "We cannot pay back our printers or our delivery crews," said editor Leann Hart, in a prepared statement whispered through my mail slot late last night. "And we have already had to banish much of our staff into the sand wastes of the desert."

She went on to explain that this budget shortfall has nothing to do with the reported lavish birthday party she threw for herself in Night Vale Stadium, featuring a lazy river made entirely of champagne and a birthday cake topped with very thin slices of moonrock. In an addendum she tapped in Morse code on my bathroom window, she said that the *Journal* is considering all new sources of income, including creating additional advertising space and mugging Night Vale citizens, and that I shouldn't mention the whole birthday party thing after all, because she was never even born, so how could she have had a birthday party? She spent the rest of the night tapping out the phrase "Birthdays are a fake idea," which actually was a pretty relaxing sound to fall asleep to.

Hey kids and parents! Time once again for our Children's Fun Fact Science Corner. Today we are exploring common birds and their meanings.

An eagle indicates that an important phone call is impending.

A sparrow says that you should beware the sea and sell any stocks invested in food-based companies.

A pigeon means that your mother has died, or that all is well. It's a bit uncertain.

A hummingbird tells us that the physical constants of the universe are slowly degrading and may someday shift, invalidating the laws of physics and instantly wiping out the universe as we know it, while simultaneously creating an entirely new universe in a single transcendent moment of genocide and genesis.

As for hawks, well: No one knows what hawks mean, or if they are real. Have you ever even seen a hawk? Of course not. No one has.

This has been our Children's Fun Fact Science Corner.

And now for a word from our sponsors. Today's program has been sponsored by the physical act of gulping. For thousands of years, gulping has been there for human beings when they needed an expressive gesture of the throat. Whether you want to indicate nervousness about an upcoming test or appointment, fear of the Faceless Old Woman Who Lives Secretly in Your Home, or just want to ingest milk faster than with regular swallowing, gulping is the way to go. Forget sweating. Never mind shivering. Sneezing? Ugh! When you think physical actions, think gulping.

Gulp now and receive a complimentary prize package, which will be conveniently buried in an unmarked spot somewhere in the scrublands. Find it and it's yours!

This just in. The Sheriff's Secret Police has just issued an important request, related to our earlier story. They ask that all Night Vale citizens be on the lookout for a man in a tan jacket carrying a deerskin suitcase. He is about five- or six-foot something, probably with hair and normal human features. He was last seen early this morning on the unlit, gravel-paved stretch of Oak Trail, near Larry Leroy's house, out on the edge of town. The man in the tan jacket was reportedly seen in the moonless black, standing next to a refrigerator engulfed in flames. He was smoking a cigarette.

Witnesses claimed he stared at them as they slowly drove by on the darkened country road. But despite the prolonged eye contact, the witnesses still could not describe his face to police.

Two days prior, the man in the tan jacket was seen standing in a park. No one can remember which park, but they're fairly certain it was a park. Or maybe it was in the Old Navy outlet store or near the Invisible Clock Tower. It wasn't quite clear. Either way, the man was definitely standing with his deerskin suitcase and staring up at the sun for hours. He followed the bizarre glowing orb, which is somehow the source of all light and life and—oh God, the sun! "Are you kidding us with this thing? We don't even have time for that mystery," the Secret Police then interjected.

Secret Police officials added that if you see a man in a tan jacket carrying a deerskin suitcase, write down what you see immediately. The City Council has temporarily lifted their ban on pens and pencils, so that citizens can help law enforcement on this matter. Once you write down your encounter, call 911 immediately, or simply say "Hey Police" out loud. We're all being monitored almost twenty-four/seven, so they'll probably hear you just fine.

Let's go now to traffic.

There is a car. It's not in Night Vale, or even in the desert that cradles our little town. It's out somewhere beyond that. There are many cars there, but I'm speaking only about one. Blue, squarish, with tires and windows and an engine that works most of the time. A woman is driving it and she is also glancing whenever she can at the child in the passenger seat. He is a child but he is fifteen. You understand. She is glancing at him, but she is not saying anything, and he is not saying anything either. She wants to cry or she wants to push him out of the car or she wants to go back in time and insist on using a condom, only she would never do that, she wouldn't change any of this really, not for all the money, piles of money, some of it defunct money from defunct and absent governments, she wouldn't give any of this back. So she drives her car, blue, squarish, with tires and windows and an engine that works most of the time. And she glances at the fifteen-year-old child, and neither of them speaks. This has been traffic.

And now, the weather.

WEATHER: "Movement 1: Invocation of the Duke" by daKAH Hip Hop Orchestra

Ladies and gentlemen, during the break I received a call from someone claiming to be an angel. Now I don't know if this was a prank or not, as nobody has ever actually proven that they've talked to an angel. (Even Old Woman Josie's word is just that—her word.)

But, listeners, I think this had to have been an angel, because my face became hot, and the voice filled every part of my body, and tears were flowing down my face the instant I touched the phone receiver, and the whole room was lit up in, well, how can I describe this... a bright black beam illuminating every atomic detail.

And the angel, if that is indeed who called, the angel said that the man in the tan jacket with the deerskin suitcase was from a place underneath the earth, underneath our knowledge, a vast world right below our feet.

I asked for more, but the angel, if that is indeed who called, whispered only "A flower in the desert," and it filled me with ecstasy and dread. Then the call ended, and the black ray of truth was gone, and I was breathless and alone. And, dear listeners, the silence. Well, it was unlike any silence you have ever not heard.

So our mystery man remains unfound, and I'm still not sure why an angel would have to use a telephone. But for now, we can only know what we know, and that is that we don't know.

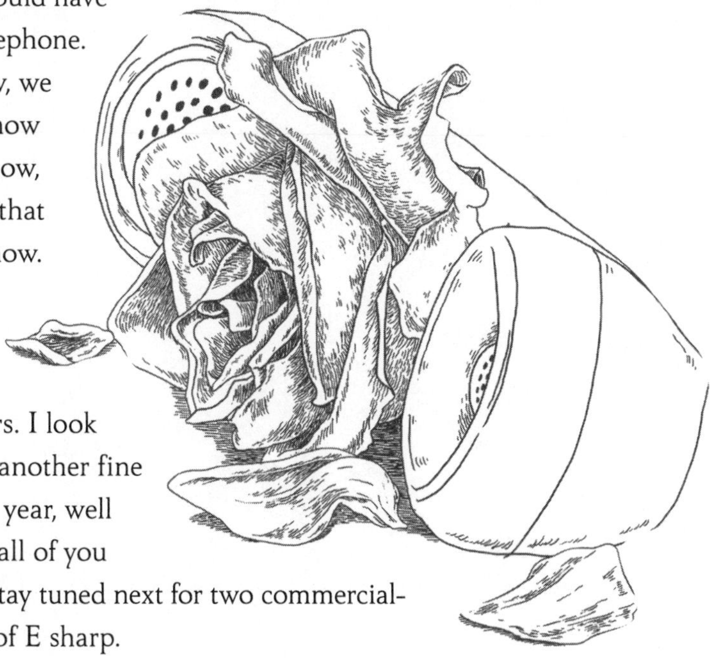

Thank you again for listening, listeners. I look forward to another fine year, a new year, well spent with all of you out there. Stay tuned next for two commercial-free hours of E sharp.

Goodnight, Night Vale. Be alert, and write down everything you cannot comprehend.

Until next time.

PROVERB: Biologically speaking, we are all people made up of smaller people.

EPISODE 15: "STREET CLEANING DAY"

JANUARY 15, 2013

THE MISSION OF *NIGHT VALE* HAS ALWAYS BEEN TO MAKE THE MUNDANE terrifying and the terrifying mundane.

At the time I wrote this episode I was living in Brooklyn, and there is nothing more constant and mundane in Brooklyn than street cleaning. The game of alternate side of the street parking and street cleaning is a big part of owning a car in the city, which my wife did. It's an ominous game, with the threat of towing and tickets if one hapless car owner mixes up their dates and times.

I took this mundane threat of the street cleaners and blew them up into full-fledged monsters. This must have resonated with people, as this episode is one that I see referenced more than almost any other by fans. It seems to be one that, if nothing else, sticks in their memories as representative of what we do on our show.

More recently, the script of it would be featured in the *Best American Nonrequired Reading 2014* collection, our first published work, beating our novel by about a year.

This post-weather section of the episode was a bit of a gamble. We often end our shows with the horrible catastrophe from before the weather section having worked itself out and leaving a peaceful and relieved town, and I wanted to expand that moment and zoom in on it. It's a lovely, peaceful moment. And lovely, peaceful moments are nice to linger on, especially in a town as terrifying and unpeaceful as Night Vale.

—Joseph Fink

Bananas are hardly that slippery. But watch your step, anyway.

WELCOME TO NIGHT VALE.

Ladies, gentlemen, you: Today is Street Cleaning Day. Please remain calm. Street Cleaners will be upon us quite soon. We have little time to prepare. Please remain calm. The City Council has issued a statement in twenty-point all-caps type, saying, "RUN! RUN! FORGET YOUR CHILDREN AND LEAVE BEHIND THE WEAK! RUN!" We have contacted those experts who have not already gone underground or changed their identity, and have been told that Street Cleaners focus on heat and movement, and so the best strategy is to be dead already. Then the experts all swallowed pills and fell, mouths frothing, at my feet. If you have doors, lock them. If you have windows, board them up. If you still have ears, cover them, and crouch, wherever you are. It is Street Cleaning Day. Please remain calm.

John Peters, you know, the farmer? He reports finding an old oak door standing unsupported by any other structure out in the scrubland. He says that he's sure it wasn't there yesterday, or pretty sure anyway. As sure as he can be since the accident. Apparently, there is knocking from the door, as though there were someone from some other side that does not exist in our narrow, fragile reality, trying to get in. He has added several deadbolts and chains to the door on both sides, unsure which direction the door opens. Which is, by the way, a huge design flaw. One should always know which way a door opens merely by looking at it if the designer has done their job, and this holds true whether it's a bank of glass doors at the local mall, or an unspeakably old wooden door leading to other worlds than these. John, meanwhile, says he will keep a sleepless vigil upon the door, as any sleep merely leads to dreams of blurry shapes in the dim distance, advancing, hissing, upon this vulnerable planet. He also says the imaginary corn is coming in real good, and we should have a nice crop to choose from soon, especially now that it will be available for sale at the green market.

The staff of Dark Owl Records announced today that they are only listening to, selling, and talking about Buddy Holly. If you want to buy music at all, you had better like Buddy Holly. If you dress like Buddy Holly, that's cool, too.

They also announced that Buddy Holly will be performing live there this Saturday night at eleven to promote his newest album, which is called *I'm Trapped in Between Worlds, Existing Only in the Form that You Knew Me; This Is Not Who I Am; Leave Me Alone and Just Let Me Die, Please.*

Organized crime is on the rise, Night Vale. The Sheriff's Secret Police and the Night Vale Council for Commerce are cracking down on illegal wheat & wheat by-product "speakeasies."

Two months ago the City Council abolished forever all wheat & wheat by-products, but a black market appears to have formed for those depraved addicts who can't get enough wheat, nor its by-products.

Big Rico's Pizza was cited this week for hosting an illegal wheat & wheat by-products joint in a hidden basement space. Big Rico's, in light of the new laws, has had to alter its menu to mostly just bowls of stewed tomatoes, melted cheese wads, and gluten-free pizza slices.

His storefront seemed to be the model of a wheat-free & wheat by-product–free society, but even the most honest businesses can turn to crime when their livelihood is on the line.

Fortunately for Big Rico, he is a very nice person and apologized to the City Council in a way that did not include blackmail or secret campaign contributions or special favors. Big Rico is just truly sorry for what he has done.

The Sheriff's Secret Police say they are upping their efforts to stop these illicit wheat & wheat by-product manufacturers. They are mostly just sniffing the air until they smell bread. It's pretty easy, actually, the sheriff said from his hoveroffice in the clouds.

More information now on Street Cleaning Day, which has come upon us just as we always feared it would. The information is that Street Cleaning Day is terrifying, and that we should all perhaps fall to our knees, letting out moans and rubbing our forearms absently. The City

Council has issued a statement indicating that they forgot they had vacation plans this week, and so are currently on a plane to Miami, as they had been planning and looking forward to for some time. They said their vacation, since it was definitely planned, has a pre-established end date, but that they cannot tell anyone what that end date is until the Street Cleaners are completely gone. In the meantime, they are leaving Paul Birmingham in charge. Paul, the vagrant who lives in a lean-to behind the library, could not be reached for comment, as he has faked his own death in an elaborate scheme to escape Street Cleaning Day unscathed. More, if there ever is more for any of us.

And now a word from our sponsors. Today's broadcast is sponsored by Target. Target is a great place to shop, and they would like you to consider the variety of silence in this world. The deathly silence when an argument has reached a height from which neither party can see a safe way down, and the soft, wet silence of post-coital breath catching. Silence in a courtroom, moments before a man's life is changed completely by something so insignificant as his past, and the silence of a hospital room as a man, in front of everyone he loves, lets the heat from his clenched hands dissipate into the background hum of the universe. The quiet of outdoor distances, of wilderness, of the luxury of space, and the quiet of dead air on the radio, the sound of a mistake, of emphasis, of your own thoughts when you expected someone else's. [*Pause*] Shop at Target.

From time to time, listeners, I like to bring a little education to our show, throw out some interesting facts, or "mind fuel." Today, I'd like to share some fascinating facts about clouds.

[*Struck out words should be read normally but will be beeped out*]

Clouds are made up of ~~tiny water droplets~~.

Rain clouds are formed when ~~large amounts of moisture accumulate above dense air~~. When the density of the humid air (a.k.a. the cloud) becomes ~~denser than the air below~~, that's when it rains.

Lightning is ~~caused by static electricity~~, and it's important to ~~stay~~

~~away as lightning~~ can kill you, or at least cause you a great deal of body-altering pain and regret.

But take some time to stop and look at the clouds. They are beautiful, wondrous creations.

Wait. I've just been handed a red piece of paper by one of the Sheriff's Secret Police officers. [*Whispering*] I can tell that's what he was because of his short cape, blow dart chest belt, and tight leather balaclava.

Dear listeners, I've been told to inform you that you are to stop looking at the clouds immediately. Stop knowing about the clouds. Intern Stacey tells me in my headset here that they've also been censoring my broadcast. Well, I back our public protectors, and if they say to stop knowing about whatever it was I was talking about, then I'll stop knowing about it.

Let's go now to the sounds of predatory birds.

[*Sound of predatory birds for thirty to forty-five seconds*]

Sirens have been going off in central Night Vale, as a warning about sirens going off in Old Town Night Vale. These sirens indicate that sirens might occur in the general Night Vale area over the next few hours, which would be a declaration of a current "Siren Watch." Please check that your Siren-Preparedness Kit is fully stocked and easily reachable.

Lieutenant Regis, of Unit 7 of the local National Guard Station and KFC combo store, said that, "It always seemed that the only way to live without regrets was just to never regret anything you did. And that seems to be the only hope for the future, anyway. Regrets just bear us down. Regrets just bear us down."

This wasn't related to today's Siren Watch. He said that a few years back and it just always stuck with me.

And now traffic.

Southbound HOV lanes of Route 800, near Exit 15, have large glowing arrows. Drive over the arrows and get a boost in speed. Save time and gas, and get your high-occupancy vehicle to work on time!

There's a stalled car at the downtown off-ramp of Eastern Expressway. Tow trucks are on the scene to euthanize the vehicle and chase away scavenging vermin.

There are several accidents to report. In fact, infinite accidents. Everything is an accident. Or at least, let us hope so. This has been traffic.

Ladies and gentlemen, it is not possible for us to exactly do another news report on Street Cleaning Day, as no information can get through the barricades and seals that are keeping us safe within our broadcasting bunker. Instead we offer the following impressionistic list of what we believe is happening outside our secure perimeter: screaming. A slow movement downwards. The crunch of items made of wood and items not made of wood. A quick movement upwards. Char. A smell like rotting seaweed, or a poisoned ocean. The song "La Bamba," only faster. You know that feeling when you realize you're not alone? Only more so. Screaming. Screaming. Screaming. Ladies and gentlemen. Ladies and gentlemen. The Street Cleaners are upon us. What can we do? What is there to do? Besides, perhaps, taking you in a haze of terror and heat, to the weather.

WEATHER: "A Little Irony" by Tom Milsom

We return you now to a safe place. The Street Cleaners have passed. Street Cleaning Day, as so many other days, is behind us. We emerge from hiding spots, from secret locations, from places under other places. We step out into the street, and it is as though it is brand new to us. Certainly, it is cleaner now, but that is not all. We have survived all the way from birth to this very moment, and we look at each other, and some of us start laughing and others start weeping and one or two of us break out into a wordless humming song, and all of us mean the exact same thing.

Look at us. Look at us out in the honey light of the finished day. Look at us and rejoice in our sheer being.

One of us turns to another, clears his throat, and puts a gentle hand upon the other's gentle arm.

"I've never told you this," that one says.

"What is it, Wilson?" says the other.

"Amber, you are all to me. Will you marry me?"

"Wilson, we've spoken maybe twice. Do you think we could start with dinner instead?"

"No, yes, no, you're right. I was confused," says the one, although he was not confused.

"Think nothing of it. It's forgotten," says the other, although she thought many things of it, and had forgotten nothing.

And then a gradual movement toward Mission Grove Park, no orders or even suggestions given, and yet we all file to that central meeting place, put our arms around each other, grip tight, and then grip tighter. Some of us are not here. We leave space for them, space that has been emptied by time.

"I suppose I should say a few words, to mark the occasion," says one of us, tall, toward the front. He says nothing more.

The City Council arrives, back from their long-planned Miami vacation, nudging those near them and talking about silver sand beaches and the food, oh those Cubans know how to do it. Even they are accepted into the gathering, despite our usual fears, and we grip them too as friends.

Night has arrived, ladies. Night is here, gentlemen. Night falls on our weary bodies.

And night falls on you too. You too have survived, survived everything up to this moment. Grip tight, hum, laugh, cry. Forget nothing and think many things of it.

Goodnight. Goodnight. Goodnight.

PROVERB: One incorporeal being said to the other, "I'm not here too! Make friends?"

EPISODE 16: "THE PHONE CALL"

FEBRUARY 1, 2013

GUEST VOICE: JEFFREY CRANOR

THIS WAS OUR FIRST EPISODE WITH A VOICE OTHER THAN CECIL BALDWIN'S. That voice was mine. I played Carlos, the scientist.

It was a short-lived acting gig.

Not that I did a bad job. (I mean, I didn't do a bad job, did I? You liked it, right?) But as Carlos's significance grew in the first year of *Welcome to Night Vale,* so did our desire to actually voice him on the show.

At episode 16, we just weren't there yet. We weren't thinking long term. Carlos was still a significant character, but we hadn't really started considering what it meant to cast a person in a role in an ongoing series. First and most importantly, casting a voice means you are pretty much stuck with that person, so they better be talented and delightful.

Not that I'm not talented or delightful. (Right?)

But here's the other thing, I'm a straight white man playing a gay man of color. So by the time we started performing *Welcome to Night Vale* live shows and writing more parts for Carlos on the podcast, it simply didn't make sense to not cast Dylan Marron, who is way more talented and delightful than I (or anyone) could ever be.

Plus, *not* casting white people in roles for people of color is the correct thing to do. It's not a noble or laudable thing to do. It is what you are supposed to do, so we corrected this, by casting a person of color in the role.

It wasn't until episodes 19 A and B where we really started casting professional actors to play other voices than Cecil's. As a playwright, nothing is more helpful to the writing process than hearing your words performed. Actors inform characters just as much as writers do, and Dylan has taken Carlos in directions I never thought possible. It's been an absolute joy to work with him.

—Jeffrey Cranor

Your existence is not impossible,
but it's also not very likely.

WELCOME TO NIGHT VALE.

In light of the ever-declining sales of newspapers and the rise of competition from digital media, the *Night Vale Daily Journal* announced that it has developed a new business model. Publishing editor Leann Hart, speaking to television and Internet reporters outside the burned-down shell of the *Journal*'s former distribution plant, said their new mission as a newspaper is to kill news bloggers with hatchets.

In this bold new initiative, a game-changing strategy by one of the industry stalwarts, the *Daily Journal* plans to just go to bloggers' homes and places of employment, with hatchets, and then chop them up (the bloggers), until they (the bloggers) are dead.

She added that the *Journal* still plans to use the *AP Style Guide*, and they are working to design a newer, more modern-looking masthead.

Several *Journal* reporters and ad reps then began swinging blades at the nonprint reporters in attendance.

The Sheriff's Secret Police is issuing an urgent message to all citizens. Attention all citizens: Memorize this list. Memorize it now. It will not now, nor ever, be repeated. Memorize this list for your safety and protection. We cannot tell you when or where you will need to know it, but when you do, you will be safe. Here is the list. Memorize. Now.

Hazelnut. Mystify. Cuttlefish. Lark. Lurk. Robert. Anglican. Pheromone halter top marmalade hardware laser pepper release kneecap falafel period chase chaste leggings wool sweater heartbeat heartbeat heart beat. Heart. Beat. Beat. Beat. Beat. Beat.

Memorize that list, citizens. In order. Secret Police warn that if you miss even one word or transpose a couple of words like *lurk* and *lark*, there could be unpleasant consequences.

This has been a special announcement from the Sheriff's Secret Police.

Listeners, guess who called me this weekend? . . . Well, hey. I don't like to talk too much about my personal life here. This is your community news station, not Cecil's personal life station, right? Okay, fine, I'll just say it. Carlos! Carlos, the dark, delicate-skinned scientist who came into our little town and our littler hearts several months ago.

Well, I gave him my home phone number quite a while back and he never called. And I didn't think anything of it, right? I mean, sometimes people just don't call and that's okay. Well, to the point. Carlos calls, and I'm like "Hello?" (like I don't even have caller ID) and he's like "I need to talk to you. This is important." And I'm like "Um . . . okay."

I mean, that's pretty forward, right listeners? But I can't tell exactly what he wants yet.

And he said, "Cecil" (just the sound of his caramel voice: "Cecil"). He said, "Cecil, I think time is slowing down in Night Vale."

And then I said, after a slow sip of Armagnac, "Oh?"

And perfect Carlos said, "Last week. Seven Days. Twenty-four hours each day. Sixty minutes in each hour. That's 10,080 minutes in a week, right?"

"Uh huh. Go on," I said, trying to sound like someone with a normal pulse and whose palms were not sweating.

"Well, I ran some figures, and during that same amount of time in Night Vale, 11,783 minutes elapsed everywhere else in the world. That's more than a full day longer. I don't know what's happening."

So that's what Carlos said.

Listeners, what do you think? I feel like time always slows down when we're together, Carlos and I. Is that what he's trying to say? I feel that way, too. But I didn't say that. I just said. Oh this is bad. I just said: "Neat."

Oh how embarrassing. I mean, Carlos is so smart, and he says so many smart things. And I'm not dumb. I like science and municipally approved books just as much as the next guy. So I can't believe that's all I could say to him . . . "Neat."

But I did manage to ask if he wanted to get together sometime and talk some more about this really fascinating subject. He said no, but he needed me to help get the word out and see if anyone has noticed a massive time shift. So that's what I'm doing now. Anything for the scientific community. I'm very into science these days.

Wow. Can you believe he called *me*?

Update on the impending invasion from the underground city. The Sheriff's Secret Police has reviewed Teddy Williams's grainy security footage from the Desert Flower Bowling Alley and Arcade Fun Complex, and they say that the nearly indiscernible gray blotch making a slight movement near the cheese dispenser definitely proves that a lost city is moving toward war with Night Vale.

A balaclava-clad man wearing a miter, cloak, and a giant silver star and speaking through a vocoder—you know, the man we all believe to be the sheriff of Night Vale?—announced this morning that all citizens should prepare their town for war. This includes fortifying porches with sand bags, training children to detect land mines, and not taking off our gas masks for meals, even though it is considered polite.

We talked with Teddy himself. He told us that during last night's league bowling tournament, the jukebox malfunctioned and would not stop playing "Mr. Brownstone." Teddy says this could be a code, some kind of threatening message or maybe even a subtle call for peace. He also asked that Night Vale citizens learn their shoe sizes. Shoe rentals are taking way too long, and it's really not that hard to memorize a one- or two-digit number.

The Sheriff's Secret Police also asks Night Vale residents to please help in their Neighborhood Watch program. Secret Police are in every neighborhood, watching everybody, so here are some tips on how you can help this invaluable community surveillance program:

1. Keep all windows open during clement weather. And if you must close them during rain, dust, or coal storms, please keep them clean and stand near them so cameras and microphones can clearly identify you.
2. When having any private conversation, whether via phone or with those in your home, turn down the TV and radio to cut back on noise pollution. Also, please try to keep your conversations lively—maybe some local gossip or polarizing sports opinions. Too much boring talk about plans for your garden or where to buy good LaserDiscs can make the Secret Police tired and less effective at their jobs.
3. Do not wear tinfoil hats. This hackneyed technique doesn't work at all. Helicopters could mind-scan you through twenty feet of lead. You shouldn't wear these homemade hats because it draws unnecessary attention to yourself. It's pathetic and paranoid. The Secret Police are embarrassed for you.

And as always, if you see something, say "something." That's the code word to call a special raid on a neighbor or stranger. If you see something, say the word *something.*

Now in the news: After several months of protests from ordinary Night Vale citizens of stout and sturdy character, the City Council has announced several improvements for the public library. These improvements are the following:

- An entrance is being constructed at the front of the building so we will no longer have to enter by waking up between two shelves in a dizzy haze, unsure of how we got there, and then wandering around, trapped, until we wake with a start in our own beds, covered in sweat and with a few books we checked out on our nightstand.

- Drinking fountains are being installed in the lobby, as well as dunking chambers and a state-of-the-art fainting pool.
- Librarian repellent dispensers are being placed throughout the building. Remember, if approached by a librarian, keep still. Do not run away. Try to make yourself bigger than the librarian.
- Finally the children's section is getting beanbag chairs.

That is all. Is it? Yes. But is it? Yes.

And now traffic.

All roads lead to somewhere, and all roads come from somewhere, and in between they are a snarl and a curve, a twist and a bend. Where are we going? I mean, metaphorically. Where are we coming from? I mean, literally. Is it possible to stop or turn around, and if not, what does that mean for the latest polls and economic reports? Ladies and gentlemen. Ladies and gentlemen, Route 800 is looking clear in both directions. The old dirt road to the small wooden shack is backed up at least thirty minutes. There. Now you know. Has that filled an emptiness for you? Are you any happier now? I hope so. This has been, and will always be, traffic.

Listeners, I can hardly stand it any longer, during the past few stories, my phone has been silently buzzing. You guessed who!

Given that I am a radio host and it is therefore my duty to read you the news, it would be completely inappropriate for me to answer my phone regardless of how much I want to soak my ears in the oaky tones of our community's most significant outsider.

But. Well, he left me some voice mails.

This may be a bit unorthodox, but I need your help, dear listeners, to determine where Carlos is going with all of this. Let's listen to these together, okay? What do you think he's trying to say?

[*AUTOMATED FEMALE VOICE: "Start of message"*]

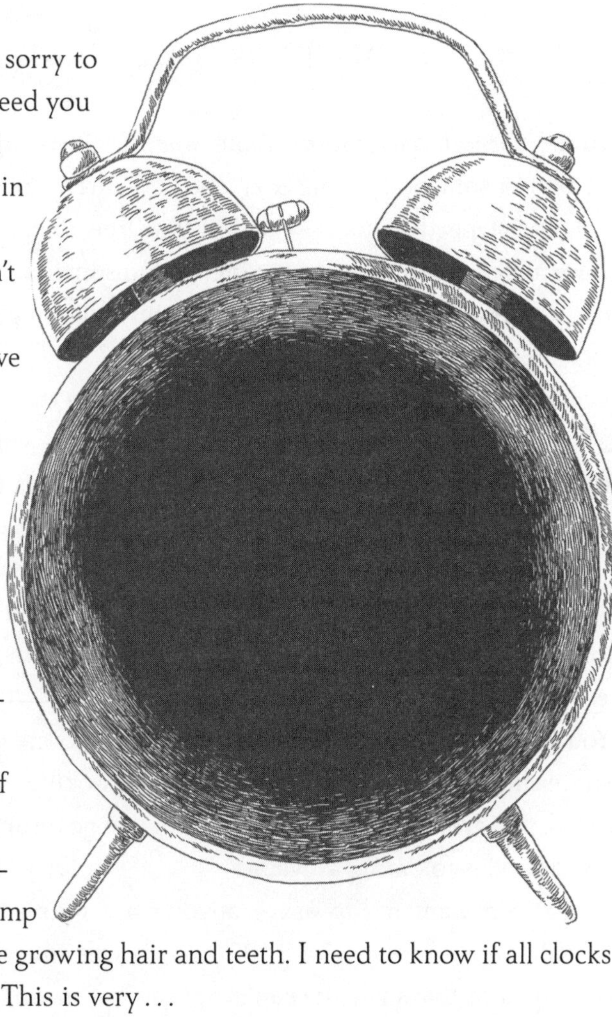

CARLOS: Cecil, sorry to bother you. I need you to get the word out that clocks in Night Vale are not real. I haven't found a single real clock. I have disassembled several watches and clocks this week, and all of them are hollow inside. No gears, no crystal, no battery or power source. Some of them actually contain a gelatinous gray lump that seems to be growing hair and teeth. I need to know if all clocks are this way, Cecil. This is very . . .

[*Whispering*] There's something at my door, Cecil. I. I need to go, okay. Call you back in well, I don't know.

[*AUTOMATED FEMALE VOICE: "Start of message"*]

CARLOS: [*Whispering*] There's a man in a jacket, holding a leather suitcase outside my door, Cecil. He's not knocking. He's just standing in front of my door. I can't make out his face. I'm peering through a crack in the living room blinds. I. Oh no, he saw me.

[*AUTOMATED FEMALE VOICE: "Start of message"*]

CARLOS: [*Normal voice*] Sorry about that, Cecil. I forget what I was doing. I think somebody came over, but I don't remember who or what for. Anyway, I need to meet you. Are you free tomorrow afternoon? You have a contact number for the mayor and someone with the police, right? It's important I find them. And again, can you get the word out on your radio show about the clocks?

Did you hear that listeners? A date! Let's go to the weather.

WEATHER: "Those Days Are Gone and My Heart Is Breaking" by Barton Carroll

Well, I just got off the phone with Carlos, listeners, and we have a date. Tomorrow afternoon! It's just coffee, but maybe it's more. Maybe lots more. Who knows?

You know, they always say, "If you're trying to meet someone, you may never find them. But it's when you're not looking, that's when they find you." I've always heard this in reference to government agents, but I think it applies to dating as well.

Carlos did want me to ask if anyone has ever actually seen the Night Vale Clock Tower. I told him that it was invisible and always teleporting, and that's why he can't ever see it. I mean, that seems sort of obvious.

Okay, that was unfair. Carlos is a very smart man, and I shouldn't roll my eyes just because he doesn't comprehend basic architecture. He obviously has a lot of other intriguing interests, though. Like clock making! And seismology. And who knows what else.

Oh, happy day listeners. Thanks for listening and for helping me through this. I'm so very excited.

Before we go, Intern Stacey just handed me this. The Sheriff's Secret Police would like to issue a correction to their earlier special alert. In their warning, they stated that memorizing a very specific list would keep you safe. This is incorrect. According to the new statement, quote: "We are not safe. We are all being hunted by time and our own deceitful bodies. Memorizing the list will merely prevent additional external pain beyond that which you experience daily just by being alive. The Sheriff's Secret Police regret the error." End quote.

That's it for our news. Stay tuned next for a community-wide frisson of cosmic fright.

Thank you again, Night Vale. May you, too, find love in this dark desert. May it be as permanent as the blinking lights and as comforting as the dull roar of space. Goodnight, Night Vale. Goodnight.

PROVERB: If I said you had a beautiful body, would it even matter because we are so insignificant in this vast incomprehensible universe?

EPISODE 17: "VALENTINE"

FEBRUARY 15, 2013

Valentine's Day is a disaster. Any day that is designed to perfectly encapsulate something as messy and personal as two people in a romantic relationship would have to be. But in Night Vale it also kills people. This is called satire.

Subsequent Valentine's Days in Night Vale have passed with other stories being told, and no mention of any great Valentine's disaster. This is because, while continuity is cool, it would be really boring to make this same joke every year.

There is an interesting moment in here that involves Night Vale sending for help to their state government, and the state government thinking it's a joke. This is the start of a relationship between Night Vale and the outside world that only gets darker and more complicated as the years go on.

This episode also features the first mention, I believe, of Night Vale's many weirdly named housing developments. My homeland of suburban Southern California is a goldmine of stupid housing development names. And the names are always put on some lavish sign with a big logo right by the entrance to the development, to remind you that you don't just live in suburbia, you are a resident of The Luscious Cleft or whatever.

The best Valentine's Day my wife and I ever spent was at a dog show. So, if you want to have a good Valentine's Day, maybe go to a dog show. Flowers are good. But petting dogs is better.

—Joseph Fink

Trust everyone.

WELCOME TO NIGHT VALE.

Hello, citizens of Night Vale. I bring you now to our ongoing coverage of the Valentine's Day aftermath. Emergency workers have been at it since early this morning, starting the long task of cleanup and recovery. Reports are still hazy, but we believe that the housing developments of Marshall's Gorge and Golden Dunes have both been wiped completely off the map, while Coyote Corners and Cactus Bloom are reporting extensive damage to structures and power lines. Please, if you are not directly involved in the recovery and cleanup from Valentine's Day, stay off the roads to make room for those who are. This Valentine's Day, as all Valentine's Days, will not succeed in bringing our city down. This Valentine's Day, as all Valentine's Days, will soon recede into painful memory, fading with time until another foul Valentine's Day is upon us again.

In other news, the Randy Newman Memorial Night Vale Airport has announced some schedule changes due to multiple severe weather conditions, including the existence of an atmosphere, and that strange fiery orb that appears for approximately half of every twenty-four-hour period. Many of today's flights will be delayed for several hours while the rest will be moved into the past and will have already happened last week. All arriving flights have been canceled except those from JFK, LAX, and XTA, which will continue on the usual routine of unsched-

uled arrivals that are a complete surprise to both the pilots and air traffic control, based on routes that appear to violate the simple laws of physics and geography.

In addition, Martin McCaffry, local TSA representative, reminded all travelers that security measures are in place for their own safety, and we should respect the sacrifice needed to keep our lives and our country secure.

Martin said: "I know going through both a metal and full body scanner, as well as crawling through a lengthy pitch-black tunnel while a recording of a monotone male voice lists possible ways of dying, are all inconveniences, and I know that many travelers are concerned with privacy issues involving the voice of a small child that comes through strategically placed ceiling grates, asking them to name every person they have ever kissed, but these are all necessary evils."

Mr. McCaffry then went on to draw a quick sketch of a strange, elongated dark figure crawling out of a kitchen refrigerator, after which he immediately insisted that he had no memory of creating the picture and no idea what it could mean. More on this eventually, probably.

Hey! Here's a health tip from the Greater Night Vale Medical Community. It's possible you won't be able to kill it. If it manages to burrow under your skin, stop fighting because it has already become part of you. Welcome your new body mate. Listen to what it has to say, and see where the new symbiotic lifestyle takes you!

Emergency workers report that the damage from Valentine's Day is worse than previously projected. They describe bodies strewn upon the ground, covered in glitter and paper cupids. Entire buildings collapsed, leaving only rubble and chalky candy hearts. And of course there is the sad fate of those chosen to be another person's valentine. Little can be said to help the families of those unfortunates, except that the process is, while exactly as ghastly and excruciating as feared, apparently not as horribly slow and drawn-out as it appears to outside observers.

As usual, no aid has come our way from either the state or national government. The statehouse even went so far as to send a formal reply, the entirety of which reads: "Sorry. We can see what you were going for, but maybe we just don't 'get' that kind of thing. Anyway, creative stuff and have a happy valentines." Those monsters.

If you or anyone you know has any footage or photos of the events of Valentine's Day, please send them directly in to the station, so that we may put the images and video on the radio. Thank you and be safe.

The City Council recently moved to name "dance" as the official town language. This measure has been met with tense debate and raised voices over the past several weeks. Proponents say we need a unified language, as it will save money on municipal signage and documentation, not to mention bring us together as a community. The poetry of the human body, they said (while quickly pulling in their elbows and turning their bowler hats down over their eyes in an obvious tribute to Bob Fosse), mates physical being with mental necessity—a marriage that brings purpose to our quickly rotting, living corpses.

Opponents say that this move, if voted into law, is discriminatory against the physically handicapped. Also, less than ten percent of Night Vale citizens have ever even taken a single dance lesson, let alone achieved lifelong mastery of one of the most ethereal and difficult-to-grasp art forms. One opponent, who asked to remain nameless out of fear of retribution, told us the bill was entirely funded by lobbyists from Cheryl's Little Princesses Dance Studio. "Just follow the money," they said. Then the anonymous insider's pupils grew until they eclipsed the whites, their tongue slid out from their knife-gash of a grin, and their hair would not stop graying and growing.

A final vote is expected on Tuesday.

And now traffic.

A representative from the Sheriff's Secret Police, waving vaguely at a map in our studio, said that there are street closures, quote, "All over."

"Just all over the general area," the representative said, tapping the edge of the map with two knuckles, "a bunch of them in different places." We asked if he could be more specific and he nodded, but did not say anything more. We tried naming a number of streets, to see if any of them were included on the list of closures, but the representative only replied with an "Oh yeah, I mean, probably," and an ambiguous head waggle to each one. He added that anyone caught on a closed road would be dealt with in the usual manner, and then he winked and gave me a thumbs-up. It is possible he was merely a vagrant who wandered into the studio. We didn't bother to check his credentials. Just to be safe, though, look out for road closures all over in the general area, listeners. They're in a bunch of different places, probably. This has been traffic.

And now for corrections. We offer the following corrections to previous reports broadcast on Night Vale Community Radio:

1. Blue, not green.
2. A low whirring sound was heard only by those to the west of it.
3. The witness's name was Henry Greggson, and not, as we reported, Crystal Souleater.
4. We were feeling, at best, fine, and not, as we stated on the record, "pretty good thanks."
5. No! No! Do not do what we advised! We were so terribly, terribly wrong. If you have done it already . . . well, our heart goes out to those who miss you. Please forgive us. Please forgive us.

This has been corrections.

More post–Valentine's Day news. The Night Vale Mall's planned Valentine's Day art installation, involving footage of actual beating animal hearts projected on a vivisected teddy bear, was canceled due to the entire mall being flooded with poisonous gas. This gas was described as difficult to breathe, and a major cause of death to those who stood in it. Mall PR officials expressed regret at the cancellation, saying "Man, it's like every time an artist has a bold new idea, the system has to come in and shut them down." They concluded by muttering, "It stinks, man, it stinks," before going off to sulk in the Red Cross medical tent.

Emergency workers, meanwhile, report coming across a stash of unactivated Valentine's Day cards, forcing them to cease operations until a specialized team could be called in to deal with the danger. Three workers died before they could retreat. Also Night Vale Community Radio Intern Stacey died a couple of months ago, soon after our last mention of her. Our sympathies to the loved ones of those who are lost, especially Stacey. Sorry that I didn't get around to telling you until now. That was totally my fault.

Mayor Pamela Winchell issued the following statement today, in regards to the increasing public support for her ouster, and replacement by dashing inmate and blogger Hiram McDaniels. Winchell said:

> The mayor smells of olives. The mayor burns like a match tip and casts her flickering light upon the darkened path of fate. The mayor does not have keys to the stone door; the mayor *is* the stone door and all that quivers behind it. The mayor is forgiving. The mayor makes no mistakes. The mayor clutches tightly to your lungs, all six arms embracing your savory breaths. Let the mayor out. Let the mayor out. Let the mayor out.

There were no follow-up questions, but the press pool did let out a simultaneous "omm" as fire burst forth from the podium, and the conference room ceiling flew away revealing a midday night sky that had grown cancerous with blinking stars.

McDaniels is still in jail awaiting trial for insurance fraud and evasion of arrest. He has previously announced interest in becoming mayor of Night Vale and is a 3,600-lb., five-headed dragon.

In other news, several alert citizens have reported that the Night Vale Post Office, closed since the strange and probably supernatural attack that it suffered several months ago, now appears to be open for business once again. This is good news for all of us, as we as a city have been unable to send or receive letters and packages since the closing. All private delivery companies, of course, refuse to enter the greater Night Vale area because, a FedEx spokesperson explained, "It is cursed."

Witnesses say the post office has opened its doors and looks to be full of activity. There have been a few changes. For instance, all clerks behind the counter are now strange cloth-wrapped figures, who hum tunelessly and turn in place instead of doing any sort of official postal business. In addition, the entire customer line and lobby area is full of more of these cloth-wrapped figures, all similarly turning and humming. Those who have tried to enter the building have reported an immediate wave of dizziness and nausea, followed by visions of strange jagged peaks and a churning black ocean. Also, they say, stamps now cost two cents more than a few months ago. It is not enough, apparently, for the postal service to violently assault our minds with visions, but they are also intent on bleeding our wallets dry. For shame. But hey, at least everyone can get Amazon deliveries again. As their slogan says: "Amazon.com. The only website now. Where did the rest of them go? Do not ask. Do not ask."

And now, the weather.

WEATHER: "Neptune's Jewels" by Mystic

Ladies and gentlemen, emergency workers report that they have reached Old Town Night Vale, and further report that it is a scene out of a nightmare, assuming you have had the usual nightmare in which Old Town received minor structural damage and debris, with no serious injuries.

Emergency workers report that they have treated those who need treating and have cleared away what needed clearing away. They report that the usual stress of day-to-day life was worse, but now it seems better, and that later, they project, it will be worse again.

Emergency workers report that they are feeling good about stuff in general, for once. Emergency workers report that they are smiling and they don't even know why. Emergency workers report a cloud. Just that, a cloud, and isn't it funny how we often don't notice little things like that, they report.

Well, listeners, it seems perhaps that we have come through this day and reached some other side. Not unaffected, no. Not unchanged. But here.

After all, this Valentine's Day, as all Valentine's Days, will not succeed in bringing our city down. This Valentine's Day, as all Valentine's Days, will soon recede into painful memory, fading with time until another foul Valentine's Day is upon us again.

Stay tuned next for me saying, "Goodnight, Night Vale. Goodnight."

Goodnight, Night Vale. Goodnight.

PROVERB: Werner Herzog is the most interesting person.

EPISODE 18: "THE TRAVELER"

MARCH 1, 2013

COWRITTEN WITH ZACK PARSONS

I WAS HONORED TO BE THE FIRST GUEST WRITER JOSEPH AND JEFFREY INvited to share the *Welcome to Night Vale* experience. I had worked with Joseph for years as a writer at Something Awful and contributed to his fictional anthologies, including *A Commonplace Book of the Weird: The Untold Stories of H.P. Lovecraft*. He knew my works of fictional weirdness and I had been enjoying *Welcome to Night Vale*'s first episodes when he contacted me in September 2012 and invited me to contribute some writing. I heard the geniuses at work and I didn't have to be asked twice.

My starting point for writing "The Traveler" was to insert a character into the richly strange world of Night Vale who would be completely self-contained. The traveler was his own beginning and his own end, as mysterious as the town, and yet by the time he departed it was my hope it would seem as if he had always been there. I was also amused by the idea of presenting a closed loop of a character: a complete quantum impossibility, who contradicts science and yet feels perfectly at home under the glowing light of the Arby's sign.

The traveler was not the only character I created, and I seeded in the mentions of a few other strange events and persons who might be useful in future scripts, like the Black Dauphin and Megan Wallaby. It was exciting to contribute to this world and a pleasure to collaborate with both Joseph and Jeffrey on the writing. I believe it was around the time the episode aired that the show had grown into a huge hit on iTunes, for which I humbly and fully take credit. You're welcome.

—Zack Parsons

The optimist says the glass is half full. The pessimist says the glass is half empty. It is only the truth seeker who wonders: Why is the glass there? Why is there water all over the floor? Why is it covering every other surface of the house? Who, or what, is doing this to us?

WELCOME TO NIGHT VALE.

Listeners, a new traveler has arrived in Night Vale. This is not uncommon, perfectly located, as we are, between several vertices, but this traveler is not one who will be mistaken for those other travelers. You know the ones.

This traveler is said to have a foreign face and a handsome but terrible beard. He is reportedly wearing a uniform with silver epaulettes, golden braid, and buttons of a metallic alloy not describable in our limited color language. This is all very similar to the marching band uniform of the Desert Bluffs Cacti, prior to The Incident, but the traveler's uniform is not scorched and soaked with blood.

"I cannot say that I trust this interloper very much, and his actions do not give me reason to trust him," suggests the *Manual on Interlopers* published by the Sheriff's Secret Police. According to the manual, citizens are advised to not speak with the traveler and to dig a shelter in their garden or, if they do not have a garden, to make themselves into a metaphorical shelter through vigilance and a positive outlook.

Who can say what agenda the traveler might have? He drives a large and expensive truck, he digs in the desert late at night, he does not seem adequately respectful of forbidden areas, and he has already married Night Vale's third most beautiful woman, Cactus June. He persuaded her to come down from her cactus and he has married her. I am looking at a photograph of the wedding in the newspaper at this very moment. Now I am drinking something. [*He does.*] Now I am [*crunchy chewing*] eating an enchilada that was just handed to me.

Mayor Pamela Winchell called an emergency press conference today, her fourth this week. After the usual crowd had gathered around, minus those arrested at previous press conferences, she began proceedings by vibrating slightly and staring at the sun for five straight minutes. Once these usual pleasantries were over, she read her statement, which was the following:

> THE FENCES IN THE CAVES. A HEART THROBBING FOR WHAT IT CANNOT HAVE. A HEART NOT HAVING WHAT IT NEEDS TO THROB. THE FENCES IN THE CAVES. HEAT FROM BELOW AND ABOVE BUT ALL IS COLD BETWIXT. THE FENCES IN THE CAVES. THE FENCES IN THE CAVES.

Then she vanished in a puff of green smoke. Several follow-up questions were asked, but since no one was at the podium, none of them were answered. Many of the questions were rhetorical anyway. After the round of questioning, a few arrests were made and the chosen journalists were led away to wherever journalists are taken when they disappear forever. All in all, a relatively uneventful press conference.

And now, a public service announcement. The Night Vale Psychological Association recommends that you spend at least thirty minutes each day believing what you see. The NVPA cited a study showing that more than sixty percent of all working citizens live in a self-created dome of obstinance, distraction, and surreal fantasy. When confronted with actual things outside of their own understanding (referred to by the psychologists as "real life") most test subjects closed their eyes and pretended there was a spider or something on the ground.

The study does warn that trusting your own eyes can lead to some dangers. For instance: poltergeists, robots, and humidity *may* create visual illusions, tricking you into unsavory activities like gambling and eating nonfoods, so that they can gloat at your misfortune.

But the NVPA assures us that taking what you see at face value (even if only for a few minutes daily) is the most efficient way to live. It saves the mind from the emotional stress of self-fiction and skepticism.

The NVPA statement adds that you look good in that shirt and that you should wear tighter clothing. People want to see what you look like under there. They also ask you to just touch their back. You don't have to rub it, just touch it. Just put your hand there. God I miss you so much, the report concludes.

This just in. The traveler and his wife, Cactus June, were seen shopping at the Ralphs just moments ago. He was shaking his head at the fashion of our clothing, and clucking derisively at our telephones and grocery scales. "We have much better when I am from," said the traveler, according to one report, which I am choosing to believe. He added, "That's right, I said 'when' and not 'where.' " He then winked.

The Sheriff's Secret Police meanwhile are more than a little interested in the sudden reopening of Jerry's Tacos, located on the corner of Ouroboros Road. You will recall that Jerry's Tacos was encased in amber last summer with Jerry inside. Now it is as if Jerry never transgressed against nature with his enchiladas.

The traveler has been spotted in the vicinity of Jerry's Tacos. If I were you—and I do not believe I am—I would be very careful about ordering anything off the secret menu at Jerry's. Definitely do not order anything off the forsaken menu.

And now for corrections. In a previous report, we at Night Vale Community Radio were talking about the commonly held belief that there is such a thing as "mountains." We scoffed at this belief, and bellowed repeatedly "IT IS FLAT ALL THE WAY ROUND. IT IS FLAT ALL THE WAY ROUND." We wrote lists of friends we knew to believe in mountains and sent the lists to the City Council, recommending that all of them be put into indefinite detention. We got physically violent with an effigy labeled "Mountain Believer," punching it repeatedly before burning it in our station's bloodstone circle. In fact, we devoted a full day of our programming to getting together the entire station staff and screaming in unison "MOUNTAINS? MORE LIKE NOTHINGS" into the microphone.

Recently one of our previously mentioned friends, who thankfully had not yet been apprehended by the council, took us for a drive out to a mountain. We looked at the mountain and even touched it, and it was definitely real. Therefore, we are forced to admit, there is indeed at least one mountain in this world, and we apologize for our previous energetic assertions to the contrary.

I'm still not completely sold on there being more than one mountain. It's possible that the mountain apologists built a single mountain in order to prove their skewed worldview. Not certain, listeners. Not certain. But possible. This has been corrections.

Here, now, is an update. We're getting reports that the traveler was just seen standing on the tailgate of his truck and addressing a small crowd of curious people.

"I have traveled here from the future. I have saved Night Vale from destruction and I will save it again," the traveler reportedly said to the crowd. "You do not know this because your memories have been changed along with the course of events. Now that I have altered the past I cannot return to my own time. I am staying here. I will show you the way. I hope you enjoy my enchiladas."

The Sheriff's Secret Police said they can bring no charges against the traveler, as Night Vale recently voted to decriminalize time travel.

Just what did the traveler mean when he said he saved our town?

How will he save it again? We have always trusted in the unknowable purposes of the hooded figures. Can we afford to abandon what we presume is their wisdom and follow this new prophet of tomorrow?

And now, a paid editorial, sponsored by Yelp.com.

[*Wordless humming and whistling*]

This has been a paid editorial, sponsored by Yelp.com.

Here's a look at the community calendar.

Eight p.m., Thursday, at Dark Owl Records: Curtis Mayfield reads from his new book, *Where Am I? I Cannot See, Cannot Feel, Do Not Know Who I Am or How Long I Have Been Here: A Memoir.*

Friday afternoon is free admission day at the Children's Science Museum. After school, take the kids to the newest exhibit: "Frogs: Truth or Legend." They've also installed a new interactive learning room, where young scientists can play freely with such scientific items as paint thinner, nail polish remover, glass cleaner, and a half-empty bucket of grout starter.

Saturday has been merged with Sunday to create Superday.

Monday will not harm you, but you should stock up on latex gloves nonetheless.

And Tuesday is hornet-free dining at the Olive Garden.

More news soon, but first, the weather.

WEATHER: "Jews for Jesus Blues" by Clem Snide

Ladies and gentlemen and those of you not clearly falling into either category, it is my ambivalent duty to report that the traveler is suddenly gone. His photograph has disappeared from the front page of the newspaper. His truck is missing. Some who reported seeing him have called back to say that they must have been mistaken and that they have never seen anything, that they don't even know how to open their eyes.

Perhaps he has leaped again through the stream of time or passed to an alternate dimension created by the changes he has made to our world. Or perhaps he was surrounded suddenly by the hooded figures, speaking in voices that only the traveler could hear. Perhaps they closed in on him and he panicked as their circle tightened and tightened around him until all that could be seen by horrified onlookers were the hooded figures. And perhaps just as suddenly the hooded figures were gone and nothing remained of the traveler except for a pile of indescribable buttons from his uniform, left scattered around the hole in the vacant lot out back of the Ralphs.

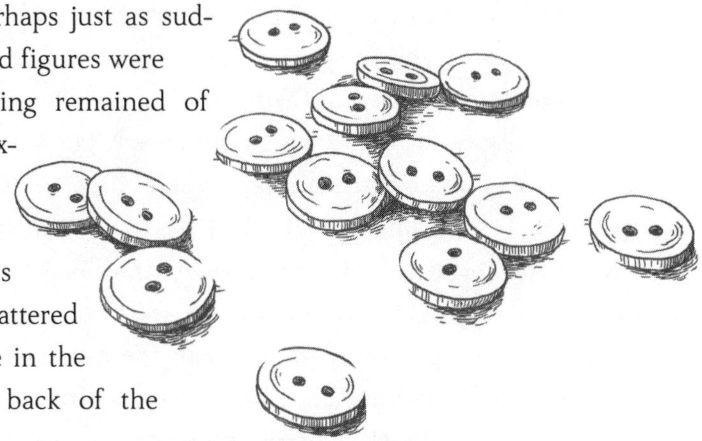

Whatever happened, I can only say, Farewell, traveler.

In other news, Jerry's Tacos now and forever shall be under the management of the hooded figures. Plants in the vicinity of the restaurant have already begun to wilt, and animals and insects are avoiding the area. The restaurant has been renovated to resemble a nine-meter-high black monolith with no visible entrance. If we learn of any change in the menu or pricing, you will be the first to know.

Finally, we are pleased to end today's broadcast with some happy news from Night Vale's hospital. There have been several additions to the community.

Tock Wallaby's wife, Hershel, has given birth to an adult man's detached hand, which they have named Megan.

The Black Dauphin has given birth to a smooth metallic pellet of astonishing density. It joins three previous pellets with similarly curious properties currently being kept inside a safe in the Sheriff's Secret Police's secret police vault.

And the beautiful widow, Cactus June, whose husband we no longer remember at all, is glad to bring into this world a baby boy she has named Champ. The birth was attended by several agents from a vague yet menacing government agency. Champ is said to be a child with a foreign face and a handsome but terrible beard.

Well listeners, this has been another day, another night, another bit of time in this bit of space. I'm sitting at my desk, feet planted on old, thinning carpet, but in my mind I am anywhere but. I am above, in the sky above, looking down at our little Night Vale. I see the lights, in grids and curves, and the places where there are no lights, because they are off or missing or invisible. I see roads with cars, and the cars have people in them, and the people are traveling through the dark in the comfort and light of the cars, and I see all of this from above. I see where the town gives way gradually to the desert, the last few lights from the last few homesteads like stray sparks from a campfire, tossed out into the absolute black of the scrublands and the sand wastes. I see the orbit of citizen around citizen, all these ordinary Night Valians about their ordinary lives in this singular, extraordinary place we call home. Moving higher, into the cold, thin air of the upper atmosphere, I see below me the crisscrossed lines of contrails and chemtrails, the signature of air machines that have long since moved on, the footprint of our civilization upon the night sky. And, looking up, I see only the stars and the void, all a little closer than they were before. All still so unreachably distant.

I have something of urgent importance to tell you, but I will tell it to you later, or I will tell it to you not at all. Certainly, I will not tell it to you now. Now I merely look, from the vantage point of my own imagination, down at a town busy with its own existence. And, for now, existing is enough.

Stay tuned next for an exact word-for-word repeat of this broadcast that will seem to you imperceptibly but unshakably different, although you will never be able to explain why.

Goodnight, Night Vale. Goodnight.

PROVERB: Find more ways to work *plinth* into daily conversations.

EPISODE 19A: "THE SANDSTORM"

MARCH 15, 2013

GUEST VOICE: KEVIN R. FREE

BEFORE *WELCOME TO NIGHT VALE* BECAME OUR FULL-TIME JOB, CECIL and I were active writers and performers in the performance-art collective the New York Neo-Futurists. We did a weekly late-night show in the East Village called *Too Much Light Makes the Baby Go Blind.* (You can still see the show: www.nynf.org. It's been ongoing and ever changing in New York since 2004.)

In late 2012, about ten or twelve episodes into the run of *Night Vale,* Cecil and I were chatting one night after doing a *Too Much Light* show, and he did something he rarely does: made a suggestion for *Night Vale.*

In this case, he said he wanted to do a really scary episode.

I had already been working on this idea for a double-episode told from two different points of view about the same event, and Cecil—a true fan of horror films and novels—made his case for a horror story. It was the catalyst for me to finish writing the Sandstorm episode drafts.

This was also the first casting choice we'd need to make (outside of Cecil, of course, and our little blip of a Carlos scene in episode 16). Like any resourceful artists, we decided to poach talented people from the

New York Neo-Futurists. For this one, we hired Kevin R. Free to be the voice of Kevin in Desert Bluffs.

The beautiful thing about Kevin—besides Kevin himself—is how his voice is so different from Cecil's. It worked perfectly for the duality in this episode. Cecil's voice is deep, dark, serious. Kevin's is bright, light, and smiling. So much smiling.

He appears only briefly in this part of the episode, but the first time I heard the audio file, it really did bring tears to my eyes. Kevin's character is so utterly horrifying and with such a chipper, sunny voice. I didn't know whether I was laughing or crying.

—Jeffrey Cranor

Blinking red light in the night sky. The future is changing, but it's hard to tell.

WELCOME TO NIGHT VALE.

Listeners, the City Council announced moments ago that a sandstorm will be arriving in Night Vale in just a few minutes. They apologized that they did not announce this sooner, but they just kind of let their morning slip away from them.

"You know how it is," they said in unison, "you think, 'Oh, we should announce this dangerous sandstorm. That's priority one!' but then you have to get some coffee, and you run into your coworker friends, and then you check your e-mail, and maybe a glance at Facebook, and you just lose track of the time. *You* know," they concluded.

The sandstorm is projected to be the largest in decades, and meteorologists warned that high winds and debris from the desert could cause millions in damage. They also said that if you're not already inside with windows closed, doors locked, and eyes shut tight then your future will probably be very different.

Meteorologists then warned that raccoons are actually pretty dangerous animals despite how adorable they seem, and never, ever feed baby raccoons because the mother raccoon will definitely attack you. Have you ever had rabies shots? Oh, it is the worst, the meteorologists continued, as the press corps got restless and hoped the meteorologists would shut up soon. God, meteorologists just don't know when to stop, the entire press corps moaned.

So, take cover, Night Vale. Hide in your homes and offices and pretend that mere walls are enough to protect you from nature's might and life's brevity and meaninglessness. Keep your radios tuned in here. We'll keep you up to date.

Hey, sports fans! Assuming we're all still here after today, it's time for baseball season! This Saturday is the minor league home opener for the Night Vale Spider Wolves. They'll be taking on bitter rivals, the Desert Bluffs Sunbeams.

The Spider Wolves are fielding a very young, but promising pitching staff this year. Fans are especially excited to see twenty-year-old hometown hero Trevin Murphy get his first chance in the starting rotation.

Murphy graduated Night Vale High School two years ago and immediately joined the Spider Wolves after they discovered he could use his telepathic powers to cripple batters emotionally, often sending them into weeks-long slumps and fits of crying, even while playing in the field.

The Sunbeams have some changes in their team as well. This off-season, they got a new owner and a new manager, because they're terrible. Just terrible. Who even cares?

And now traffic.

Highway officials are warning all Night Vale residents to stay off the roads. The sandstorm is making travel nearly impossible. We are told that several cars have stalled near the southbound off-ramp at Exit 6 on Route 800. Traffic officers reported that each car screeched to a halt, and through the rushing sand they could see dozens of drivers and passengers running into the road, pairing off and then fighting. They noted that each fighting pair seemed to be of the same build, gender, age, and were wearing the exact same thing.

Also, unrelated to the sandstorm, all stop signs and traffic lights have been taken down for their bimonthly polishing. They'll be back from the cleaners on Tuesday, officials said.

Listeners, thank you for your calls and e-mails. We're getting word that the sandstorm has already begun to hit. Larry Leroy, out on the edge of town, called moments ago to say that the sand was thick and really flying fast, but that when it touched his skin he could hardly feel it. He could hardly feel a thing, that the past was a fiction and that consequences were a choice. He saw colors and shapes instead of familiar things like stoves and ponies. He shouted a bright confirmation of life up toward the sand-covered sun before gasping and screaming "No! Not you! Not you!" and then hanging up the phone.

Well, thank you, Larry, for that informative report. We'll certainly keep that in mind. Old Woman Josie has not called, but Intern Dana said that Josie updated her Facebook page with an Instagram of some rune stones. Dana has been furiously translating these symbols and her best guess is that they say: "They come in twos. You come in twos. You and you. Kill your double."

There's also a link to this amazing cat that keeps jumping in and out of boxes, and oh my god, that is the cutest thing I have ever seen. Dana, you have got to post that on my wall. Oh my god, he loves those boxes so much.

And now, a look at financial news. A fallow wheat field, gray sky, cut by black *V*s of black birds. There is a child dragging a hatchet. His eyes cast down. His eyes tight. His eyes white and red and superfluous. He knows not what he sees, but he knows what is there. A single black-wingéd beast, beak cracked, feathers rotting, alights roughly on the child's shoulder. They stop. The bird picks at the cartilage of the boy's ear, as if biting secrets into it. The boy groans, not unpleasantly. Heavy, slow clouds roll and rise, starkly contrasted against the flickering daguerreotype hills, which stoically keep the poisonous rains at bay. A sudden little river, partially walled by palsied shafts of grain, rolls by. The boy walks to it. He bends forward. His blank eyes stare into his reflection. Neither he nor his mirror knows the other is there. But the bird. The bird knows. The bird cackles. Or perhaps cries. Even the bird is uncertain. The boy takes a palmful of the dark water. Most of it runs out through his long, zigzagging fingers. He licks the remainder from his dusty skin. A sound. Like thunder. Like drums. Like steps. The boy turns and hurls his hatchet behind him. The bird flies up and away. There is a hideous thump. The boy knows not what he has hit, but that it has been wounded. He waits for its retort.

This has been financial news.

This just in, Night Vale: Mayor Pamela Winchell has declared a state of emergency. She has asked that if you are still outside, you return home immediately. A second announcement, shortly after, says that she was lying and that you shouldn't listen to her. She's not the real mayor. I am. A third announcement followed requesting that you give me that microphone and get away from the podium. This is my press conference, you replicant clown! The press conference then erupted into shouts of "Phony!" and "Impostor!" as the press corps suddenly doubled and began fighting itself.

Night Vale, do be careful. I fear this sandstorm to be quite a terrible event. Please stay safe inside, and should you see yourself, I cannot condone murdering yourself. I just do not believe violence is ever the answer. (It is a question. The real answer is far more terrifying.)

So make peace with your double, Night Vale. Do not be tempted to draw swords or guns. We can get along.

[*Muffled thump or crashing sound*]

Oh dear. What was that noise?

Dana? Is everything okay in there, Dana? Who are you fighting?

Dana, put down the letter opener. Dana put away the—

[*Muffled crashing sounds, more intense*]

I'm coming in there! Let's go to a word from our sponsor.

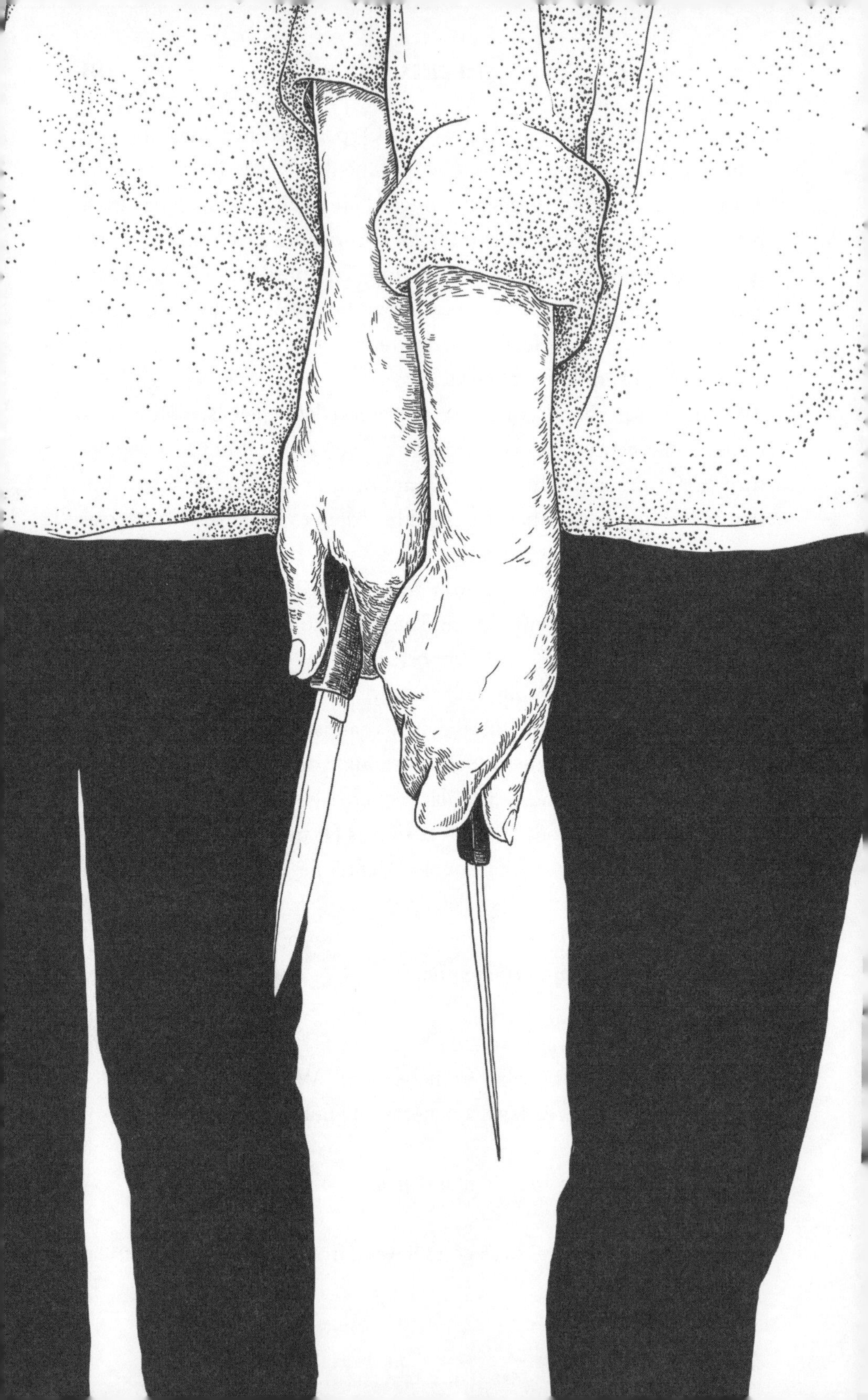

[*Sudden shift in sound/ambient music/tone of voice*]

Got a home improvement project? Need help? Incomplete? Having feelings? Strange feelings? Feelings you've never felt? Incomplete? Is your body filled with hot blood, waving curves of sinew and skin? Can you feel all that blood? Is it even your blood? How can you be sure? Incomplete? Are you dizzy from it all? All of this? What are your hands doing? Incomplete? Where are your hands now? Where have they been? Where are they going? Where are you going? Have you ever broken the surface of something with a hammer? Ever channeled sublime thought into sandpaper? Ever wanted to touch something because you feel things? Because touch is the only sense you trust? Incomplete? What is trust? Is making a thing proof that you exist? Is fixing a thing proof that you have transcended mortality? History? Incomplete? Feel things? Feel things? You can do it. We can help. The Home Depot.

[*Back to original ambience*]

Listeners, I have some bad news and some good news. Dana is dead. But the other Dana is alive. I don't know which is the original and which is the double. Right now, one of the Danas is standing above her own corpse, panting. I cannot tell if she is grinning or grimacing. When I went in, she had clutched in one hand a broken stapler and in the other a printout of this e-mail from . . . oh god, and this is the bad news I was talking about . . . an e-mail from Steve Carlsberg.

I don't even want to read an e-mail from that jerk, but if printing it out was one of the Dana's final actions, I must honor her efforts. Steve (ugh), so Steve writes: "This sandstorm is clearly a cover-up. I believe this was a government-created project. Our government has long been participating in cloud-seeding experiments and trying to suppress the people with pharmaceuticals. I believe that this government will stop at nothing in order to—"

Now, you listen here, Steve Carlsberg. You're not saying anything new, Steve. Of course the sandstorm was created by the government! The City Council announced that this morning. The government makes no secret that they can control weather and earthquakes and monitor thoughts and activities. That's the stuff a big government is supposed to do. Obviously, you've never read the Constitution.

Okay, sure, government can be very inefficient and sometimes bloated and corrupt, but the answer is not to complain about everything that they do. Without government, we would never have schools or roads or municipal utilities or helpful pandemics or black vans that roam our neighborhoods at night keeping us safe. So please, Steve Carlsberg, I've had enough of your government-bashing.

[*Deep hum*]

And with that dear listeners, let's go to the—

Oh my. Look at that. Listeners, there is a black, almost indigo, vortex that has formed along my studio wall. Listeners, words fail me. It is so beautiful. I can't leave you, as our show is not yet over. But. There must be something beyond this something, Night Vale. I must see what it is. I must go. I will try not to be long, listeners.

[*Last line, voice fading away from the mic, shouting as he runs away*]

I will try not to be long.

[*Long silence, just the hum*]

KEVIN: Hello. Hello, Desert Bluffs? What is this studio? Hey there, Desert Bluffs, I don't know if you can hear me. Kevin here. I don't know where I am. It's a radio studio, but the walls are darker, the equipment looks much older. Certainly much dryer than it should be. This microphone was made . . . when? Have I gone back in time? Vanessa, are you in the booth?

Listeners, if you can hear me, I am in a strange place. I do not know if I am in Desert Bluffs or if anyone can hear me. The sandstorm rages outside. The vortex is still there only it's black, almost a deep blue. There's a low hum: I do not know if this is the portal or the storm or my own body. There is a photo here on the desk. It is a man. He is wearing a tie. He is not tall or short. Not thin or fat. He has eyes like mine and a nose like mine. And hair like mine. But I do not think he is me. Maybe it is the smile. Is that a smile? I can't say.

I do hope he is safe, whoever, wherever he is. I hope I am safe wherever, whoever I am. It is night. I think it is night. It is night. You may not know me, nor I you, but we have this mic, and this voice, and your warm ears blossoming open to hear comforting secrets and the vibrations of a voice that pulse so deep into your body your heart relaxes for a time.

And we have this sitting right here on this odd and bloodless desk. So now, dear listeners, whoever you are, I give you: the weather.

WEATHER: "Eliezer's Waltz" by The Ventura Klezmer Band

[*Cecil's voice again. Humming is gone.*]

CECIL: Hello. Night Vale? I told you I would be back. It took longer than I thought, but I have returned from whatever horrible place I have gone. Along the way, in the vortex, I saw a grotesque man. A foul devil of a man. And he attacked me. I tried to choke him to death, but I remembered. I remembered what I told you. And I let him live. I let that woeful beast live.

I am sure he is not without his wounds and bruises, and I pity that he must return to that awful, awful place from whence he came and to where I most unfortunately visited. But, somehow, I am happy he is alive. That I am alive. That you are alive. That we are alive.

Outside, the winds are subsiding. The sun is sweeping away our pains. I am sure there is blood staining the streets. The graffiti of our sins, the writings of an immoral but necessary battle, I presume. The bodies of some, replaced by others who were, we were, all the same to begin with.

And we are healing. Those of us, whoever we are, who survived. Those others of us, whoever we are, who conquered. Whoever you are now, you are home. We are home, Night Vale. You and I are together again. My mouth, your ears. We have each other. And for now, and always, goodnight, Night Vale. Goodnight.

PROVERB: Step one: Write down the names of everyone you know.

Step two: Rearrange the letters.

Step three: This will reveal a great secret of time.

EPISODE 19B: "THE SANDSTORM"

MARCH 15, 2013

GUEST VOICE: KEVIN R. FREE

Monday, December 17, 2012 at 12:03 PM
From: Jeffrey Cranor
To: Kevin R. Free
Subject: Ahoy!

Hi Kevin R. Free!

Hey, so you know the podcast Joseph and Cecil and I have been doing for the past few months? I don't know if you've listened to it before, but I was interested to see if you wanted to do a little (actually kind of big) reading for it?

So I finally sat down and listened to the podcast and got my world rocked.

To me, Desert Bluffs was so like Night Vale: Steve Carlsberg made an appearance? there was an old woman named Josephine? there were dying interns and there were cats. But it was also clear from the writing that it was so different: They wanted someone sunny and nice and pleasant to be the radio host of this newly corporate-run town. A cast member, not an employee. A friend, not a teacher or a student. Someone who equaled much less than the sum of the town's parts. This town where cute pets include puppies *and* spiders? where benched baseball players pore over spreadsheets? where people's doubles are welcomed to help increase productivity? and where hugging and fighting are very similar. And still, all roads lead to Internet cat videos. I knew I could do this. I had waited tables in a bunch of corporate establishments. I knew how better than any of their other friends named Kevin to hide all my black rage with a smile. AND THEN FOCUS IT INTO A MIC.

I made one decision: make my voice higher than it already is to contrast with Cecil's basso profondo. Joseph recorded me in his apartment. Then, listening to the episode, Jeffrey sent me a text about how he was crying at his desk. I have chosen to believe that was a compliment.

It was lost on me until I listened to episodes 19A and B that it was a DOUBLE episode about DOUBLES. But I think that's the power of all the *Welcome to Night Vale* episodes: so much is lost on us till we listen to them again. Each episode has more layers than an angry black ex-waiter.

—Kevin R. Free, Voice of Strexcorp's Kevin

KEVIN: The future is what you make of it. Just know that your supplies are limited.

WELCOME TO DESERT BLUFFS.

Good afternoon, Desert Bluffs! This is Kevin bringing you all your news and good spirits for another gorgeous day in the Bluffs. But before we get too comfortable, there is some news about that gorgeous day. We're getting word that a sandstorm is moving in toward us. Authorities are telling us that it is a doozy, and that we should all stay indoors. Nothing to worry about. Just stay out of the way. It will pass. As with life, and as with all things, it will pass. The sun will be upon us again, and it will be like two mornings in a day. Yes. A two-morning day! A rebirth! A reawakening! What do you think of that, Desert Bluffs?

Intern Vanessa did point out that sandstorms can do a lot of damage to cars, and if you have access to a garage, you should bring your car in. Also, get those pets inside, Desert Bluffs! We don't want all those cute little puppies and spiders and baby raccoons getting lost out in the sandy breeze. Bring those loved ones inside.

A little factoid for you . . . Ted, our staff weatherman, says that no one really knows what causes sandstorms. God, he thinks. Or maybe they're just big gusts of wind that carry big things of sand. How much sand do you think there is in this world? There's got to be a lot, a lot, of sand. Who even counts it all? Wow, big questions today, Desert Bluffs. Big questions.

So, keep your radios tuned in here, as we'll bring you all the latest reports from today's sandstorm and how you can make up for all this lost time. Hiding from nature is taking away a lot of business productivity, Desert Bluffs, but I'm sure you'll find time to get done what needs to get done. You won't disappoint your town, your home. I believe in you. So mark down the time you spend cowering from the weather, okay? And we'll work that time back into your schedule. Great!

And, listen, get all that time in before the weekend, because this Saturday it's baseball season again! Desert Bluffs has just a great team this year. New manager Samantha Figgins is not only the first manager to get hired straight out of business school, but she also brings a powerful ethos of teamwork, fun, and responsibility.

Last year's Sunbeams team had some excellent games, but they spent a lot of time just sitting on the bench with nothing to do, because only one person gets to bat at a time. This season, Figgins plans to keep her boys active with customer orders and accounts receivable spreadsheets.

Baseball is not an individual sport. They're all in it together. As Figgins says, "It's not about winning and losing or who you're playing. It's about building the strongest possible team brand."

The Sunbeams also welcome a new owner in 2013—Strexcorp Synernists, Inc. Look around you. Strex. Look inside you. Strex. Go to sleep. Strex. Believe in a smiling god. Strexcorp: It is everything.

Let's have a peek at traffic.

The Highway Department says all roads are running smoothly. Smooth roads. Smooth concrete. Smooth tires. The slow, undulating buzz of cars over slight hills. Hardtop streets gently gliding us all to our jobs and back home. The beat, beat, beat of society's healthy heart as we all play parts in its exquisite body.

Oh, I am getting one report that there are several stalled cars in the northbound lanes of Route 800, near Exit 66. Police are on the scene dealing with fistfights in the middle of the road. Now, I can't imagine why in a beautiful town with so many kinds of yogurt stores and pony-petting stations, anyone would want to fight his neighbor, so hopefully that gets cleared up soon with a song and a hug.

I want to thank all you listeners for your calls and e-mails. The sandstorm came to town more quickly than expected. Lawrence Lavine, out in the Edgertown Development, called in to say that the sand was like sand but slightly different. That if you touched it, you could feel it . . . twice. Lawrence said he took a scoop of sand into his soft right hand and it was as if he had two right hands. He then held the sand with both soft palms and felt four hands, like one of those foreign gods or radioactive four-armed deer that seem to be attracted to the new Strexcorp distribution center. Lawrence said he was making a sand angel and then he saw himself. He said he just walked right up to himself and started making two sand angels. He said that there were two of him just making sand angels, and that he would happily double his sand angel production today. He hung up the phone laughing like Vanessa had never heard him laugh.

Well, thank you, Lawrence. That was a useful report. Intern Vanessa also tells me she's keeping an eye on Facebook to see if our other neighbors have any news of the storm. I see Grandma Josephine posted a photo of a lovely bouquet of white lilies outside her door. Very pretty. Oh and look at this video, Vanessa! This cat just jumps in and out of boxes. That is adorable. Vanessa, can you tweet that to me?

Let's have a look at financial news. The markets are jumping today. Really jumping. The markets are up and down, but then back up again, like gravity and our fight to break it. The violent force of impact: ground to heel, heel to shin, shin to knee. And then back up again, muscular might and the threat of flight. A young boy heals his wounds as quickly as they form, jumping and pounding and hitting and soaring. He reaches skyward, the drift of the body disconnected from its earth gives the flutter of wings not just on the back but in the belly. The moment between knowing you are mortal and bound to the ground and then dreaming you have awakened a great power to fly like those hollowed-out rodents that clog our skies with feathers and fluids. It's in that moment of knowing and unknowing, consciousness and bliss that the boy sees all that can never be. Upon his return to the flat,

hard truth, he sees things, himself, others as they should be seen: as his equals. He gives the jumping one more go. But the magic is gone. Another. Still none. One more for old time's sake. No. It will never be the same. Well, maybe. One more. Still another. He jumps and jumps and jumps. The jumping makes a sound. Like thunder. Like drums. Like steps. Soon he is old. The ups and the downs lack even the memory of the magic. They have replaced nostalgia with creaking, painful bones. He is old now, still jumping.

This has been financial news.

This just in, Desert Bluffs: Mayor Pablo Mitchell has declared today Sandstorm Day. This massive sandstorm has already damaged several apartments and malls in the northwest part of town and it seems to be on course for even more costly wreckage. So Mayor Mitchell announced that we can all take today off of work. Today is a citywide holiday. A second announcement, coming from a man that looked and dressed like the mayor said that we can make up some of our lost hours by teaming up with our doubles. The two joined together for an inspirational call to work together with these magical doppelgängers.

Is this true, Desert Bluffs? If so, what a blessed and wonderful event to bring us doubles of ourselves. I am stuck inside—doing a job I very much love, of course—but if I were you, I would run outside into the sandy afternoon air and try to meet your other. How exciting.

So make friends with your mirrored colleague, Desert Bluffs! Think of what we could accomplish if there were two of all of us!

[*Muffled thump or crashing sound*]

Oh dear. What was that noise?

Vanessa? Is everything okay in there, Vanessa? Who are you talking to?

Vanessa—Oh! There are two of you! What are y—

[*Muffled crashing sounds, more intense*]

Oh you're building a new shelving unit! Let me help you with that. I'm coming in there. Let's go to an important message from our parent company.

[*Sudden shift in sound/ambient music*]

Got something to say? Need to say it? Unfulfilled? Never made sense of what you are? Who you were? What you will be? Unfulfilled? Do you forget sometimes about your own skin? Your own hair? Other people's hair and skin? Can you make more hair? More skin? Do you need more hair and/or skin? Unfulfilled? Are you satisfied with it all? Do you see it all? What room are you in? What room do you want to be in? How big is your room? Unfulfilled? Have you ever said a thing inside your brain and then sent it to your hand to move a pencil to write it into symbols onto a paper, which used to be a tree, and then used your eyes to translate those symbols back into the thing you just said inches away in your brain and then re-said it with your mouth into an ear? Whose ear was it? Unfulfilled? Ever eaten things that made you think differently? Breathed things? Unfulfilled? Feel things? Felt things? We are you. Strexcorp.

[*Back to original ambience*]

Welcome back. Listeners, I have some bad news and some good news. Vanessa and her other Vanessa broke one of the parts of the new shelving unit, and I don't think we have anything to replace it. One of the Vanessas cut her head pretty badly. When I went in, Vanessa—I think our original Vanessa—was standing over her with a staple gun and a clean, wet rag.

She also handed me a printout of an e-mail from one of our listeners. Well, I presume he's a listener, I've never heard of him. He claims to live in Night Vale. I had no idea those folks down in Night Vale could get our tiny little radio station, Vanessa. How wonderful. You know, in all my years I have never gone to Night Vale. I bet it's beautiful. Really, this whole desert is beautiful. I mean, when it comes right down to it, why would you ever leave Desert Bluffs? How can it get better, really? I wouldn't risk it.

So Steve writes, "This sandstorm is clearly a cover-up. I believe this was a government-created project. Our government has long been participating in cloud-seeding experiments and—"

Let me stop you right there, Steve Carlsberg. You have hit the nail on the head. Say no more. The government is indeed covering up their involvement, or should I say lack of involvement in this sandstorm. Honestly, I don't think the government even knows how to orchestrate a project of this magnitude and of this quality. You need a well-run private business like, say, Strexcorp that has not only the faculties and materials to execute a massive geologic and psychedelic storm but to do so inexpensively and without tax dollars. Why, without Strexcorp, and companies like it, we wouldn't have trade schools, or regulated behaviors, or insurance, or helpful pandemics, or black helicopters. Thank you for your e-mail, Steve. What a great guy!

[*Deep hum*]

And with that listeners, let's go to the—

Oh my. Look at that. Listeners, there is a white, almost pink, vortex that has formed along my studio wall. Listeners, words fail me. It is so beautiful. I can't leave you, as our show is not yet over. But. There must be something beyond this something, Desert Bluffs. I must see what it is. I must go. I will try not to be long, listeners.

[*Last line, voice fading away from the mic, shouting as he runs away*] I will try not to be long.

[*Long silence, just the hum*]

CECIL: Hello. Hello, Night Vale? What is this studio? What is this damnable studio? Night Vale, I do not know if you can hear me. This is Cecil, and I do not know where I am. It is clearly a radio studio, but the walls are covered in blood, and instead of dials and buttons on the soundboard, there is just animal viscera, glistening under the green LED lights. I hope this microphone works. Am I in hell? Dana. Dana, can you hear me?

Listeners, if you can hear the sound of my voice, please contact the Sheriff's Secret Police. There is so much blood; it is seeping into my shoes. There are—oh master of us all, no—teeth scattered across the floor. The window into the control booth is shattered and there is a swath of skin and a fistful of long, clumping hair hanging from a sharp glass point. I do not know if this is even Night Vale. I know that I can hear the sandstorm raging outside. There is a low buzz and deep hum that might be my own heart ready to tear itself from my chest in horror or grief. I cannot know which. There is a photo, a single photo of a man on the desk here. He is wearing a tie. He is not tall or short. Not thin or fat. His hair and nose are like mine, but his eyes. His eyes are black as obsidian, and his smile. No. It is not a smile. He must be wicked, this man.

Dear Night Vale, please pray in your bloodstone circle for me. And pray, too, that no one should ever have to meet this vicious wretch of a man. I want to be home, Night Vale. Oh Cecil, you fool! The vortex! The vortex is still there (only here it is white). Okay, dear listeners, from this vile, vile place, I leave you to your prison. But before I go, because I am a radio professional, and it is sitting right here on this blood-splattered desk, I give you: the weather.

WEATHER: **"Eliezer's Waltz" by Disparition**

[*Kevin's voice again. Humming is gone.*]

KEVIN: Hello there, Desert Bluffs! It is Kevin again. I told you I would be back. I don't know where I went, but I think that I met my double. The vortex is gone now, but as I was returning, I passed a man, a man who looked just like me. I smiled and said "Hello there, friend!" I hugged this man, and he hugged me back. We shared a moment in this otherworld.

I am not sure to where that spiral of space and time took me, nor through where I traveled, but I am certain that there must be more to us than just us, and that there is another place, another time where things could have been different. Better. Worse. But let's think not on woulds, coulds, and shoulds. I am just happy I am alive. I am happy my other is alive. You are alive. We. We are alive.

Outside, the winds are subsiding. Our doubles have left us as the sand has left us. The sun is rising again just as it is setting. Our second sunrise collides with the sunset. Let's reflect on this.

Let us reflect on our lives and where we will be tomorrow. We lost our other selves, Desert Bluffs, but we gained new perspective. Tomorrow, we'll wake again, work again, live again. We are home. All of us, together. My mouth, your ears. We have each other. And as always, until next time, Desert Bluffs, until next time.

PROVERB: Step one: Separate your lips.
Step two: Use facial muscles to pull back corners of mouth.
Step three: Widen your eyes. This is how to be happy.

EPISODE 20: "POETRY WEEK"

APRIL 1, 2013

CONTRIBUTORS: KATHERINE CIEL, DANIELLE DUBOIS, VANESSA IRENA, ERIKA PASCHOLD, RUSSEL SWENSEN, AND TRILETY WADE

TWITTER WAS GREAT FUN WHILE IT LASTED.*

When we created the Night Vale twitter account (@NightValeRadio, if you're not too far in the future, and the satellites haven't burned out and there is still electricity), we mostly used it as a place to make weird jokes, because as far as we could tell, that's what you did on Twitter.

And through that account, we met a lot of funny and fascinating people, a few of whom I wrote to in early 2013 asking if they'd write a poem for the *Night Vale* podcast.

I didn't really have an idea what I would do with those poems, just that I knew I wanted to write an episode called "Poetry Week." So Russel Swensen, Vanessa Irena, Trilety Wade, Katherine Ciel, Erika Paschold, and Danielle DuBois all submitted some lovely words, and I patched a story around it all.

*Is it still around? When are you reading this book? I assume civilization has crumbled, or at least changed beyond recognition. If so, Twitter was a website (do you know what a website is? I don't have much space, so you'll have to look it up on your own if you don't.) where people could write short messages (no more than 140 characters, or maybe 10,000, hard to say) to other people.

I heard Joseph say once that this time is the best time to be an artist because there are so many resources and lowered barriers to entry. We have Twitter and Tumblr to help us find communities of talented people and to disseminate original art.

Here were these six people I knew only as people who wrote really good tweets, and they all contributed something really wonderful to our show.

As a side note, a fan on Tumblr sent me a photo of a tattoo she'd gotten on her back. The tattoo is the entire text of this episode's traffic report. I immediately forwarded the photo to Katherine Ciel, who wrote that passage. I hope Katherine feels the same way, but it was one of the prouder moments of my life.

—Jeffrey Cranor

"You'll be safe here," says a whisper behind you.

WELCOME TO NIGHT VALE.

Listeners, today begins Night Vale Poetry Week—one of our most sacred town traditions. As you know, every citizen is required to write hundreds of poems. Nonstop poems. During this time, the City Council lifts their bans on writing utensils, thesauruses, and public descriptions of the moon. And they mandate that everybody use their municipally granted free will to join in on the fun.

Last year, over 800,000 poems were written by Night Vale residents and then eaten during the Poetry Week's closing ceremonies by real, live librarians who were chained to thick titanium posts inside double-locked steel cages. (Honestly, listeners, I don't think it's a good idea to ever have librarians out in public no matter how secure the posts or cages are. I know there were no serious injuries last year, but some of you older listeners may remember what happened in 1993, when an unchecked librarian population resulted in the loss of many innocent and screaming booklovers.)

But that was twenty years ago. Let's not dwell on our corpse-strewn past. Let's celebrate our corpse-strewn future. On the show today we'll be featuring some poems sent in by listeners from all over Night Vale. We'll start with this one. Last night, Night Vale's poet laureate, Trilety Wade, with clenched teeth and frightened eyes, delivered the opening stanzas for the Poetry Week festivities. Here is what she read:

I fell in love with a hooded figure
who tied my tongue with an ink ligature,
and silently urged I write this po-em.

Please believe me, I wasn't forced,
through bone telepathy or the code of Morse,
to pen this uncoded, unsubversive gem.

On the desert farms, the ghost-eyed maidens make the cheese
while a maelstrom of thick milk falls with ease.
Our punishment? Hot-blooded clotted cream.

The days here pass like cancerous sunspots.
And black metal trees can't compare to car lots.
You are in Night Vale—Welcome.

Wade capped off her reading by screaming, "It is lies. It is lies!" before separating into minute white particles and fluttering away on a swirling breeze. Like soft snow, she covered our hair and light coats and, like snow, it smelled of fennel and meat. Then a voice announced over the PA: "Everything is perfect in our little town." Poetry Week has begun, Night Vale! It's going to be a great one!

This weekend the Night Vale Zoo finally reopens after last month's renovations. Among the new features are fences and Plexiglas to separate the animals from each other and from zoo patrons. Zoo officials promised that they focused especially on the tiger, bear, spider, and snake areas in this regard. Another new feature is the Sensory Extraction Room, where a randomly selected zoo-goer will be dropped into a pitch-black, soundproof booth for two straight days while zookeepers harvest their scent and teach it to genetically improved predators. They've also unveiled a new logo featuring a swan being eaten by a giraffe and a new slogan: "You go to the zoo so the animals can watch you."

So come join in on the fun this weekend. Slow-moving children with more than fifteen percent body fat get in free!

Oh, I can't wait anymore, listeners. Poetry Week has to be the most wonderful time of the year. Let's get back to the fantastic poems that have been sent in. Some of them are even from our city officials, like Mayor Pamela Winchell, who put her quill to parchment and sent us this lovely stanza:

No one will
Have to be
Anyone
Ever again, in fact
It will not
Be
Allowed.

That poem also doubles as recently enacted legislation, enforced by the Sheriff's Secret Police. Thank you, Mayor! And now—and this is very special—a poem written by the sheriff himself! Here goes:

The town criers have cross-stitched their mouths shut and stapled
their eyes open.
The benches are all broken.
No one sits down anyway. No one can fit their broken wings
beneath their cloaks.
A skin condition that makes its victims appear timelessly sad
afflicts most.
Prominent citizens drown in the carpool lane.
Their makeup floats to the surface. Wineglasses clink together.
They hate each other.
They clink.
Until one breaks and then the other.

There is no such thing as vagrants.
There is no such thing as home.
The sun has a tic.
No one can afford flowers but the children stand very still in the garden.
Until the cold snap cracks.

Very pretty. Thank you, Sheriff.

And now a poem sent in by Irena Panchyk, a third-grade teacher from Night Vale Elementary. It is called "Street Cleaning Day":

Run Run
Remain Calm
Run

Where are my children?
Do I have children?

Run Run
Remain Calm
Run

I know
I know where
they will not go

But what way?
Again the announcement:
Run Run
Remain Calm
Run

They are coming
I must choose
I have chosen
Save myself

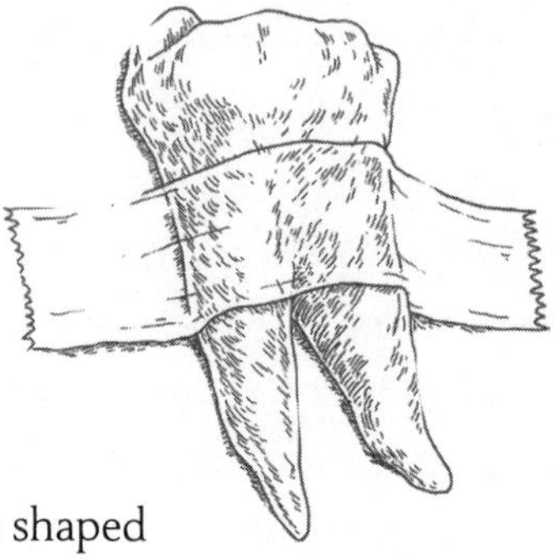

Thank you, Mrs. P. You did the right thing.

Madeline LaFleur, executive director of the Night Vale Tourism Board, sent in a piece of paper that just reads, in all caps:

TOURISM IS IMPORTANT

Below that is a reddish-brown smudge shaped like an underfed hawk alighting on a mesquite tree. She also Scotch-taped what appear to be three human molars to the page. You know at first I thought, this is *not* poetry. This is visual art, but that's mere semantics. We are all poetry, Night Vale. Every breath or branch or sigh before another hopeless night of uneasy slumber is itself a verse in a great poem.

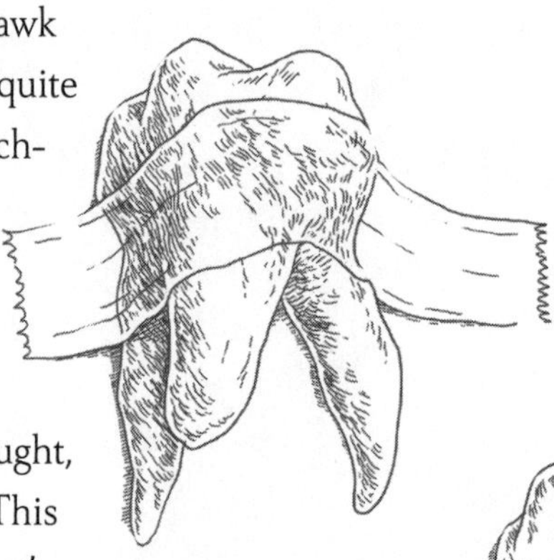

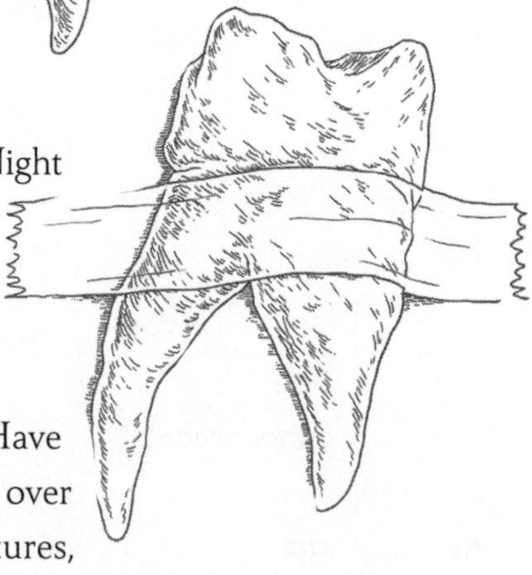

Here's a question, listeners: Have you seen those new billboards all over town recently? They have no pictures, just hyper-bright and colorful text that reads "20% OFF EVERYTHING! WE'RE GOING TO TAKE 20% OFF EVERYTHING!

EVERY THING. WE'RE CRAAAAZY!" There's no store or brand associated with the advertisements, and the Highway Department said that there's no record that anyone owns the billboards or that they were ever put up. "They just appeared one day, and we all sort of accepted that they were there," a representative from the city told us.

The Sheriff's Secret Police warned that the advertisement appears to be completely literal, and that soon twenty percent of everything might, indeed, be gone. They are still investigating as to whether or not we have a choice of which twenty percent gets taken off and where that twenty percent goes.

Scientists say that the twenty percent must go somewhere because of something to do with something called "thermodynamic laws," but police officials reminded us that scientists are comedians and that they should stick to comedy.

Let's have a look at traffic.

Old Town Night Vale resident Katherine Ciel just sent in the following report of what's happening out there on the roads. Katherine writes:

On Sunday, a lambent crevice opened up in the street outside my house.
By Tuesday birds were flying into it.
"I probably won't miss you," my mother said.
"I'm only interested in the end of the world," I replied.

Many find it difficult to breathe
without the atmosphere
but we knew how. We just stopped breathing.

We're at the Moonlite All-Nite Diner and they're serving up fruit from the plants growing out of the waitress.
The CLOSED sign whispers, "Please, don't touch me."
We watch bodies fall to the ground outside like deep-sea creatures surfacing.

You turn to me and ask, "Do you ever think about suicide?"
I look away from you and close my eyes,
eat the raspberries to confuse the blood in my mouth.

Now you're in the only car in the parking lot at midnight and you're watching me throw stones at the moon,
which hangs low in the sky so that he can look into your house.
Your sister tried to touch him from her bedroom window once, and he flinched; now he and the oceans watch her with a quiet concern.
The lilac sky is trying to rest her head on his shoulder, all trees gradually growing through her.

A hummingbird whispers to you, "Be careful, under her dress is her skin," and then builds his nest in the middle of the highway.
I look back to you, and you close your eyes.

So, Night Vale, it sounds like you should use some alternate routes today. Thank you, Katherine, for that report. This has been traffic.

An update now on Poetry Week. A strange thing has happened, listeners. A note was posted at the entrance to the Dog Park. I'm told the note is on paper that is black like the ocean of space, and the text is—well, it's not white, really, more resplendent—radiating its strange free verse message from the dark page. The message reads:

Today they scratched me from sleep.
Nails unhinged, carving

my name in cement. Ash stains
my pillow and bruises the shape
of spiders climb my neck.

Sunlight catches dust
and broken glances between strangers
dodging desert puddles of something metallic.

I'm highly contagious, quarantined
to another body I've since infected.
I will seep into you
if you hold me too tightly.

I assemble your letters, left
torn in the pocket of a hospital
gown. I stain the paper
with sweat. I'm beginning
to steal your voice.

The voice that lies
dying
in the Dog Park.

The poem is signed with just the letter *E*. Listeners, while I certainly love luxuriating in the lush language of a good poem, I do not condone entering the Dog Park. It is forbidden. Dogs and dog owners are not allowed in the Dog Park. Please disregard this renegade poet's radical lies and stay away. Oh, I fear the damage is done, listeners. Whoever this "E" is must know we are all now in grave danger.

And now a word from our sponsor. With low interest rates, now is the perfect time to buy a home. Just name your amenity. Every house in Night Vale has a luxurious view of the void. We also have great schools and plenty of spiders. Who wouldn't want to settle down in Night Vale? Seek a licensed Realtor to help you find the house of your dreams. Realtors live inside deer. When you find an undersized stag or ailing doe you can catch, simply wrestle it down and knife open the chest cavity. Then let the Realtor inside help you achieve your American dream.

The head of the Greater Night Vale Realty Association, Russel Swensen, says, "No one has lived here for years. You're one of them.

One of the no ones. A woman is a fire and no one is invited. Anyone can watch. No one can help." [*Beat; off mic*] Dana, is this a poem Russel wrote for us, or . . .

[*Beat; shuffling papers; back on mic*] So start looking today for your new Night Vale home. As the old saying goes, "Streets swallow their own tails and choke."

Listeners, oh this is bad news, the gates to the Dog Park have been opened for the first time anyone can recall. In fact, no one even knew there were gates. We've only ever seen tall black walls with no visible entrance or exit. But there are gates, and apparently they're just standing wide open. Witnesses said that inside you can see a couple of old tennis balls, some Frisbees, and a black stone monolith that is humming a hum that makes anyone who hears it feel calm and ever so slightly more sensual.

The City Council issued a statement moments ago which was just a series of ancient glyphs. Nobody could read the language, but we all understood what it said. It was a dire warning. A warning to the mysterious "E." A warning to those by the Dog Park. A warning to all of Night Vale. A great pain. A great piercing. A great scream that will soon break apart our sky and our lives if this insolence does not stop.

If you are near the Dog Park, listeners, do not enter it. The monolith (or whatever you think you see) is not for you to know. Public property is not for citizens. Stay home, Night Vale. Write your poems. This should be a fun and festive time to write government-mandated rhymes. Not storming the shores of hell and bringing us all to war with you.

I've just sent Intern Dana (or Intern Dana's doppelgänger, I am still unsure) to the park to warn those who are standing so near to their demise. I only hope Dana is in time to save them.

Let us go now, possibly for the last time, to the weather.

WEATHER: "Get Me Home" by Robin Aigner

Old Woman Josie called during the break and said that the mysterious "E" is one of the angels and that the *E* stands for Erika. "Erica?" I asked. "No, no, Erika. With a *K*," she said. "Oh, Erika, with a *K*," I said. And then there was a weird pause, and then she said, "All angels go by the name Erika," and then I was like "Right, right," and I felt dumb, because that's like the first thing you learn in seventh-grade Transmigration Studies.

Anyway, the City Council in a press conference said, "Oh, an angel wrote that? Well, okay then! Never mind. Sure, we'll show you the monolith. Come in."

And so those on the streets outside the Dog Park entered. And the City Council showed them the monolith, welcoming all with friendly upturned palms. But some witnesses resisted, and their conservatism served them well, for the tall black gates soon closed, vanishing into the smooth onyx walls, taking the Dog Park visitors with them. No entrance. No exit. There may never be either again.

Sadly, Intern Dana (or her double) was inside the Dog Park when it was sealed. And listeners, I hesitate to tell you, but as a journalist, I think I must. Intern Dana (or her double) texted me a photo of the monolith just before the gates closed. Did you know there is an inscription at its base? And get this, right here, on this, the first day of Poetry Week . . . the inscription is a poem.

According to the plaque, the poem was written in 1954 by former Night Vale mayor Danielle DuBois, quote, "in honor of nothing that should never not be unknown." The poem reads:

the gentle man, in glowlight
is a candle in his maybes.
his face is a loamy bog.
do you ever stop to look at
all the blood you gather?
metal halos spring

from your attention. she said:
watch with all your eyes
lest chance again escape you

said: chalk's wasted
on blind children,
wrote TODAY'S SPECIALS
on the board.

What's blessed entry
in this weather? i heard it
tapping, but it doesn't leave
a trail. when you catch a beating
heart in the wild, you hold it
squirming, & say:

that is that.
but the damn thing
keeps on moving
till you squeeze
it in your hands.

I know not what the monolith's poem hides, Night Vale, nor if there will be consequences for my actions today. But I do know it is Poetry Week. It is only the beginning of our fun and festive favorite time of year. Let's not think about what we're not allowed to know. Let's think about what is safe to know. And let's start with the beauty of our words. So get out those pens and dust off your iambs and couplets.

Also, Intern Dana (or your double), you will be missed. I tried texting you back, but now there's just blood seeping up through some newly formed crack on my touchscreen, so I think that's a no-go. Good-bye, Dana.

And for the rest of you, good-bye too, but with the hint of a future hello. Stay tuned next for the sound of some helpless thing being eaten.

Goodnight, Night Vale. Goodnight.

PROVERB: Pain is just weakness leaving the body, and then being replaced by pain. Lots of pain.

EPISODE 21: "A MEMORY OF EUROPE"

APRIL 15, 2013

I REGULARLY SEE COMMENTS THAT WE MUST BE ON SOME POWERFUL DRUGS to write *Welcome to Night Vale*, or at the very least that we must be constantly stoned.

Comments like this both ignore the power of the human imagination and also misunderstand the quiet, boring concentration that is needed to get anything written and edited, even the weird stuff. Not to mention, it overestimates the productivity of marijuana and other narcotics.

Which is all to say that even the strangest moments of *Night Vale* were written while we were sober, in our respective offices, during a planned work time, and with the primary motivator of word counts and episode deadlines to get us moving. The creation of any kind of art is rarely glamorous, but there's a reason why short stories and novels, especially, rarely have behind-the-scenes footage. No matter how exciting the end product, the process is rarely fascinating to watch.

This is all a roundabout way of saying that I wrote an important section of this episode while very not sober. It might be the only thing I've written not sober that has made it into the show.

One drunken night in Spain, as I was falling asleep, I thought,

"Time is like wax dripping from a candle flame. Fluid and falling in the moment, and then solidifying into a record of whatever it happened to land as." This seemed like an interesting enough idea that I got back up, not without some struggle, and wrote it down along with some notes expanding on it. Then I passed out.

Luckily, this thought turned out to still be interesting to me when I was no longer drunk, and so it turned into the passage that ends this episode. So this show was never written on drugs, but I cannot say that it has always been written completely sober.

It's still a pretty boring and unglamorous process.

—Joseph Fink

Hang a map of a place you'll never go on your living room wall. Draw new streets. Tear off bodies of water. Wait for news crews to arrive.

WELCOME TO NIGHT VALE.

Teddy Williams, owner of the Desert Flower Bowling Alley and Arcade Fun Complex, has reported that he is starting an around-the-clock militia watch on the entrance to the buried city beneath the pin retrieval area of lane five. This watch will consist of a line of patriotic volunteers, armed to the teeth and forming an unbroken perimeter along the whole of the bowling area. Teddy admits that this will make bowling slightly more difficult than usual, and league games may have to be rescheduled or made illegal, but he adds that this is a small price to pay for safety. The other price for safety is $2.25, which is how much he would like every single good Night Vale citizen to pay him for this important defensive service against the unknown but presumably fearsome and dangerous aggressors from the buried city.

Witnesses have reported seeing the Apache Tracker out back of the bowling alley, in fervent discussion with a man in a tan jacket. Sheriff's Secret Police report that the conversation was too quiet for them to hear, and reminds all citizens to please hold conversations in a loud declamatory manner, facing outward, and making dramatic gestures to increase both the ease and excitement of their surveillance duties. The man in the tan jacket was described as impossible to remember, but presumably a man of some kind, with facial features and limbs. The Apache Tracker was described as a real jerk, just now, by me.

Listeners, the coming of the first gentle winds of spring has brought me back to my college years, and to the late spring I spent backpacking through Europe. Truly this is a milestone in the life of any young person able to afford it, and I am thankful for the opportunity.

I remember spending a wonderful period in the country of Svitz. Svitz, of course, land of low rolling hills and off-key tones heard on the breeze, is perfect for the visitor with a strong constitution and a low tendency for hallucination. My traveling partner and I stayed in a lovely two-bed hostel, situated in a plywood shack on a steep hillside. The incline meant that my partner kept rolling into me, and then we would both roll out of the shack and tumble down and down until we came to rest in a ravine full of thorns and fragrant, violently blue flowers, at which point we would trudge up the hillside, settle in, only to have it happen over again. Oh, we laughed and laughed. The situation was made stranger by the fact that I don't remember having a traveling partner before or after Svitz. Who was he? Who knows? It all seemed perfectly normal at the time. I also don't know how long I stayed in Svitz, rolling down that hill and climbing up again. What with the tones on the breeze, the intoxicating smell from those flowers, and the fact that it was never any time but the middle of the night, it was difficult to keep track. But it couldn't have been more than a decade or so. Eventually I was knocked out on one of our falls and when I awoke it was in a different country, I had aged by years, and no one I talked to knew where the country of Svitz was, or even had heard of it. Anyway, it was a lovely place and I would say it's a must-see for any European traveler that can find it.

Trish Hidge, from the Mayor's Office, called a press conference today, in which she stood in front of a large truck painted in bright neon colors and decorated with flashing lights, and resolutely denied the truck's existence. She continued this denial for several minutes and through a lengthy round of questioning from the gathered reporters, although it should be noted that many of the questions took the form of just pointing at the trunk and raising an eyebrow. Ms. Hidge admitted afterward that the conference was simply a workout of her denial skills, which she says she must keep sharp through constant practice, and which she also says do not exist. She was then heard to deny the sky, the existence of a loving deity, and eggs. Eggs aren't real, she said. Nah uh. Show me an egg. That's not an egg. What's an egg? Who let you in here?

Simone Rigadeau, the transient living in a recycling closet in the Earth Sciences building at Night Vale Community College, released a statement today saying that the world has ended. "The world ended three or four decades ago," she scrawled on a Subway sandwich wrapper. "I don't know what this thing is that we're living in, but it's not the world. Scientists won't investigate it because they're not real. Turkey with extra Swiss." I think that last bit was already written on the wrapper by a Subway sandwich artist or one of their familiars.

Well, provocative stuff from one of the foremost minds in the Earth Sciences building ever since it was condemned by the city as unsafe and left vacant. Has the world ended? What would the world ending even mean? And how did Simone get this Subway wrapper, given that all Subway restaurants have many entrances but no exits? As their motto goes: A thousand ways in, no way out, eat fresh. Eat so terribly, terribly fresh.

Terribly, awesomely, gruesomely, terrifyingly fresh.

For more on this world-ending story, we now go live to the sound of an aquarium pump:

[*Sound happens as described*]

Returning now to my hazy and sepia-toned European memories: Another country I recall with great fondness of course is the nation of Franchia. Franchia, land of arches. It is fascinating to see how other cultures live, shaking you out of your locked-in Night Valian ways, and

Franchia is a prime example. To see a culture that doesn't even have any people, a country with no population, just ancient stone arches, hundreds of square miles of arches, intertwining and leaning against each other. The wind hollows through the narrow alleyways as the lone traveler, camera in hand, explores the vast, empty cityscape. One doesn't need to be able to speak another language to be able to try your hand at communicating inside the borders of Franchia. Merely call out "Hello?" after long silent intervals, and hear your call echo back to you from the depths of the knotted, crumbling arches, unanswered. The beauty, oh listeners, of intercultural exchange.

Of course, despite the fun times I had, curled up with a blanket through the long nights of Franchia, looking up at the stars in a haze of cheap wine, no visit can last forever. Eventually I became convinced that I was not alone in the labyrinth, that somewhere among the arches was a beast, stalking me. I would stand still for hours, listening to that wind, searching for the slightest sound of movement off in the distant halls of arches. I fled Franchia, running desperately for the border, finding dead end after dead end before, heart pound-

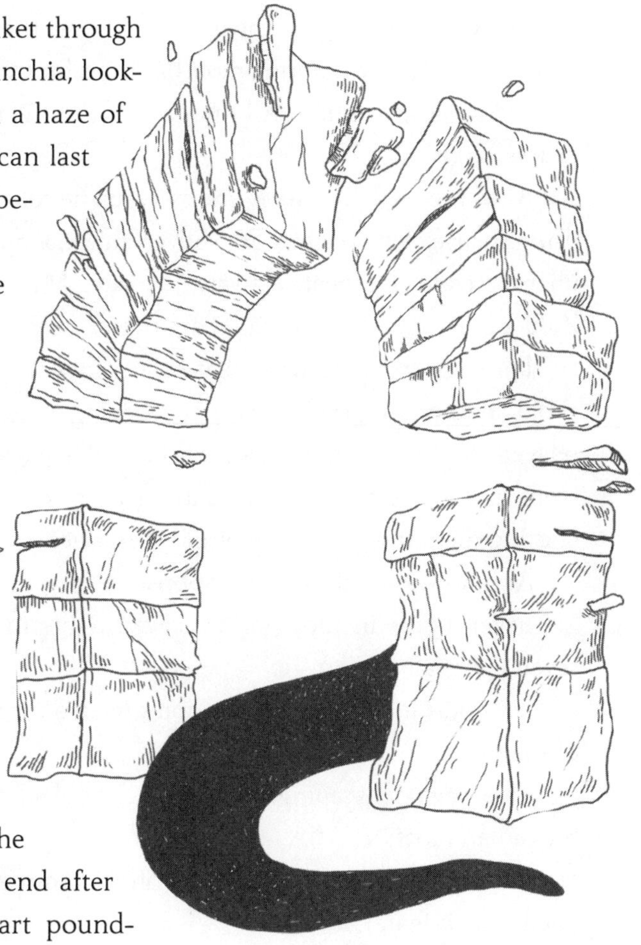

ing, I crossed into the next country and fell to my knees on the grassy hill of the countryside, the arches having stopped completely at the border. And I swear listeners, I swear, that in the moment of crossing I felt a single claw graze against my back. I swear I felt the endless wind of Franchia turn hot and wet, the breath of the beast inches away from my neck. So visit Franchia! But, you know, watch out for the monster that I may or may not have only imagined!

Now: traffic.

The Night Vale Department of Transportation has advised us that work crews are slithering on certain sections of Route 800. Commuters are advised to drive slowly in these marked areas as construction-hatted workers will be roiling on the ground all over the place, a heaving mass of limbs and lolling, panting mouths. Fines for traffic violations in these marked areas are double. All fines outside of the marked areas are quadruple, as usual.

Also, the DoT has asked me to read the following advisory notice, using their exact wording. So: "Silver Hawk, Copperhead, and the Gopher, activate. I repeat, activate. Execute Mission Alpha-November-Zulu-Zero-One-Three. Lethal Parameters Acceptable."

I'm not sure quite what that means, but if you understood it then avoid an annoying traffic ticket by obeying whatever dictate was being relayed. And remember: wear seat belts. They are a cool fashion statement and easily obtained by cutting them out of your own car and crafting them into any number of accessories.

And now a word from our sponsors.

Seven lights in the window, seven lights in the hall, seven lights seven lights all in all.

Six notes in the melody, six notes form a dirge, six notes to rid you of the urge.

Five ways of escaping, five ways all blocked off, five ways each one broken and lost.

Four words in a whisper, four words in your ear, four words that fill you up with fear.

Three taps of a finger, three taps on a wall, three taps as you try to stall.

Two eyes wide and desperate, two eyes squinting scared, two eyes open yes but nothing there.

One light in the window, one light in the hall, one light one light all in all.

Taco Bell. Live más.

To return once more to pleasant reminiscence: Europe is not just about looking at monuments and talking to monuments and licking monuments. It's also about the people. One memorable interaction happened in the little alpine country of Luftnarp. It had been a long day of train travel and searching for then checking into a cold and dreary hostel, and I was in desperate need of a warm meal and some good company. I remember heading down to the local alehouse, where the proprietor stared at me frozen, with a gaping mouth and gray, ashy skin. So did everyone else in the place. All of their mouths were stretched to almost cartoonish dimensions, outside of the bounds of known medical science. I asked for a plate of whatever they found most delicious, adding a quick "please" in the local language to indicate that I was trying to blend in and was not the usual ugly American tourist. They graciously responded by letting out a guttural rattle, in unison, and by not moving as I walked into the kitchen and devoured some of the less moldy potatoes and a few mysterious and slightly sour sausages. I left them, rattling away in their local tongue and frozen in a caricature of human terror, feeling like I had not only gained a good meal, but a few new good friends.

Big news in the science world! Scientists announce that they have discovered the world's deadliest spider, a previously unknown species that is as hard to spot as its bite is hard to survive. Apparently the specimen was found when your dead body was examined. They say you were a portrait of agony, your skin a myriad of pulsing, angry colors. Oh, you know what? I'm sorry. This report is from next week. Things have gotten so confusing ever since the wire services started using time

machines. Never mind. No need to worry about that report for a few days.

And now the weather.

WEATHER: "Sni Bong" by Dengue Fever

Thinking back, ladies, looking back, gentlemen, thinking and looking back on my European tour, I feel a heavy sadness descend upon me. Of course, it is partly nostalgia, looking back at that younger me bustling around Europe, having adventures, and overcoming obstacles that, at the time, seemed so overwhelming but now seem like just the building blocks of a harmless story.

But here is the truth of nostalgia: We don't feel it for who we were, but who we weren't. We feel it for all the possibilities that were open to us but that we didn't take.

Time is like wax, dripping from a candle flame. In the moment, it is molten and falling, with the capability to transform into any shape. Then the moment passes, and the wax hits the tabletop, and solidifies into the shape it will always be. It becomes the past, a solid, single record of what happened, still holding in its wild curves and contours the potential of every shape it could have held.

It is impossible, no matter how blessed you are by luck or the government or some remote, invisible deity gently steering your life with hands made of moonlight and wind, it is impossible not to feel a little sad looking at that bit of wax, that bit of the past. It is impossible not to think of all the wild forms that wax now will never take.

The village glimpsed from a train window, beautiful and impossible and impossibly beautiful on a mountaintop, and you wondered what it would be if you stepped off the moving train and walked up the trail to its quiet streets and lived there the rest of your life. The beautiful face of that young man from Luftnarp, with his gaping mouth and ashy skin, last seen already half-turned away as you boarded the bus, already turning toward a future without you in it, where this thing between you that seemed so possible now already and forever never was.

All variety of lost opportunity spied from the windows of public transportation, really.

It can be overwhelming, this splattered, inert wax, recording every turn not taken. What's the point? you ask. Why bother? you say. Oh Cecil, you cry. Oh Cecil.

But then you remember, I remember, that we are even now in another bit of molten wax. We are in a moment that it is still falling, still volatile, and we will never be anywhere else. We will always be in that most dangerous, most exciting, most possible time of all: the now, where we never can know what shape the next moment will take.

Stay tuned next for . . . well, let's just find out together, shall we?

Goodnight, Night Vale. Goodnight.

PROVERB: Ask your doctor if right is left for you.

EPISODE 22: "THE WHISPERING FOREST"

MAY 1, 2013

LISTENING TO THESE EARLY EPISODES IS A BIT LIKE LOOKING AT OLD MIDdle school class photos—there's a feeling of embarrassment at ever being so young and fresh-faced, mixed with a degree of pride of having made it through those "awkward years" intact. This episode came out near the end of our first year of creating *Night Vale*, when we were just beginning to see people other than our friends and family discovering the show. There's a lot to this episode that marks it as "classic *Night Vale*," an episode that does not necessarily forward any overarching plot, but helps build the world and ambiance of the show with a terrible glee.

The "teaser" at the beginning of the episode remains one of our most quoted lines from the podcast as a whole, and has inspired many a great piece of fan art. Many of the characters featured in this episode are perennial favorites who would appear in later episodes—Diane Crayton, the Glow Cloud, the Night Vale Psychological Association. It is strange and delightful to go back and listen to the adolescent appearances of these characters, unknowing at the time what they would mature into. Diane would have an entire novel written about her; the Night Vale Psychological Association would make an appearance on stage in over eighty performances in *The Investigators*; and I still sneakily tag coffee shop, dive bar, and backstage theater walls with Glow Cloud graffiti icons as my personal "Kilroy was here."

And then there's the Whispering Forest . . . The voice of the Whispering Forest was, I think, a surprise to Joseph and Jeffrey. I don't know what they heard in their mind when writing the voice of this hive-mind forest, but I am pretty sure it was nothing like the Pinocchio-sounding final product. The genesis of this character voice is both pragmatic and enigmatic. One of the lessons I learned from doing classical theater was to throw away presupposed notions of who a character is or how they appear—instead, take note of what is actually said about them or by them, and allow your own imagination to come up with original solutions. In this case, the text for episode 22 says this forest has a "small, ungendered voice" that doles out rather benign compliments with child-like enthusiasm. Pretty simple, right, but what does that sound like? I have no logical explanation for where the inspiration came from, but all these components added up to sound very similar to South Park's incarnation of Michael Jackson. Random, I know, but it made me giggle and was fun to perform . . . and that is usually the sign you are on the right creative track.

—Cecil Baldwin, Voice of Cecil Palmer

There's a thin, semantic line separating weird and beautiful, and that line is covered in jellyfish.

WELCOME TO NIGHT VALE.

Ladies and gentlemen, several of you have noticed the new forest that has formed just to the east of Night Vale. It's hard to say how these dense, piney woods have cropped up in a vast desert wastescape, nor how they have grown in only a couple of days, but these woods are encroaching quickly on our little town.

Botanists from Night Vale Community College said that this beautiful, lush woodland is called the Whispering Forest and that, while lovely, should not be approached. Officials from the Night Vale Parks Department agreed with this sentiment in a prepared statement wherein they just wrote the word *No* on a single piece of paper but with hundreds of *O*s and maybe two dozen *N*s so it reads kind of like Nnnnnnooooooooooooooooo [*read in slow-motion style*] or maybe it's more of an echoey scream. It's hard to say. They did not include stage directions in their press release.

What we do know is this: There is a Whispering Forest just outside of town and it should not be approached under any circumstances.

The Night Vale School District announced that schools will be closed all of next week because nothing really matters and is anything even real? They cited the ever-widening night sky as the impetus for this decision. "How can we place any importance on something so insignificant as math or spelling or history when the void has already swallowed our tiny existence? We are ants, crushed daily by the indifferent feet of the universe and it's just no good anymore. We can't carry on like this," the school board said, swigging on a bottle of table wine and bobbing their heads weakly.

The school board president, an enormous Glow Cloud that drops animals from great heights and casts a looming fog of despair over all it covers, added, "GROVEL MORTALS. PUT YOUR TONGUES TO THE SOIL AND BEG FOR YOUR WORTHLESS LIVES."

Some parents, of course, are very upset by the decision to close schools, saying that we can't let the vast incomprehensibility of the unknowable universe stop us in our tracks. We have to keep pushing forward. Treasurer of the Night Vale PTA Diane Crayton said, "School is a meaningful part of a child's life and to just shut it down because you're scared of your own insignificance is ridiculous. See, I'm looking at the sky right now," Crayton continued, "and I'm saying, 'You can't hold me back sky! I can do anyth— . . . I can . . . I . . .'" Crayton then stopped speaking, lowered her loosening fist to her side, and sighed audibly. She added: "Nothing is real, I don't think. Whatever. Who cares?" She then stared back up at the sky and a single tear zigzagged down her right cheek and she mumbled something about trees having the right idea.

And now a public service announcement. The Night Vale Psychological Association, in conjunction with a vague, yet menacing, government agency, has asked that all citizens start keeping dream journals. Dream journals can be a spiritually satisfying exercise in understanding your unconscious mind, helping you to fully examine your being and balance your emotions. They also can be rife with useful data for government officials and corporate marketing executives.

Of course, dear listeners, many of you are saying, "This sounds fantastic, Cecil, but how do you keep a dream journal?" Good question. I have kept one for years now, and I must say I agree with the NVPA on this. It seems hard at first, because you have to get in the habit of writing first thing in the morning, and also because the City Council's ban on all writing utensils is still in full effect. But once you learn how to create a makeshift non-pen out of a cocktail straw, some cotton, and any number of colorful municipal food pastes, you'll be good to go.

In an effort to educate Night Vale citizens about dream journaling the NVPA has created this helpful how-to.

Step one: Find a foreign dictionary or hymnal. It is strongly preferred that you choose something in Russian or Ukrainian, but German will work, too.

Step two: Carve out several pages, creating a secret compartment in the book.

Step three: Write down your dream, in great detail, the moment you wake up.

Step four: And this is the most important step of all: Eat the paper you wrote your dream on and then place a bird skeleton in the book.

Finally, bury the book near a magnolia or willow tree and repeat each day.

The sooner you start this process, listeners, the sooner you can start actualizing your existence, exploring your inner self, and the sooner the Sheriff's Secret Police can track down and arrest those vile miscreants who keep dreaming about horses.

More on the Whispering Forest. Larry Leroy, out on the edge of town, said that he went out to the Whispering Forest this morning just to see what all the fuss was about and said that as he neared the woods' edge he felt a terrible sense of fear and began to tremble and sweat, but then he heard a small, ungendered voice whisper, "YOU LOOK SO NICE TODAY, LARRY. I LIKE WHAT YOU HAVE DONE WITH YOUR BEARD. AND JUST LOOK AT THAT BELT. IS THAT NEW?"

And of course, Larry's beard is looking very good, listeners. He finally grew out his old goatee and stopped dying it black. It's now a full, even blanket of soft-looking, peppery wisdom comforting his wise, noble face. The forest is totally right.

So Larry said he entered the woods and all his angst just melted away. He felt young and carefree in a way he'd never felt and the woods told him they loved him. "WE LOVE YOU LARRY," the Whispering Forest reportedly whispered, "YOU ARE GOOD. AND YOU LOOK GOOD. DO YOU WANT TO HANG OUT MORE? LET'S HANG OUT AND TELL SOME JOKES AND MAYBE PLAY GAMES. YOU ARE A GOOD FRIEND. LET US BE FRIENDS."

Larry said he wanted to stay but that he remembered that he had cable TV and didn't want to miss anything just because there was some beautiful nature he'd never explored, so he went back home to catch an *Iron Chef America* marathon.

So, listeners, it sounds like the Whispering Forest is actually pretty nice. I can't imagine what all those academic types and bureaucratic pen pushers were going on about. Larry made it sound like a really friendly place. I'm going to send Intern Richard out there and see what else we can learn about this fascinating new addition to our landscape.

And now a look at the community calendar.

Monday is the opening of the new exhibit at the Children's Science Museum. The exhibit is called "THE MOON IS A LIE." It explores how the moon is a government-created myth to keep us all from knowing about the ancient alien machinery that controls the oceans. In the Hands-on Learning Room, children will be able to make their own moons out of Styrofoam and aggressive propaganda, just like the Masons did.

Tuesday, Buddy Holly returns to Dark Owl Records. There will be no performance or book signing, and no one will see him. He will just hover over music lovers' shoulders and disapprove of their misguided musical tastes. Incorrect shoppers will receive a bout of uncontrolled sobbing and a horrifying chill up their spine from the legendary rock and roller himself.

Thursday is recycling pickup day: paper goes in blue bags, plastic in clear, and any teeth you have lost because of last week's public water mishap should be gently placed in a wooden box and set afire.

Friday at the Night Vale Recreation Center are cooking classes for beginners. Amateur chefs can learn about knife skills, the basics of baking, and a seminar about whether or not deer feel pain or are just sad.

Saturday afternoon is a secret parade. You will know where and when it is, if and when you are chosen to see its secret floats and hear its secret songs.

Sunday is the day we decided last fall we would clean up around here. You promised. We need to clean up, okay. And that's this Sunday. Don't make other plans. You always do that. You always are doing that.

And now a word from our sponsor.

You cannot see. You grope around, wildly, as your footing is also unstable. You feel a thin liquid filling your shoes. It is not water, you can tell. A pungent smell of brine or anxiety. Your hands strike something solid. A wall, you think. It is soft, leathery, but also wet. You keep your hands to the surface and it is moving in and out. Like it is breathing. No, more like spasms. You hear a dull rumble from above, a gurgle from below. You still see nothing. The walls jerk back quickly. You lose your balance and slide down to the floor, which is the same surface, but now the liquid is sloshing past you. Something grabs your leg. Something is grabbing your leg. You are being pulled down. You cannot see. Which way madness. "WHICH WAY MADNESS" you scream but no sound comes from your stubborn lips. Your impudent throat. You reach, for what you do not know, only that you reach. A blinding flash. A moment of understanding. You are in an empty storeroom. Tied to a chair. There are others but they are hooded and limp. You recall this living nightmare. You take comfort in its familiar pain. You smell fermentation and can hear a dull, unending beeping. Someone shouts in a language you do not know. You love your family. You love them. Welcome to Red Lobster. Come see what's fresh today.

More on the Whispering Forest . . . Intern Richard called to say the woods are stunning and the moment he arrived they were so welcoming. "RICHARD, YOU HAVE LOVELY GREEN EYES. I CAN'T BELIEVE I JUST NOTICED THEM. THAT SHIRT REALLY BRINGS OUT THOSE PIERCING GEMS. YOU ALSO HAVE NICE SOFT HANDS. DO YOU PLAY GUITAR? WOULD YOU LIKE TO PLAY GUITAR? DO YOU LIKE MUSIC?" the forest apparently whispered.

Richard reported to me that he wanted to stay in the forest, but I told him that he still has intern tasks to do here at the radio station, like filing ad contracts and renaming the wingless insects. But he insisted on staying. Richard told me that his feet started itching at first, then tingling, a very pleasant tingle. He then noticed gray-brown patches forming along his feet and legs and he couldn't move. Richard assured me that this was exactly what he wanted, but I have already sent for help.

Ladies and gentlemen, for your safety, please stay away from the Whispering Forest. Do not listen to its hollow compliments, its sappy flattery. Learn from Larry Leroy, stay inside and watch television. There is no reason to go explore nature. No reason. So, as I try to find out what has happened to our station intern, let us go to the weather.

WEATHER: "Winifred" by Seth Boyer

Well listeners, there's good news and bad news from the Whispering Forest. The bad news is that Intern Richard, as we know him, is lost to us forever. As are the dozens of first responders, concerned citizens, and curious nature lovers who all went to the Whispering Forest today. To the family of Richard, let me say I am terribly sorry for your loss. He was an excellent intern, and he will be missed.

The good news is that none of those we lost today are technically dead. According to Simone Rigadeau, from the Earth Sciences building at Night Vale Community College, the Whispering Forest is a place where we can all plunge our feet and hands into the cool, soft soil, allowing our fingers and toes to grow and spiral into the earth, quickly and deeply intertwining with themselves, each other, snaking in and through a complex organic network to become one. In the Whispering Forest, everyone is one everything. They share each other now.

I know Simone is only a transient who lives in an unused storage closet in the Earth Sciences building and not an actual scientist, but I thought that was a beautiful story and it brought some meaning to the otherwise meaningless life of an intern.

Rest easy, Night Vale, knowing that we have lost no one today. They have gained each other. They share the soul of the Whispering Forest now. And we will have them, always, or at least however long trees live, which I think is fairly long. I'm not really sure. I had a hamster as a child and it died in, like, two weeks, so what do I know?

Stay tuned next for the sound of a rapidly beating heart.

As always, goodnight, Night Vale. Goodnight.

PROVERB: If you love someone, set them free. Set them free now. This is the police, and we have you surrounded.

EPISODE 23: "ETERNAL SCOUTS"

MAY 15, 2013

THE CONCEPT OF ETERNAL SCOUTS STARTED AS A QUICK JOKE IN THE FIRST episode, and then was briefly mentioned again in episode 10. And, looking at the concept, I started thinking, "Well, what does an 'Eternal Scout' mean? What does that even look like?" This episode is me attempting to answer that question.

I was never in the Boy Scouts. My parents once took me to a Cub Scouts meeting, but I was a terrible and stubborn child and when I didn't want to do something there wasn't much of a way of making me do it, so that only lasted one meeting. My dad was a Boy Scout, and so was always in charge of building the fire when we went camping. I never really learned how, and now my wife is in charge of making the fires at home.

None of that has anything to do with this episode.

As mentioned in the introduction to this book, the first project that Jeffrey and I worked together on was a play called *What the Time Traveler Will Tell Us*. Because it's not likely a play that will ever be performed again, certain scenes from the script have been mined for *Night Vale*.

The passage at the end here, which attempts to define a number of important words, is lifted directly from the play. It was a passage I liked a lot, and I wanted more than the one hundred or so people who saw the play to hear it. The play had a motif of toast and the smell of toast, thus the bit about toast in there.

This episode also marks the introduction of what would much, much later become an important side character voiced by Wil Wheaton: Earl Harlan. Here he is a fragment of Cecil's past, mostly characterized by the semi-romantic regret he held for Cecil. When we brought him back, we wanted him to be much more than a crush he perhaps once held, and so we developed a number of story lines for him that are not at all foreshadowed here. People are always much more than the first impression they make.

—Joseph Fink

**We report only the real, the semi-real,
and the verifiably unreal.**

WELCOME TO NIGHT VALE.

Here at the station we have been receiving many calls and e-mails over the last several months asking us about Khoshekh, the cat found hovering in the men's bathroom. Well, he is doing just fine, and thank you very much for your concern. In fact, he recently gave birth to an adorable litter of kittens. How does a he cat give birth? Well, how does a he cat hover in an immobile spot in a radio station bathroom? Some things just aren't meant to be questioned. Most things, actually.

We slipped a note under Station Management's door asking if we could keep all those adorable floating kittens. Management responded with a great thrashing behind the closed door of their office, and a localized rainstorm in the break room. We are still working with the station oracle to understand their message, and we will let you know soon what we do with the kittens.

Exciting news from the Night Vale chapter of the Boy Scouts. Two of their members, Franklin Wilson and Barton Donovan, have achieved all the necessary requirements to advance from the rank of Fear Scout to that final and most terrible of ranks: Eternal Scout. The ceremony will take place at an unspecified time today in the hole in the vacant lot out back of the Ralphs, and anyone is invited to attend. Those who wish to view the ceremony should wear loose-fitting clothing and tell

everyone they know that they will be going on a long trip, oh, just somewhere, to clear their heads, you know? And that they don't know when they'll be back but it won't be for a long time probably. I just really have to find myself, and I think the open road is the place to do it, you should say. Don't look for me, you should continue, taking hold of your loved one's shoulder and maintaining an intense eye contact. Don't look for me.

The City Council voted this week to make death a meritocracy. For all of human existence, death has been a "communistic sort of event," the council said in a prepared statement, and that "we live in America where it is not the government's job to give death to every single citizen."

The council noted that from now on death would be earned through hard work and productivity, not just as a handout for every resource-sucking freeloader on the street. If you want to die, the council said, you will have to achieve death yourself. Not everyone gets to die, and that's just how it will be.

The vote won by a small margin with the opposition split between keeping death universal and others pushing for banning death altogether.

Listen, Night Vale, I don't know about you, but I am for this new merit-based system of death. If everyone gets to die, then no one will really value death. I used to be young and idealistic and think that death was a human right, that everyone deserved to die, but now I realize that dying is very hard work. I'm working hard every day trying to die, but you don't hear me complaining, "Oh government, where's my free death." No, when I die, I want to have earned it.

I don't mean to sound insensitive to those less fortunate who don't have the means to die without government help, which is why I support our local non-profit shelters that help ease our more down-on-their-luck brothers and sisters toward the death they truly want but just can't yet afford.

At her regular daily press conference today, Mayor Pamela Winchell extended a warm congratulations to Franklin and Barton for their Eternal Scout achievement.

"FIRE IS ACTUALLY COLD," she shrieked. "IT IS THE COLD THAT BURNS YOU."

She went on to produce several colorful balloons from her mouth, which she presented to strange, mute children in the audience, children whom none of the reporters remembered having been there just seconds before, and whom none of them recognized. The children thanked the mayor by vibrating and dissolving.

The Scouts, meanwhile, have continued preparations for the ceremony. The vacant lot out back of the Ralphs is now covered by a thick burlap tent, and Scout leaders were seen rolling several oil drums into the tent, drums that rattled as they moved. They also have put up streamers and a hand-painted banner over the tent entrance that reads "GREAT JOB FRANKIE AND BARTIE."

Great job indeed. Oh, this is so exciting. What a wonderful little town we have.

After a long battle with parents over the controversial soda machines in the recently reopened Night Vale High School, the school board has finally capitulated to pressure from the PTA. While the school board, led by the ethereal and menacing Glow Cloud, refused to remove the machines because of the much-needed extra revenue, they concurred that so much corn syrup was simply not good for students' health.

As a compromise, the school board agreed to booby-trap the machines with swinging blades and an electrical maze to promote healthier drink choices and physical activity, which can help burn off all that sugar. To make up for the potentially lowered income from fewer purchases, the school board said they would raise soda prices, remove all water fountains and sinks in the building, and double up the salt in all cafeteria dishes.

The school board concluded their announcement with the following: "ALL HAIL. ALL PRAISE. ALL SUBMIT BEFORE THE GLOW CLOUD." Then they sprayed themselves and reporters with shaken-up two-liters of warm Sierra Mist.

Agents from the vague yet menacing government agency are having their annual recruitment drive at the abandoned missile silo outside of town next week. Those interested in joining whatever vague but important work it is that they do should submit résumés and headshots into one of several secret drop spots around town. At the event itself, the candidates will be ruthlessly interrogated to determine how they found out where the secret drop spots are, what exactly they know about the agency, and who told them.

A representative for the agency, speaking through a representative, who in turn spoke through a heavily drugged proxy, said, "Oh, you know, it'll be a lot of the standard job interview stuff. Asking you to name your greatest weakness so that we can use it to turn the screws on you even tighter, breaking you slowly through a series of hypnotic light pulses and disruptive sound patterns, stuff like that."

Those who make it through this rigorous process will vanish forever from our lives, presumably to join the vague yet menacing agency in some capacity. Those who fail the process will also vanish. Eventually, given enough time, we all will vanish, even the memories of us corroding and fading. The recruitment drive includes a potluck lunch, and the agency mentioned that they usually are overstocked on desserts and do not have enough main courses, so keep that in mind.

If you want to witness the Eternal Scout ceremony, now is the time to run to the burlap tent over the vacant lot out back of the Ralphs. Scout leaders indicate that the ceremony will be starting any second now, although much of the ceremony is out of mere human control and so they could not give a specific time.

Scoutmaster Earl Harlan said, "I'm proud to be the first Scout troop to achieve this rank. I'm also terrified to be the first Scout troop to achieve this rank. The two emotions are mixing inside my body, and it's confusing. It's confusing." He shivered. "We could have had something, Cecil. Always remember that," he concluded, clutching my arm, before walking, head bowed, out of the studio.

Well, I think we're all both proud and terrified most of the time, and that's because we live in the best town in this county, in this state, and in this nation. That's where the pride comes from. The terrified part is because life is terrifying. It just is.

And now a word from our sponsors.

Losing hope? Hard to see a way out? Hope? Losing it? Lost? Lost in a cave? Lost in a cave that spirals around a single obsidian column, lit dimly by a source that does not seem to be either above or below? Hard to see? Scrabbling among the rocks for any landmark that might tell you from whence you came, to where you should go? Depressed? Suffering from depression? Suffering? Tripped on a rock and tumbling for a painful eternity down the evenly lit featureless spiral? Losing hope? Six Flags Desert Springs. Just off Exit 64 in Night Vale.

The Night Vale Medical Board announced today that they can't help you. Not if you're going to keep screaming like that. They also asked that you clean up a bit before you come in. They don't want to get sick.

"One of the major problems we face as doctors is the sheer amount of blood," said Suzanne Thurgood, publicity director for the medical board. "We get so much blood all over our floors and jeans and copper magnetic bracelets, it becomes nearly untenable."

Thurgood added that the best thing to do if you are unable to stop bleeding is to first take a few breaths. Calm yourself. This should help you concentrate on not bleeding. Then, once you have finished bleeding, come to a doctor's office. "It's not a matter of medical training," Thurgood said, "it's simply a matter of respecting other people."

Thurgood then lit a cigarette and placed it expertly into the mouth of a low-flying hawk. As the bird flew away, a distant clock tower chimed the quarter hour, and a gentle rain began to fall.

This has been Community Health Tips.

Reports are coming in that the Eternal Scout ceremony has started, and that herds of strange, mute children are streaming out of the burlap tent, filling all public and private spaces and standing silently as though awaiting an order from some unknown higher source. The Sheriff's Secret Police advise that the children are creepy, and that they are creeped out by them. I myself count five in this recording booth with me, exactly half of them boys and half of them girls.

Who knows for what purpose these children have come to us, and to what end their actions will take us? Who knows anything, actually, for sure? Let's go, surrounded and confused, vulnerable and trembling, to the weather.

WEATHER: "Too Much Time" by John Vanderslice

The ceremony is over, dear listeners. The children are gone.

It seems we have come through this crisis, as all crises before, safe and sound, the alarm only a false alarm.

The children that had surrounded us were not the threat we imagined. After their period of ominous silence, all they did was attack savagely, dragging many citizens with them into the tent over the vacant lot, out back of the Ralphs. Secret Police indicate only ten or so people were taken, and maybe a dozen more killed. How foolish we were to worry. How much of our lives we spend building complex prophecies of fear when the world itself is just the world we have always known and gotten along in.

Scoutmaster Harlan was one of the ones taken. I hope that he continues to be both proud and terrified in whichever new reality he finds himself. I think often about the last moments with him, and the things that were said. I think often about many things. Other things I think less about.

Franklin and Barton, now and forever holding the rank of Eternal Scout, have been preserved and placed in glass cases out front of the city hall, a reminder to all who pass of the risks and rewards of bravery, of loyalty, of being a Scout. May all children who see them feel a swelling of pride, except that hoard of mute children from some other world. Those children hopefully we will never see again.

Listeners, listeners out there, listeners out in the vacant night, clinging to my voice as a simulacrum of companionship, remember:

Fear is consciousness plus life. Regret is an attempt to avoid what has already happened. Toast is bread held under direct heat until crisp.

The present tense of regret is indecision. The future tense of fear is either comedy or tragedy. And the past tense of toast is toasted.

Stay tuned now for more voices, more reassuring noise in this quiet world.

Goodnight, Night Vale. Goodnight.

PROVERB: Mamas, don't let your babies grow up to be cowboys. Show them pictures of cows when they're young and administer brief electrical shocks.

EPISODE 24: "THE MAYOR"

JUNE 1, 2013

People sometimes ask us, "What is your favorite line from the podcast?"

I have a few answers for that. Usually I go with one Joseph wrote because 1) there are numerous good ones to choose, and 2) it feels a bit self-serving to choose one of my own. (Here's a good one: "All tattoos are temporary tattoos.")

Well, the "Stay Tuned Next" at the end of this episode is one of my favorite lines, and I wrote it. You hear me? I wrote a funny joke. It was so funny that even I thought it was okay to admit that it was funny.

Beyond it being funny—which after this buildup, it no longer is—I loved this joke for being that perfect combination of funny, easy/obvious, and original. It's hard to do all three. That's usually one of those triangle drawings like "Fast, Cheap, Good: Pick only two."

Original and funny is not always the easiest and most obvious joke. Often an obvious joke is not funny and is almost never orig—

What? What do you mean you looked ahead at the joke and you've heard it before?

No you didn't. You absolutely did not. It is fresh and orig—

Oh, you thought of this joke a long time ago?

Well, you should have written it down in a script and then recited that script into a mic and put it out as a podcast instead of just muttering it to your friend Devon while driving to get more tacos for the party. Too late. It's my joke now.

—Jeffrey Cranor

It's worth noting that it is also one of my favorite jokes in *Night Vale,* and my favorite "Stay Tuned Next" we've ever done. I'm still waiting for the full episode based on the idea.

—Joseph Fink

The sun has risen. You are awake. This symmetry is not without meaning.

WELCOME TO NIGHT VALE.

Listeners, I'm receiving word from the Sheriff's Secret Police that Mayor Pamela Winchell has gone missing. After this morning's press conference where she updated the media on standard mayoral news—stuff like her favorite kinds of rocks and a demonstration on hatchet sharpening—she walked to her office and then disappeared.

Trish Hidge, one of Winchell's staffers, said, "Mayors can disappear. It's not a big deal. She disappears all the time. She can fly and turn into a horse, too. It's perfectly within her rights as a mayor to turn invisible, to disintegrate into a thin cloud of imperceptible existence." Hidge continued, "In fact, I can disappear if I want to. Because I work for the mayor I have all of the mayor's powers. I just don't use them all the time. Out of respect for the mayor."

When pressed by reporters to show her powers, Hidge reluctantly agreed, saying "Just this once," and then standing in place, visibly straining, eyes bulging, cheeks reddening. There was a long, uncomfortable silence before Hidge said, "Well I can't do it with everyone watching. Turn around, okay?" But then, before anyone could turn around she vanished, leaving behind only a light white puff, like baby powder, a faint smell of olives, and an echoing voice that said, "No wait. I got it. See?"

If anyone has any information on the mayor's whereabouts, please contact the Sheriff's Secret Police or just speak into any phone. They are all bugged, of course.

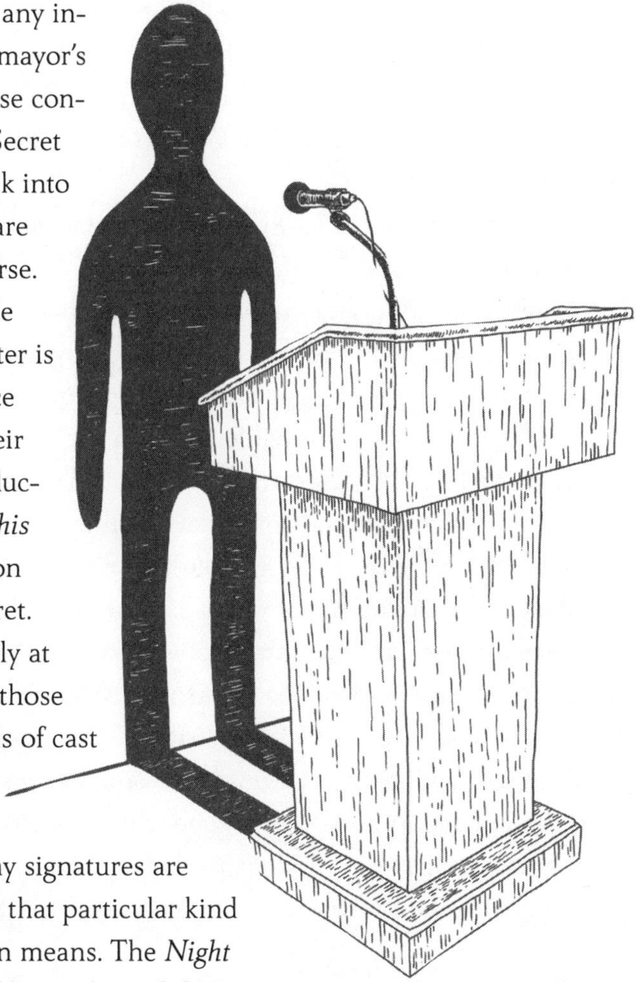

The Night Vale Community Theater is proud to announce the opening of their long-awaited production of *Once on This Island*. The location and cast are a secret. Curtain is promptly at eight o'clock, and those seeking autographs of cast members after the show should ask themselves why signatures are valuable and what that particular kind of transaction even means. The *Night Vale Daily Journal* has indicated their intention to review the musical, as soon as they can find out where the performances are taking place. They are interrogating anyone who might provide them the necessary information.

I am, myself, an aficionado of the theater, having once played the role of Pippin in a high school production. The musical being produced was actually *South Pacific*, but our director had a real flair for experimental theater and felt the addition of characters from other famous plays would spice things up. He also hid dangerous traps all throughout the set, in order to keep us on our toes. Oh, it was a wonderful couple of months, preparing for and performing in front of parents and friends, and those of us who were left at the end of it felt like we had truly been through something, something we would never forget, not even in the middle of the night, staring blankly into the darkness, sweaty, pallid, trembling.

Students and seniors receive a ten percent discount on all tickets to the hit musical.

Here's a public service message to all the children in our audience.

Children, the night sky may seem like a scary thing sometimes. And it is. It's a very scary thing. Look at the stars, twinkling silently. They are so far away that none of us will ever get to even the closest one. They are dead-eyed sigils of our own failures against distance and mortality. And behind them just the void, that nothingness that is everything, that everything that is nothing. Even the blinking light of an airplane streaking across it does not seem to assuage the tiniest bit of its blackness, like throwing a single stray ember into the depths of a vast arctic ocean. And what if the void is not as void as we thought? What could be coming toward us out of the distance? Insentient asteroid with a chance trajectory? Sentient beings with a malicious trajectory? What good could come of this? What good, children, could come of any of this? Fear the night sky, children. And sleep tight in your beds, and the inadequate shelters of blankets and parental love. Sleep sound, children.

This has been our Children's Fun Fact Science Corner.

More on our missing mayor. Listeners, this might be worse than I could have imagined. I'm receiving word that Old Woman Josie and a gentleman that may or may not be an angel friend of hers (depending on whether or not angels are real, or if they are real but aren't really friends with Josie, or not real but suddenly became real because Josie willed them into existence). However it is, Josie and her exceptionally tall, wingéd friend saw Mayor Winchell earlier this morning near the Moonlite All-Nite Diner talking to a man in an offensively cartoonish Native American headdress.

Listeners, that is most certainly the Apache Tracker. And, look, I don't know what he is up to, but everywhere he goes, nothing good happens. For instance, last time he went to the post office they had to spend months cleaning the blood off the walls and hire who knows what kind of specialists to stop the disembodied screaming coming from every darkened corner. I mean, what kind of contractor even specializes in removing screams (besides Shriektronics, of course, but they moved their offices to several miles deep underground and mostly just generate earthquakes for the government these days).

The point is that the Apache Tracker, despite his recent, unexplained transformation into a real Native American, is not who he claims to be and is not a trustworthy individual. I can only fear the worst for Mayor Winchell. Old Woman Josie said she saw the two in a heated discussion that culminated in the Apache Tracker opening a leather briefcase, which in turn released a thick cloud of black flies, more than you would think could fit into a normal-sized fly briefcase.

The man with the insensitively feathered headdress then got into the backseat of a black sedan. Josie said she saw the driver clearly and recognized him but could no longer remember any details about his face. Josie did not see where the mayor went though, as her possible angel friend was spending a lot of time explaining why an unassisted triple play in baseball is so rare and she got distracted because it seemed like a really important story and she didn't want to seem rude.

Listeners, we have contacted the Sheriff's Secret Police. If you see this black sedan, the mayor, or have any other information, including light and citrusy dessert recipes for our upcoming special on fresh summer cuisine, please contact us immediately.

And now a word from our sponsor.

Listeners, are you lost? Don't know where to turn? Might I recommend THE BROWN STONE SPIRE? Do you need cash? Cast your eyes to THE BROWN STONE SPIRE. Alone? Drowning in back taxes and legal problems? Look at THE BROWN STONE SPIRE.

Night Vale's newest spire, built in the night several weeks ago by unknown agents or aliens or animals or just our collective imagination, the BROWN STONE SPIRE offers itself to all those who are down on their luck or destitute or simply being crushed by the consequences of their own malfeasance. THE BROWN STONE SPIRE DOES NOT CARE! THE BROWN STONE SPIRE DOES NOT DISCRIMINATE BASED ON PETTY MORALS.

Divorce? Out of work? GIVE YOURSELF TO THE BROWN STONE SPIRE.

You may be asking how much does it cost to receive help from THE BROWN STONE SPIRE? I can assure you it does not cost money. It costs other things, but if you're concerned about what those costs are then you are not in enough trouble for THE BROWN STONE SPIRE. You just need a lawyer. But if you are filled with glass shards of regret . . . THE BROWN STONE SPIRE . . . or screaming impotently at an indifferent moon . . . then no need to look . . . THE BROWN STONE SPIRE WILL FIND YOU.

THE BROWN STONE SPIRE has a slogan. It cannot be pronounced.

This message brought to you by Wendy's.

During the commercial break, listeners, we received several calls from drivers, saying that they saw the Apache Tracker in a black sedan but that the mayor was not with him. He and his driver, who they couldn't describe, were standing outside the Desert Flower Bowling Alley and Arcade Fun Complex still, unmoving, a swirl of dust and smoke spiraling slowly about them. A soft rumble below the sand and the visceral tension of something about to burst. So much bad news with those two men, Night Vale. Stay away from the Fun Complex if you can. Not only these men, but there is also that secret civilization living under lane five that is planning a great war against us.

On the other hand, tonight is dollar beers and free jukebox tokens.

Listen. You do what you want. It's your choice. But I'm just saying that Apache Tracker, or whatever he likes being called . . . I mean, if you knew someone who was always affecting a derogatory accent or told racist jokes, you wouldn't be friends with them, right? So who would hang around this guy? What a jerk.

Still nothing on the mayor, dear listeners. The City Council has even become upset over this. They have been on the steps of city hall pacing and howling in unison, like elephants in mourning.

Listeners, I know we don't always agree with the mayor, and that sometimes we just despise our elected officials because of the artifice of political parties, or because they don't represent every one of our very specific interests, or because they are a different species or have frightening supernatural powers and threaten violence against innocent citizens. I understand all of this. No politician is perfect, Night Vale.

But Mayor Winchell has overseen some great moments in our town's recent history. She increased funding for the cancer ward at Night Vale Hospital, and now anyone who wants cancer can get cancer, whether or not they have health care or a reason to live. She regularly visits Night Vale Elementary School classes to promote youth literacy by reading children's classics like Murakami's *The Wind-Up Bird Chronicle* or any number of Cormac McCarthy's novels.

She has been controversial, to be sure, but she is our leader. Our parent. She cares very much about us, Night Vale, and when she jails or tortures someone without just cause or due process, it is because she loves this town so much. Let us find our mayor, Night Vale. But first, let us go to the weather.

WEATHER: "Biblical Violence" by Hella

Listeners, moments ago, Mayor Winchell was found! She was holding an impromptu press conference. The press had to stay at least five hundred feet away from her, as she was standing at the edge of the Dog Park, and no one except city officials and hooded figures are allowed that close.

Mayor Winchell apparently set up a podium and quietly delivered a prepared statement without a microphone, and no one could hear what she had to say. Two hooded figures were standing behind her.

But listeners, oh listeners, do we ever have a scoop. Former Intern Dana, who I thought had been lost forever after she was swallowed up by the Dog Park two months ago, well, she texted me just now from whatever plane of existence she's on. Dana is still alive and in the Dog Park, and she heard the mayor's speech. And it turns out Mayor Pamela Winchell is stepping down by year's end.

Other reports indicated the mayor concluded by lighting the podium on fire, kicking it over, and climbing the twelve-feet-high smooth, obsidian walls quickly, gracefully, like a salamander and then shouting several things that sounded like Russian vulgarities. The hooded figures stayed outside the Dog Park and stared down reporters, who grew gray and hunched with melancholy. Many began wailing and clutching their eyes.

Listeners, first of all, it was so nice to hear from Dana. We miss her so. I tried e-mailing her back, but my thumbs began to burn and blacken and blood began trickling from my nose as I wrote, so I had to stop. Hopefully we will see Dana again. Time is weird. So is space. I hope ours match again someday.

As for the mayor. Well, this is surprising. Did the Secret Police force her hand? Some vague, yet menacing, government agency? Would this have anything to do with the Poetry Week incident, where actual Night Vale citizens, like Dana, got inside the forbidden Dog Park?

Or maybe it was simply the mayor's choice. It's actually a good way to go out. The last six mayors were all executed quite publicly and creatively. (Remember that many junior high students still learn about the skeletal system from the late Mayor Tom Garmin himself!)

So to get to announce your own retirement is pretty excellent. Maybe Mayor Winchell needed to spend more time with her family. Or maybe she has been exiled to the Dog Park, for sins yet unknown. Or maybe she plans to grow into a tree by joining the collective life force and single, shared soul of the Whispering Forest, which has become a very popular lifestyle choice these days.

All I know, Night Vale, is that we should all be so lucky to set our own futures. Dana did not. I don't know that I will. Each day the sun rises and sets. The moon pulls the tides. Our hearts beat. Our loved ones love us back. And we share our inhales and exhales with the great organism that is our tiny planet.

But as you watch the sun rise again tomorrow morning, think to yourself: "Past performance is not a predictor of future results." And then force a smile, drink another cup of coffee, and try not to look down as you walk across the soil that will eventually fill your lifeless lungs and repurpose your corpse. Each day that is . . . is a blessing, Night Vale.

And now . . . Stay tuned next for the popular radio game show *Wait Wait Don't. No Don't. Please Don't.*

Goodnight, Night Vale. Goodnight.

PROVERB: The most dangerous game is Man. The most entertaining game is Broadway Puppy Ball. The most weird game is Esoteric Bear.

EPISODE 25: "ONE YEAR LATER"

JUNE 15, 2013

IMAGINE THAT A FRIEND INVITES YOU TO A DINNER PARTY. LET'S GIVE THIS friend a name: Cheryl. You don't know anyone who will be there. Let's give you a name: Dylan Marron. You love Cheryl, so you're sure you'll love her friends. Also, you love dinner—the concept and the experience of consuming it—and Cheryl is a great cook. So you e-mail her back and say "Cher-bot!" (You've been friends for a while now and nick-names are a thing). "Of course! Count me in!" But then Cheryl really hypes you up to her friends. "Oh, jeez," Cheryl group-texts her other guests, "you are going to just LOVE my friend Dylan. He is the absolute funniest." Upon learning this you become nervous, almost cripplingly so. Nothing you say or do at this dinner party will live up to your fel-low guests' preconceived notions of what "funny" means to them. One guest, for example, loves dry comedy. Another? More of a pun master. And we all know that Cheryl owns *The Definitive Gilda Radner Box Set*. You obsess over this for a bit. "Different strokes for different folks," you recite to yourself in the mirror as you get ready to leave your apartment. You're nervous as you knock on the door, practicing the one-liners you'll deliver and the pratfalls you'll stage. But then Cheryl answers the door and hugs you. "I'm so glad you're here," she'll whisper, and she'll mean it. Cher-bot always knows just what to say. The other guests are excited to meet you. They smile when you speak, happy to finally put a face to a name. You ease into the night, and so you ease into yourself. You realize that you can't live up to the hypothetical standards of others, that superlatives are subjective, and that by being yourself people will adapt their standards to you. Everyone is happy to be there. And the meal? Oh man, the meal is the absolute best.

This is a parable of my experience being cast as "Perfect" Carlos.

—Dylan Marron, Voice of Carlos

A friendly desert community, where the sun is still hot, the moon still beautiful, and mysterious lights still pass overhead while we all pretend to sleep.

WELCOME TO NIGHT VALE.

Word is in about a disturbance at the Desert Flower Bowling Alley and Arcade Fun Complex. There has been the sound of chanting and machinery from under the pin retrieval area of lane five, and Teddy Williams has changed all the bowlers' names on the electronic scorecards to "THEY ARE HERE." This is causing some confusion and has completely ruined Jeremy Godfrey's fiftieth birthday party, which had rented out a few lanes for the afternoon. Jeremy was last seen drinking a light beer out of a plastic cup, shaking his head sadly as he swished the liquid around and looking out the window at the sky, mostly void, partially stars. Teddy Williams was last seen howling, commanding his militia to surround the pin retrieval area and prepare for an attack. And Carlos, sweet Carlos, brave Carlos, was last seen approaching the entrance to the underground city, saying he was going to get to the bottom of this, that someone had to, and that Teddy Williams was deranged. Teddy Williams was then last seen saying, "Oh yeah? Oh yeah? Say that to my face, big shot," but Carlos, my poor Carlos, was already gone. I fear, Night Vale. I fear for what we know. I fear for what we don't know. I fear for what we don't yet know that we don't know.

The Apache Tracker stood outside of the bowling alley, glowering at the entrance and shaking his head. I remind you that this is the white guy who likes to dress in a cartoonish approximation of a Native American and claims to have mystical powers. He's a real racist jerk and no one likes him. And the fact that he recently disappeared and reappeared as an actual Native American changes nothing, and neither does the fact that he can now only speak Russian. He is still the same embarrassment to our town he always was. Anyway, he's glowering at the entrance, arms crossed, wearing one of his stupid, plastic feather headdresses.

But back to Carlos. Carlos the scientist, perfect of stature and bearing, perfect of tone and taut, and, time having fixed what the barbarous barber Telly so treacherously snipped away, perfect of hair.

One year. One year later. Listeners. Listeners! One single year since two major events in our town's history. First, the opening of our lovely, state-of-the-art Dog Park, which is forbidden, and which I will not mention again. Second, and more important, it is one year since the arrival in Night Vale of our most beloved and singular citizen.

He came to us to investigate our town, because he said it was scientifically extraordinary, and downright bizarre. We had no idea what he was talking about, but with his golden voice ringing out from the bell of his mouth, who among us could argue with the content of such perfect speech?

Ah, just one short year ago.

I had arranged a small ceremony to mark this occasion and invited Carlos to attend. However, it looks like he will be delayed.

But I am not worried. I am not upset. I know that Carlos will be here for the ceremony. I have the trophy here in my hand. I am holding the trophy and I am not upset. Carlos will be here. He will. I am holding the trophy.

In other news, a commercial airliner appeared today inside the home of surprised Night Vale citizen Becky Canterbury, who said she was about to get in the shower when it roared down her hallway and then disappeared, as suddenly as it had arrived. There is no conclusive evidence that this is the same airliner last seen in the Night Vale Elementary gym one year ago, but we have jumped to that conclusion and will defend it against all naysayers, violently and without mercy. Our truths may or may not be true, but they are ours, and we stand by them, even as the experts and skeptics hold aloft clipboards and intone to us about snow and mountains. Becky added that she would like to take that shower now, and that she has no idea how we managed to arrive for an interview mere seconds after the incident occurred. "My doors are locked," she said. "My windows too. I've had my eyes shut for years. How did you get in here?"

The local chapter of the NRA has begun market-testing some possible new slogans. These include:

- "Guns don't kill people. Blood loss and organ damage do."
- "Guns don't kill people. People kill guns."
- "A list of things that kill people: 1. Conceivably anything. 2. Not guns."
- "Guns don't kill people. We are all immortal souls living temporarily in shelters of earth and meat." And
- "If you say guns kill people one more time I will shoot you with a gun and you will, coincidentally, die."

To vote on the new slogan, simply fire a gun at the object or person that best represents your choice.

Parents: Let's talk about safety when taking your children to play out in the scrublands and the sand wastes. All children in Night Vale are missing this week, so there's no current safety issues. Hope we find them!

Oh happy day! I have just received word that Carlos returned from the entrance to the city, gesturing to everyone around and asking them to follow him. He led them into the pin retrieval area, which is not an easy place for a crowd, so there was a lot of crouching and saying, "Excuse me." But soon enough they were all arrayed on the clifftop overlooking that dreaded subterranean metropolis. Teddy Williams, and his militia, and the folks who had come for Jeremy's birthday party, and Jeremy himself, still holding his plastic cup of beer and leaning morosely against the wall, pointedly refusing to look where everyone else was.

This was the first time most of them had seen the city. It seemed so distant below them, its strange spires small and far away, the windows in the buildings, alight with the fire of hostile life, were tiny dots from where they stood. They could hear the footsteps of the approaching army, the chanting. Many of them quaked with fear. But not Carlos. My brave Carlos stepped out into the pit, climbing down the slope. At first onlookers were horrified at his lunatic descent. Then they were confused, as he got to the city much faster than they expected, and then there was panic, as their eyes told them a story they could not understand, let alone believe.

"Behold," said Carlos, standing in the center of the underground city. "This is not an enormous city *miles* below the earth. It is a very small city about ten *feet* below the earth, populated by tiny people who have had to spend a year slowly climbing the ten feet to our world." He gestured at the spires, which came up approximately to his knees. "We have nothing to fear." Well, if Carlos says it, I will happily repeat it. We have nothing to fear, and never did.

The City Council would like to remind you about the tiered heavens and the hierarchy of angels. The reminder is that you still should not know anything about this. The structure of heaven and the angelic organizational chart are still privileged information. Also, angels aren't real. "I really get tired of having to say this," a City Council representative said to a group of disgruntled angels. "Angels aren't real. They just aren't." The angels became unruly and were dispersed by a thunderclap from heaven.

Oh! A truly fearful thing has happened, listeners. Carlos, standing triumphantly in the toy-scaled city, was attacked by tiny people, using projectiles and explosives. He fell back to the side of the small hole in the pin retrieval area of lane five. Blood welled through his shirt. And here I am, stuck in my booth, useless, only able to narrate, not to help. He staggered, fell to his knees. So much blood. He collapsed completely. Curse this town that saw Carlos die. Curse me. Curse it all.

Let us take this moment to . . . Let us take this moment . . . Ladies and gentlemen, let us mourn the pass . . . I can't. I can't. I am still holding this trophy. I . . . We go now to this prerecorded Public Service Announcement.

[*All grief gone from voice*] Scientists, and science in general, would like to remind you that some things exist and some things do not. Usually, you can apply the simple test of seeing if it is there. If it is there, it exists. If not, it probably doesn't, but it might just be currently existing somewhere else. Existence is tricky, the scientists say. Research shows this. For instance, there is that house in the housing development of Desert Creek out back of the elementary school, the house that doesn't exist. It seems like it exists. Like it's just right there when you look at it, and it's between two other identical houses so it would make more sense for it to be there than not. But it does not exist. They have proved this with science. The scientists still haven't gotten up the nerve to ring the doorbell and find out what happens. Do you want to do it? They'll pay you five dollars if you do. Just ring it once, okay? We'll be watching from back here. You'll probably be fine.

Ladies! Gentlemen! How wonderful! Carlos is not dead at all! It seems that the Apache Tracker ran in, crouching awkwardly through the pin retrieval area, and shouting, "Наконец моё время подошло."

He leapt into the pit, trailing his offensive feather headdress, and heaved Carlos up in a mighty bear hug, carrying him out of the pit while being attacked viciously by the miniature citizens of the miniature city. Even Jeremy, upset still about his ruined birthday party, couldn't help but cheer as the formerly false, now real Native American laid Carlos safely on the linoleum floor. Teddy Williams, who of course is also a licensed doctor, as all bowling alley owners are required to be, checked his wounds and indicated through a series of rhythmic hoots that Carlos will in fact be . . . okay.

He's okay.

Never before in my career as a broadcaster have I gone through such a roller coaster of emotion and fear. To think that I had lost that most precious thing to me, the presence of Carlos in my life and then to have it brought back, so that I could appreciate it all the more. Oh Carlos, all the words I would never have said to you.

And the news that the city is in fact only a miniature city ten feet down, that was startling as well.

But it appears that all is well, and so I say to you, with a heart singing its way from heavy to light: Goodnight, Night Vale. Good—

Oh no. I have just been handed a note. Oh, this is not good news. Ladies and gentlemen, in his valiant rescue of our beloved Carlos, the Apache Tracker was mortally wounded. He is bleeding profusely and it is getting all over his fake feather headdress, and he says that even his ancient Indian Magicks will not help him, which of course they won't, because they're not real.

Listeners, how could I have been so wrong about this man? A racist embarrassment to our town? Maybe. A real jerk? Yes. But he also was a man with Night Vale's best interests at heart, who worked closely with the angels and the mysterious man in the tan jacket to protect us from the miniature city under the bowling alley. And he, at the cost of his own life, saved Carlos. Carlos breathes, and soon, the Apache Tracker will not. Tell me nothing else, and still I will tell you: Here is a good man. Here is a good man dying. Here it is, the end of a good man's life.

The Apache Tracker spoke, not in a hoarse whisper, but with a clear ringing voice, addressing the sky hidden behind the Styrofoam panels of the ceiling: "Ладно. Ладно. Я знал, это случится. Ты можешь взять мою машину."

He said this and then he died. The Apache Tracker is dead. Teddy Williams confirmed. Jeremy is slumped into a folding chair, kicking his feet, and saying this is the worst birthday party anyone has ever had.

Goodnight, brave Tracker. Goodnight. I thought you were one thing, and you were another. It is likely I will learn nothing from this.

And, oh, a message on my phone. Carlos wants to see me. He says to meet him at the Arby's parking lot. I am not sure what scientific exploration now needs the services of my radio audience, but I will dutifully go. Dutifully meet him. And as *I* go, let us *all* go, go now to the weather.

WEATHER: "Sunday Morning Stasis" by Joseph Fink

I arrived at the parking lot to find Carlos, perched on the trunk of his car in flannel and jeans, his perfect hair mussed, his perfect teeth hidden.

"What is it?" I said. "What danger are we in? What mystery needs to be explored?"

He shook his head.

"Nothing," he said. "After everything that happened . . . I just wanted to see you."

My heart leapt. My heart soared. My heart, metaphorically, performed a number of aerial activities, and, literally, it began to beat hard.

"Oh?" I said, my voice more tremble than word.

Carlos looked at the setting sun. "I used to think it was setting at the wrong time," he said. "But then I realized that time doesn't work in Night Vale and that none of the clocks are real. Sometimes things seem so strange or malevolent, and then you find that, underneath, it was something else altogether, something pure and innocent."

"I know what you mean," I replied.

Somewhere the tiny people of the city below have arrived in Night Vale and are beginning their war against us, having already shown themselves capable of murder. Somewhere a man in a tan jacket is whispering into the ears of our mayor, and we do not know what agenda they pursue. Somewhere the body of the Apache Tracker lies cold and still, never to speak of Ancient Indian Magicks again. This all happens, somewhere else.

But here, Carlos and I sat on the trunk of that car, his car, looking together at the lights up in the sky above the Arby's. They were beautiful in the hushed twilight, shimmering in a night sky already coming alive with bits of the universe.

One year later. One year since he arrived.

He put his hand on my knee and said nothing, and I knew what he meant. I felt the same. I leaned my head on his shoulder.

We understand the lights. We understand the lights above the Arby's. We understand so much. But the sky behind those lights, mostly void, partially stars, that sky reminds us: We *don't* understand even more.

Goodnight, Night Vale. Goodnight.

PROVERB: Fun game. Say "toy boat" over and over. Do it for the rest of your life. Retreat from society and live on alms. Whisper "toy boat" as you die.

DISPARITION MUSIC CORNER

DISPARITION IS A PROJECT I BEGAN IN 2004 AS AN OUTLET FOR ORIGINAL electronic and instrumental compositions. Over the years, under the Disparition name, I have released a number of albums in styles ranging from synth-based ambient to beat-driven Intelligent Dance Music (IDM), often incorporating field recordings and live instruments, and covering topics ranging from twentieth-century geopolitics to early modern alchemy.

In 2007, I was living in California and met Joseph Fink through a humor site called Something Awful where we both worked as moderators, and became friendly due to a mutual interest in religious history and music. In 2008 I relocated to New York City and began working in the publishing industry as an online community manager for Barnes and Noble's website, and met up with Joseph, who had moved to the city around the same time. I later hired him to moderate a religious literature discussion board for B&N.

Over the next couple years I continued to work day jobs in publishing and marketing while becoming increasingly involved in sound design and composing for various experimental theatre projects at venues such as Dixon Place, NYTW, and 3LD. I kept in touch with Joseph, who was similarly working various day jobs while becoming involved in experimental theatre, specifically with the New York Neo-Futurists operating out of the Kraine on East Fourth Street, and developing his own fiction.

In 2012, Joseph told me about a new project he was working on, the fictional podcast we now know as *Welcome to Night Vale*, and asked if he could use Disparition music as the soundtrack. Joseph initially described Night Vale to me as a town "in a universe where all conspiracy theories are true." As I am a fan of and subscriber to many conspiracy theories myself (and so wrote most of my music in a world where all conspiracy theories are true), I was taken with the idea, and readily assented.

In general, I have very little involvement with the making of any given *Welcome to Night Vale* episode. Joseph takes the music from my albums (as well as random one-off pieces that I release online) and sorts it into several categories according to mood, and then inserts these as background in podcast episodes. The song that he chose for the theme, "The Ballad of Fiedler and Mundt," from the album *Neukrk*, takes its inspiration from the classic John le Carré novel *The Spy Who Came in from the Cold*, and is meant to illustrate that novel's opening sequence. Other pieces used frequently in the podcast include *Hvar*, a tribute to the tranquil atmosphere of the island of that name in Croatia, and *Nieuwe Utrecht*, a piece used for the podcast's introduction that features percussion and drones sourced from New York City's subway system—a tribute to Brooklyn's early Dutch settlements.

Now that my music has been used in *Welcome to Night Vale* for several years, it's strange to realize that there are many people out there who have heard these songs and have very different associations than my own. Fans of the podcast might strongly associate a particular song with one of the characters or major plot point, while perhaps I had intended it as political commentary or a reflection on a moment from my life. Partially in response to this, I have started writing lyrics, in order to leave more of a presence or clear statement in my music. But this has also caused me to think back on my favorite artists and what their music meant to me while I was growing up, and how much the creator's intentions can differ from the audience's experience and interpretation of a piece of art.

LIVE SHOW: "CONDOS"

AS PERFORMED ON DECEMBER 18, 2013, AT THE BELL HOUSE, BROOKLYN, NEW YORK

CAST:
CECIL BALDWIN—Cecil Palmer
DYLAN MARRON—Carlos
JACKSON PUBLICK—Hiram McDaniels
MARA WILSON—Faceless Old Woman

THIS IS THE FIRST *NIGHT VALE* LIVE SHOW PERFORMED, ALTHOUGH NOT the first one planned. We had booked the live show that would become "The Debate" (available in Volume 2) over the summer of 2013 and it had sold out in seconds. As we waited for that to happen, a variety of non-*Night Vale*–related circumstances ended with me, Cecil, and the voice of the credits and eventual emcee of our live show, Meg Bashwiner, all in San Francisco.

I decided to reach out on Twitter to see if anyone might have a place where we could do a show. Lauren O'Niell, now a good friend, who works at The Booksmith on Haight Street in San Francisco, e-mailed us offering her bookstore for the show, and we took her up on it. We put tickets up and they sold out more or less instantly. We added a second show, and that too sold out. And just like that, we had two different live shows coming up.

I wrote this script a week before the show. No script has ever made me feel more nervous and unsure. Was it good enough to be our first live show? What did that even mean? I was not very confident as we headed into the day of the show.

That afternoon, we did a read through in an apartment I was renting in the Mission. We ate snacks from Bi-Rite and I tried to figure out what Disparition songs on my iTunes to play behind Cecil talking.

And then the show started. And it's a moment I will never forget. The room was filled with 350 people who were there to see a thing I wrote, and, sitting at my laptop in the YA section running sound from my laptop, I got to watch them experience it. I had never had anything like that happen.

We have since had bigger shows, and better shows, and shows that I can't believe we were able in our lives to do. But we never had another first show. And I never got to watch an audience listen to our stories for the first time again. It was magical. It was the start of something.

—Joseph Fink

There's an amazing synthesis between writing and performance throughout Welcome to Night Vale, and "Condos," being our first official live show, is one of the best examples of how the script and actors play off each other in real time. The prose in this live show is gorgeous and lush; the dialogue is funny and quick. It is a joy to read, and even more so, a true delight to perform.

What fun it was to breathe life into this script in front of a live audience. No . . . with an audience. There's a give-and-take between actor and audience for any piece of theatre, but this has so many instances where being present in the room truly makes the show soar. For example, the traffic report with the car and lake is a real dance between the performer and spectator. Pause too much or work the joke too hard, and the through-line of the whole falls apart. Run through it too quickly or ignore the audiences' experience in the moment, and it begins to feel rhetorical.

I know you're probably silently reading this collection of *Night Vale* scripts, but just for a lark, do an experiment and read this episode out loud to yourself. Or, if you want to be even bolder, get a few friends together and take turns reading "Condos" to each other. But here's the trick—read the script in your own voice. Don't try to impersonate Mara or Dylan or me. Just take each sentence as it is written, and I promise you will begin to hear the cadence and rhythm of Joseph and Jeffrey's writing. There's a brief moment in Hiram's story of wanting to be mayor where he describes an unflappable man on the street as letting out a "loud hoot." But that wasn't the original line. At first, the line was, "He lets out a deep hoot." Just take a moment to say the words *deep hoot* out loud a few times, and you'll understand why we thought it best to do a little, tiny rewrite. Words can be silly and fun, right?

There is one other reason why "Condos" is right at the top of my favorite *Night Vale* scripts—the denouement about the nature of perfection. Yes, this is a "love conquers all" ending, but what makes it truly beautiful and chilling is Cecil's realization that perfection is unrealistic. All "squees" and "feels" aside, what kind of world would this be where absolute perfection is expected of our loved ones? Or ourselves? One filled with disappointment, to be sure—a world of expectation rather than existence. Instead, this episode leaves us with the challenge to truly look at the love in our lives, honest and imperfect, and cherish that love for what it is, rather than what it should be.

—Cecil Baldwin, Voice of Cecil Palmer

At last, we are alone. At last, we are all of us alone together. At last, every human, alone together, on this earth.

WELCOME TO NIGHT VALE.

Thrilling news, listeners. It has come to our attention that there will be condos for sale right here in Night Vale. Details on them are a little hazy. For instance, we don't know what these condos will look like, where they will be located, who is building them, and what they will cost. But, in the official brochure for the development, it does say **CONDOS FOR SALE** in a thick all-caps black scrawl.

One local Realtor, speaking under the condition of anonymity and from within the belly of a grazing deer, said that condos are a great investment.

"Invest your money in condos," said the Realtor. "Invest your time in condos. Invest your life. Invest emotion and hope. Invest your ideas about the future. Invest your disappointment with your ongoing now. Invest drops of blood. You lose blood all the time on frivolous accidents, now is the chance to imbue it with purpose and verve. Spill your blood before the condos."

The Realtor was then cut off when the deer was spooked by a passing car and ran away.

Listeners. I don't know much about condos. I don't know much about anything at all, honestly. But I do know this. Condos are coming to Night Vale. They will be for sale. And this is great and exciting news for us all!

Well, it seems that just about half the town of Night Vale is lined up outside of the condo rental office, which is located in the abandoned gas station on Oxford Street. Everyone is there! Janice Rio, from down the street, who was practically hopping up and down with excitement over owning a new condo, whatever a condo is, whatever it looks like. Leann Hart, publishing editor of the *Night Vale Daily Journal,* who was holding a bloodied hatchet in case she came across any bloggers or online journalists who might threaten her grip on the printed word. Carlos the scientist, ah Carlos the scientist, he was there, wearing a business casual lab coat and analyzing those around him with complicated devices he couldn't explain without eventually just shaking his head and muttering "Science." I don't know if I've ever mentioned this on this show, by the way, but Carlos is totally my boyfriend. Just didn't know if I had brought that up. He's very handsome and into science and he's learning to be better about calling when he needs to cancel dates to get some experiments done.

Where was I?

Ah yes. Even the dreaded Glow Cloud was there, hurling dead animals down upon those in line and intoning to all that would listen: "THE SUN WILL NOT SET AGAIN ON YOUR LIVES. ALL THAT YOU ONCE WERE NOW BELONGS TO ME. BURY YOUR FACE INTO THE BREAST OF THE EARTH AND WORSHIP THAT WHICH YOU CANNOT UNDERSTAND." You know, it makes total sense that the Glow Cloud would want one of these condos. I mean, after joining the school board and sending your kid to the local school, you need to have a nice place in which to raise whatever strange and terrible creature it is that constitutes your family.

No one could see into the abandoned gas station, so no one knew what the condo rental office looked like. There was only a bubbling dark movement, like a pot of boiling squid ink, and the occasional pinpoint of light, like distant, dying stars. People began to shove each other, trying to catch a glimpse of what the condos might be. There was shouting. Roger Singh started to point at every object in his sight, blades of grass, the rust shell of the former gas pump; Janice Rio, from down the street, asking, "Is that a condo? Is that a condo?" in a high, cracked voice.

And . . . all right, this is out of nowhere I know but: At what point in a relationship is it normal to think about living together? Is, say, buying a condo a sign that you want to move to that stage? Is that what an action like that might hypothetically be indicating?

Oh yeah, also Roger was holding a freshly separated spine of an unknown animal or possible person, waving it at the bubbling dark window and howling, "Give me a condo. What is a condo? Give me one. Will this buy me a condo?" As of press time, no one had told him whether a spine would buy him a condo.

. . . But do you know what I mean? Like could this be a sign that he wants to move things in that direction? I wish he would communicate more directly sometimes, but scientists don't communicate directly. Everyone knows that. They communicate using a series of obscure and arcane codes and signals. That is what it means to be a scientist.

Roger has started flailing at people with the detached spine. Several people have been trampled. It is still not known whether he will be able to buy a condo with the spine. Probably not.

[*Phone rings*]

Oh, I'm sorry, listeners. I have to get this. Hello?

CARLOS: Cecil?

CECIL: Carlos?

CARLOS: Yes. Scientifically speaking, that is who I am.

CECIL: I've been meaning to tell you. You sound different lately.

CARLOS: Yes. I put in new vocal cords recently.

CECIL: I didn't know you went in for surgery.

CARLOS: No, no. I'm a scientist. I put them in myself. Easy. It's important that a scientist update his or her vocal cords once in a while. Otherwise . . . throat spiders.

CECIL: No, I knew that. Obviously I knew that. I'm very into science. But listen, I'm in the middle of a show.

CARLOS: Yes, I know. You're covering the story about the condos. That's why I called.

CECIL: I . . . I . . . didn't know you listened to my show.

CARLOS: Every time you're on.

CECIL: I . . . sorry listeners, I'll be right with you. So, those condos, right? They're . . . very exciting, right?

CARLOS: Everything is exciting, particularly existence. Existence is the most thrilling fact of all.

CECIL: Right . . . So are you doing okay? I'm getting reports that it's even more fatal outside than usual.

CARLOS: By nineteen standard fatality units, I know. I have a Danger Meter in front of me. Listen, Cecil, I called to talk with you about something important. But now I don't think I have time.

CECIL: But time . . .

CARLOS: Isn't real, I know. Neither is anything else. That is the most scientific fact of all. But they're calling my name and I don't want to lose my place in line. This is important. Because . . . oh. Oh, I have to go. I'm sorry. I'll call you back later. Probably. Everything is some level of probably. Nothing is a promise. It is most likely we'll survive to talk again. Hey listen, I lov—

CECIL: [*Overlapping with hey listen*] I understand, I lov— Oh, sorry, you go.

CARLOS: They're calling my name. I have to— I'll call back when I can. Good-bye!

CECIL: Oh, okay. Good-bye! Sorry listeners. Where was I?

Let's talk about your health for a moment. Let's concentrate on your health. Let's think about your health. Do you feel healthy? Pay close attention to your body and see if you feel as healthy as you thought?

Oh! Was that a slight twinge in the muscle of your arm? That's a bad sign. That's a symptom of all sorts of diseases. Was that a slight sniffle as you breathed in? Sure, it could just be allergies, or a mild cold, but it also could be the start of tuberculosis. Does tuberculosis even start with a sniffle? You don't know. And so it might very well. Listen to your heart beating. Hear that heart beat. Feel it. Feel the one thing keeping you alive. Feel your heart beat. Are you healthy? Are you healthy?

This has been a public health announcement by the Greater Night Vale Medical Community. Their lines are open for appointments now. Please have a credit card ready.

Ladies and gentlemen, the condos are here. They arrived silently in the night. They are thoroughly modern in their design. They are so modern, it is postulated they might actually be from a few centuries in the future, which is the most modern a thing can be.

The condos are featureless black cubes. They are standing, perfect dark forms, where the ramshackle homes and dust-worn strip malls of Night Vale once stood. There are so many of them. They are a majestic cityscape. They are a nightmare and they are beautiful.

Carlos has hauled out his science equipment, of course, and is testing the cubes. The cubes emit a low level of radiation, and some sort of strange pulsing energy. This energy is difficult to describe in scientific terms, but if he had to give it language he would probably use the scientific terms "pulsing" and "strange."

The cubes do not appear to have any entrance or windows, so they are similar to many of the old tract homes built around here in the '50s, but they also do not appear to have any roof or foundation or yard or terrace or patio or any other vestige of a home. They only have their sleek lines, their contours, their corners, the sheerness of their featureless walls.

We do not yet know if these condos mean us harm or well. We only know of their presence, and so let us know that. Let us all hold on to that knowledge. The condos, black cubes of enormous size, are here. And we know it.

And now—

FACELESS OLD WOMAN: Cecil? Cecil?

CECIL: Listeners, there is a voice, but I can see no one in my studio. It is a familiar voice. Also, my coffee cup appears to be three inches to the left of where it was.

FACELESS OLD WOMAN: It's me. The Faceless Old Woman Who Secretly Lives in Your Home. Also, I put your coffee cup where it was supposed to be. For reasons of fate.

CECIL: Ah, I see. Well, while I have you here . . .

FACELESS OLD WOMAN: It is terrible, what the condos will do to you. Not to you, as in you, but to you as in all of us. But not to me. Nothing ever really happens to me. I am completely safe from harm, and this is a great burden.

Oh, while you were out this morning, I made your dining room table half a foot shorter. I thought it looked better that way. I hope you like it. It took me an hour with a hacksaw and a level.

CECIL: I'm sure that lower meals means faster digestion. Or not sure, but I'm saying it, and in saying it I am instantly believing it and then I'm going from believing it to being violently certain about it against all evidence to the contrary.

FACELESS OLD WOMAN: Thanks, that means a lot. Not to me, but your words hold a lot of meaning intrinsically. Almost everything we say does. If you looked at any single word in the English language close enough, you would see within the great glowing coils of the universe unwinding.

CECIL: Right.

FACELESS OLD WOMAN: Our language holds the key to it. The key to the unraveling of all things. I think that one day this world will simply talk itself to death and I will be left to flit about in the void. I will be the Faceless Old Woman Who Secretly Lives Nowhere.

CECIL: You mentioned the condos. Let me ask you: What do you think it means when Carlos says he is looking at condos? Did he mean that he wanted us both to look at condos? Together? Or was he communicating independence? Like: You stay here, I'm going off to look at condos alone!

FACELESS OLD WOMAN: Beware the condos, Cecil.

CECIL: Do you think that he's looking to just buy one for himself? Is that what you're saying?

FACELESS OLD WOMAN: Beware the unraveling of all things.

CECIL: Or is he looking for a shared condo? Hello? Hello? I can no longer see a fleeting image of someone just over my shoulder, no flicker of movement in the corner of my eye. I guess she's gone.

Also, there are three slow-walking gray roaches climbing out of my coffee cup. Also, I'm out of coffee.

And now traffic.

Picture a car. No, you're picturing it wrong. Try again. Picture a car. Really? That's what you picture when you picture a car? All right, look, we'll go with that. I'm not happy about it, but we'll go with your idea of a car for now. So picture that car and now picture a road. Are you picturing it? Close your eyes if you have to. If you need to, gently remove your eyes and slip them into your bag for now. Do you see the car driving on the road? Good. Now picture a destination. Any destination you want. No, that was incorrect. The correct destination was a clear and placid lake. So all of you out there picture the car. Picture the road. Picture the clear and placid lake. And what I want you to do now is put the car in the lake. It's very simple, just imagine the car leaving the road and now entering the lake. Leaving the road and entering the lake. Great. Are we all picturing the car in the lake? Okay. City Council is notifying me that the test worked perfectly, and that we successfully murdered a lone driver somewhere using the collective willpower of our minds. Wow, the human mind is a powerful thing.

This has been traffic.

Reports are in that the first condo buyers nervously approached their acquisitions, those black cubes, giant, where once stood other places. The buyers edged toward them. They reached out their hands, trembling. They touched the smooth, cold walls of the cubes. And they saw. They saw.

Janice Rio, from down the street, saw a city, a lost city, a dead city

nestled in a jungle, the kind of jungle that only ever existed in books written by people who had never seen a jungle. The city stood, and Janice stood, in perfect dread. Its doors were open jaws. Its windows were open jaws. Its roads and avenues were gaping mouths and open jaws. That dead city teetered, it rotted in its jungle tomb, but it was not empty. And she started to run, run through the thick foliage of that absurd place, she shouted and ran. And then her hand slipped away from the condo and it was all gone. She fell to her knees, weeping, as though she had lost something, although of course she'd never had anything at all.

Roger Singh—who *had* been able to buy a condo with the spine—saw a cave underwater, in an ocean, far to the north. The water around him was dark, so dark that he wasn't sure even which way led to the surface, to life, and which led down only to the deep silent. He gasped but found he had no breath, no need to breathe. And there was this cave that smoldered with a light, a light that was charged and alive. Shadows moved against the light, cast by . . . what? . . . within the cave. He swam toward it, uncertain whether he was guest or sacrifice or invulnerable dreamer. He heard a song from the cave and he knew it and it was perfect and he sang along but at the same time he had never heard that song before in his life. And what was his life? What made it his? It all seemed so small, part of a world that didn't exist anymore. Then he went backwards from the face of the condo and the ocean and the cave vanished and he stared up at the blue sky, as awash with light as the water around him had been dark. "Was that a condo?" he asked. "Was that what one is?"

Another, Samantha Guzman, only screamed, eyes bulging wider and wider, her hand clamped to the surface of the cube.

So it seems that move-in day is going smoothly so far.

Today's show is brought to you by the generous support of the following sponsors:

- The sun
- All other suns, with their own planets, and own possibilities
- A trail winding its way into a thick wood
- This gesture: [*makes a gesture*]
- This bit of melody: [*hums a quick melody*]
- A&W root beer
- The slow disintegration of your body
- Light in every form, visible, invisible, deadly, hidden

Please help our show by supporting these sponsors, using chants and simple offerings.

More now on the condo story.

HIRAM-GOLD: Excuse me.
CECIL: Excuse me?
HIRAM-GOLD: Sorry to interrupt, but . . .
HIRAM-GREEN: CEASE SPEAKING AND TURN YOUR AMUSINGLY SHAPED EARS TO HEED MY BOOMING AND IMPRESSIVE VOICE.
HIRAM-GOLD: Yes, thank you Green Head. Hi listeners, Hiram McDaniels here. Mayoral candidate, noted five-headed dragon, and completely innocent of any trumped-up insurance-fraud charges.

CECIL: Hello, Hiram. It's great to have you live in the studio, and also you and you and you and you.

HIRAM-GOLD: Great. Yes. We couldn't help but notice that you had the Faceless Old Woman on just a bit ago. That hardly seems fair.

HIRAM-BLUE: Candidates must be given equal time on community radio, it says that in section 12, clause 3 of the Fairness Code we all are born with imprinted on our hearts.

CECIL: My apologies, you're perfectly right. That was my failing as a community radio host, but it's just, I'm a little distracted. Hey, can I ask you a sort of . . . relationship question?

HIRAM-GREEN: NO, YOU BARELY SENTIENT SACK OF FLESH AND FLUID.

HIRAM-GOLD: Oh, sorry there, Cecil buddy. But we just don't have the time right now. Anyway, if it's okay with you, I'd like to exercise my right as a mayoral candidate by talking about the important subject of my favorite memory. Now, my favorite memory was when I was just thirty years old, and hardly half as big as I am today.

HIRAM-BLUE: We were forty-three percent of our current stature, give or take a decimal.

HIRAM-PURPLE: Give it or take it, blue head. Give it or take it. That's your natural right.

HIRAM-GOLD: Great. Thanks, Purple. So there I was, standing on a street in a city. Not this city. I hadn't heard of Night Vale yet. And I asked a man walking by on the street where a good place to eat was. And do you know what he said?

CECIL: I know very little.

HIRAM-GREEN: HE HOWLED IN FEAR AND SCRAMBLED TO THE FRAGILE SHELTER OF THE NEAREST BUILDING. I ROARED, FILLED WITH SHAME AT THE EFFECT MY FORM HAD ON THESE JUDGING INSECTS.

HIRAM-GOLD: Yeah, it was a real bummer.

HIRAM-GRAY: We cried and we were still hungry as we cried.

[*Pause*]

CECIL: That's . . . well, that's a nice favorite memory.
HIRAM-GOLD: Oh, ha ha, no. No that wasn't my favorite memory. That was just, what do you call it?
HIRAM-GREEN: CONTEXT.
HIRAM-GOLD: Yeah, thanks Green, context. No, my favorite memory was when I was standing in a city. This city. I was standing in Night Vale. I had heard of it by then.
HIRAM-PURPLE: Whispers. Rumors. Flying through the night on hot updrafts with vague directions in my mind and nothing but miles of flat darkness all around me.
HIRAM-GOLD: Oh right, this place was real hard to find. So I was standing on the street and I asked a man walking by where a good place to eat was. And do you know what he said?
CECIL: Again, knowledge is very limited here.
HIRAM-GOLD: He said . . . well, he said . . .
HIRAM-GRAY: He didn't say anything.
HIRAM-GOLD: Right, gray head, he didn't say anything. He just opened his mouth wider than a human is physically able to, let out a loud hoot, and pointed at the Moonlite All-Nite Diner. Then he went about his day. No screaming. No fear.
HIRAM-GREEN: IT WAS VERY DISAPPOINTING.
HIRAM-GOLD: No Green, it was magical. Finally, a place where what I looked like didn't matter. And it didn't matter that I have trouble controlling my fire breathing. Or that the diner looked a bit far and so I just ate the man instead. None of that mattered. I had found my home.
HIRAM-BLUE: We had found our home.
HIRAM-GOLD: Yes. Exactly yes. And that is why I want to be mayor. Mayor of the first city that ever made me feel normal. Night Vale. As my campaign slogan says: "I am literally a five-headed dragon. Who cares?"

Well, many, many people care, all over the world. But no one here. And that's all that matters to me.

HIRAM-PURPLE: And me.

HIRAM-BLUE: And me.

HIRAM-GRAY: And me.

HIRAM-GREEN: AND ME.

HIRAM-GOLD: Thank you, listeners. And thank you, Cecil.

CECIL: Thank *you*, Hiram. That was a very nice story, even if I did my best to learn nothing from it.

HIRAM-GREEN: GOOD-BYE, BITE-SIZED CREATURE.

CECIL: Good-bye! Wow, what a striking and charismatic dragon.

Where was I? Oh yes. More now on the condo story.

Those people who had been given terrible visions by the condos are saying that they feel they must go back, go back to their condo. That something felt unfinished about what they saw, and that even as they feel terrified, they must go back to see what it is will happen next.

The Sheriff's Secret Police are attempting to stop the condo owners by sending passive-aggressive messages via helicopter-borne loudspeaker. "Sure," they are saying. "Go ahead and touch the cube again, I guess. I mean, if you don't care about your community and your fellow citizens, then I guess you probably should. We won't miss you anyway. Like no big deal. Touch the cube if you want."

And they are. Roger, Samantha, Janice Rio from down the street. They are touching the great black walls of the condo cubes and the walls are rippling and bubbling as though liquid, like a pot of boiling squid ink, with darting light like distant, dying stars. The hands of the people are pushing through into the space within, whatever that space is. And they are, one by one, and with varying degrees of hesitancy, entering their condos.

Bystanders say that once inside, the human forms are going limp and floating up into the center of the cubes, where they stay, paralyzed, faces slack, eyes glazed.

A small sign has appeared outside of each cube that contains a person. The sign is red and says in simple white lettering: CONDOS: A PERFECT KIND OF HUMAN. A PERFECT KIND OF LIFE. GET YOURS TODAY.

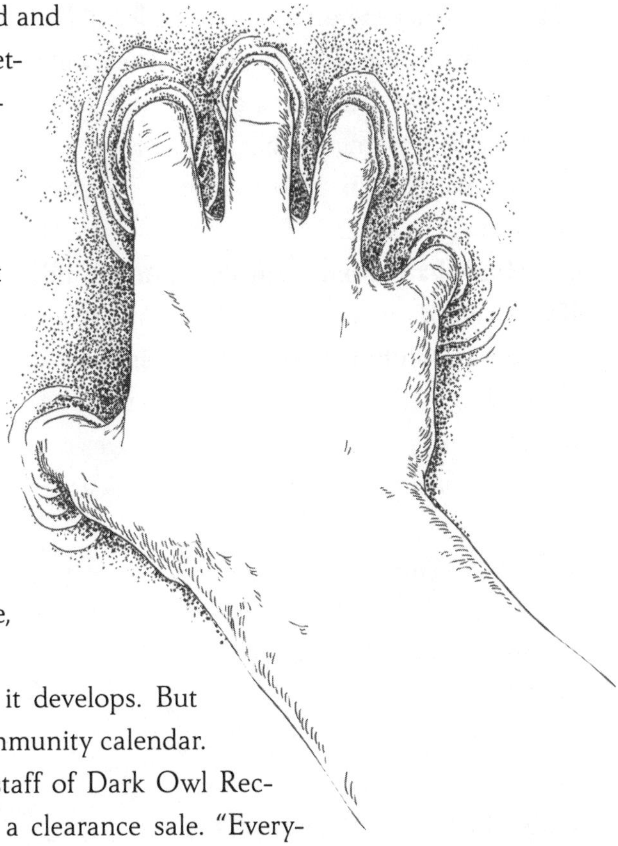

Listeners, I cannot advise getting yours today. Not until we understand fully what these condos are. And given our track record, we will likely never fully understand what they are, so best just stay away.

More on this as it develops. But first, a look at the community calendar.

This Friday, the staff of Dark Owl Records will be holding a clearance sale. "Everything must go," they will declare on a bright banner with a thick font. "Music is old. It is ancient. It cannot tell the stories of our lives, our souls, our societies any longer," the banner will read. "It cannot mean anything. It cannot give you what you need. Buy this music and eat this music," the banner will say in bright yellows and blues. "Tear it into plastic shards and swallow it. It knows not what it has wrought on our world," the banner will exclaim to excited music lovers. "Let it shred you from within as we laugh from without," the banner will announce. Forty percent off all CDs. Seventy percent off all posters. Friday only.

Saturday afternoon is the opening of the new Kids Unlearning Wing at the Museum of Forbidden Technologies. This wing *has* been built, but no one is certain where. The museum staff says that kids interested in unlearning all about forbidden technologies, as well as those kids who are uninterested—in fact, all children, the museum says—will eventually be chosen during sleep. They will wake up one late night in this new wing experiencing all the magic and wonder of Unlearning.

Sunday morning the Night Vale PTA will be holding a raffle. Tickets are only $2 each, and the winner, as usual, will never be heard from again.

Monday has been rescheduled to Wednesday, and Wednesday has been doubled.

Tuesday—oh man, you don't even want to know. Or, you do want to know, but the powers that be don't even want you to know, so you can all be properly . . . surprised.

This has been the community calendar.

[*Phone rings*]

[*He answers the phone*]

Hello?

CARLOS: Hello, Cecil, are you there?

CECIL: Carlos! Hi. Yes. I'm on the air. I'm still doing the show.

CARLOS: Right. No, I know. It's just . . . I got a condo. A condo for us. I was thinking that maybe we could . . .

CECIL: For us? We could . . .

CARLOS: But it wasn't what I thought it would be. It's a giant black cube. Featureless. Where the vacant lot behind the Ralphs used to be. I touched it and I saw . . . I saw endless rows of Erlenmeyer flasks, and every one held a liquid, and all the liquids were bubbling, and before each one was a notebook of numbers, and up above was a dial, with more numbers. I saw all of this and I understood.

CECIL: You touched the condo? Don't touch the condo! Don't touch it again. Hold on, I'll be right there.

CARLOS: I need to get to those flasks. Each liquid was bubbling. There were numbers. I'm going to go into the condo. The condo is perfect. It is perfect. I understand.

CECIL: Carlos, no! Don't go in there! Carlos? Carlos? Hello?

I'm sorry ladies and gentlemen, I have to . . . I'm going to be back as soon as I can. Before I go, let me take you now, to the weather.

WEATHER: "Remember Us" by Gabriel Royal

FACELESS OLD WOMAN: Hello again, listeners. Cecil is still gone. I guess it's just you and me now. You have no idea how often it's just you and me.

I've learned this new thing where I can silently skitter along your ceiling. It's an interesting perspective. I'd show you, but you can't see me, and anyway I think maybe it would upset you to see a faceless old woman skittering along your ceiling. There always seems to be something upsetting you.

You should relax more. It's not that there's nothing coming to get you. There's everything coming to get you. But relax anyway. Just on principle. Lie down and look up at the ceiling, a ceiling on which you can see nothing skittering, even though there *is* something skittering, there are so many skittering creatures on your ceiling, but: Forget that. Lie down and look up at the ceiling and breathe with those curiously fragile lungs of yours and remind yourself:

Don't worry. Don't worry. All is as it was meant to be. It was meant to be lonely and terrifying and unfair and fleeting. Don't worry.

Let me tell you a story.

Once upon a time there was a young woman who had a face and did not live in secret. She had a home of her own. And she always thought that her life had some great purpose. "This is not my life as it should be," she said, indicating her life as it was. "My life is different than this. This is not it at all."

And so she sought out changes in her life. She changed careers and romantic relationships. She changed houses and hair colors. And still her life was not what she was sure it should be. She changed more. She became more secretive. She watched how other people lived. Maybe one of them had the life that should belong to her. Soon there was less and less of her. She was not living her own life, and so she was not living any life. It was harder and harder for people to see her, because there was less and less of her to see.

Then she died.

Oh, that wasn't me. I see the confusion here. No, that was a young woman I watched as I secretly lived in her home. I just found her story interesting, as I find so many stories interesting.

Cecil should be back soon. I know you are hoping that he is safe and that the scientist is safe. I know. I'm watching them right now, even as I speak to you. But I won't tell you what's happening. This is because I am also slightly malicious. Sorry about that.

I should go now. I don't mean go. I am always with you. But I'm going to stop talking now. Let you forget about me. Let you find some reason to dismiss that movement in the corner of your eye.

After all, it's probably nothing. It's probably nothing, after all.

CECIL: Sorry, listeners. I'm back now. I . . . I'm sorry for . . .

By the time I got there Carlos was floating in the cube and there was that sign: "A PERFECT KIND OF HUMAN. A PERFECT KIND OF LIFE." Well, I didn't hesitate. I jumped into that black cube after him. And instantly, I saw. I saw great distances. I saw, ugh, jagged mountains. I saw a dark planet, lit by no sun. I saw shrouded figures standing on a beach, in a circle, gently swaying into each other against the backdrop of a roiling bottomless ocean. I saw all of this. And I understood.

I understood that the cubes are perfect. I understood that this is how we become perfect. I understood that what I was seeing was the way to perfection. I don't know how I understood this. Thinking about it now, nothing about it seems even good, let alone perfect. But inside the cube, within its chambers, it all made sense and I understood.

And there was a moment, there was a moment, dear listeners, where I considered it. I considered joining Carlos, and becoming perfect.

But I've come to know something after these months together with dear Carlos. Perfection isn't real. Perfection isn't human. Carlos is not perfect, no, even better, he is imperfect. Everything about him and us and all of this is imperfect. Those imperfections in our reality are the seams and cracks into which our outsized love can seep and pool. And sometimes we are annoyed, and disappointed, and that too is part of how love works. It's not a perfect system, but . . . ah well.

And so I resisted. I fought off the vision of the shrouded figures, and the dark planet, and all that was perfect and I held close to imperfection, to my imperfection, to my imperfect Carlos. I took him and I carried him out of that cube. And we came up heaving into this world that will disappoint us, finally free.

He said . . . well, actually I recorded the whole conversation, of course. I'm never without my microphone. He said:

CARLOS: Cecil, I was thinking about the series of ongoing actions that we perceive as the present. And the amassing of memories that we treat as a living record of the past. And the hopes and dreams and assumptions that we project as the future. I was thinking about time and about how it means something to so many people and about how it's so finite and also so infinite.

I was also thinking about space, about how it is nothing. And then a point, which is just a single spot within the nothing, and a line which separates the nothing into two nothings. And how a plane is a patch of nothing, and an angle just where two nothings meet. But all of those things combined, an object of points, lines, planes, and angles. An object with length and width and depth that can take up actual space. How that object becomes something made of nothing, within nothing. An object can be a wall, a floor, a roof, a bed, a table, a dog, a door, a rug, a . . . a home.

And then I thought about how a home is just a group of objects connected by a shared personal experience of time—our past, our present, our assumed future. A home is . . . I mean scientifically speaking. Speaking from the point of view of mere facts and logic and . . . What with science and all . . .

I just thought that it was time for us maybe to make a home together.

CECIL: And I said, "Yes! Yes! That would be . . . well, that would be neat. But somewhere else, okay? A duplex. Or an apartment. I don't think a condo."

And he said:

CARLOS: No. Not a condo.

CECIL: And then he said . . . listen. He thinks I shouldn't tell you everything. That I should leave something there that belongs only to us. So . . .

The cubes are slowly fading into the earth, taking those who are frozen inside with them. The Sheriff's Secret Police report that those within the cubes are becoming another thing entirely. They have become the sound that a certain type of sand makes under your feet, the tone of light at a certain time of day. Walking through where the condos once stood, you can still hear their voices, but distantly, but faintly. And if you reach out when you hear that voice, if you reach out and feel for them, you too will get a vision of some far-off place. A place that is in its own way, in a way perhaps that can never be explained, perfect. A perfect place that you will never visit and that's the best news of all.

Listeners, I send you now back out into the night. It's dangerous out there. It's lonely. It is not perfect.

Stay tuned next for a round of applause followed by a round of silence and departure.

Goodnight, all of you here. Goodnight, all of you listeners.

And goodnight, Night Vale. Goodnight.

PROVERB: "Wonderwall" is the only '90s song visible from space.

ABOUT THE AUTHORS

Joseph Fink created the *Welcome to Night Vale* and *Alice Isn't Dead* podcasts. He lives with his wife in New York.

Jeffrey Cranor cowrites the *Welcome to Night Vale* podcast. He also cocreates theater and dance pieces with choreographer wife, Jillian Sweeney. They live in New York.

ABOUT THE CONTRIBUTORS

Cecil Baldwin is the narrator of the hit podcast *Welcome to Night Vale.* He is an alumnus of the New York Neo-Futurists, performing in their late-night show *Too Much Light Makes the Baby Go Blind,* as well as Drama Desk-nominated *The Complete and Condensed Stage Directions of Eugene O'Neill Vol. 2.* Cecil has performed at the Shakespeare Theatre DC, Studio Theatre (including the world premier production of Neil Labute's *Autobahn*), the Kennedy Center, the National Players, LaMaMa E.T.C., Emerging Artists Theatre, and at the Upright Citizens

Brigade. Film/TV credits include Braden in *The Outs* (Vimeo), the voice of Tad Strange in *Gravity Falls* (Disney XD), the Fool in *Lear* (with Paul Sorvino), and *Billie Joe Bob*. Cecil has been featured on podcasts such as *Ask Me Another* (NPR), *Selected Shorts* (PRI), *Shipwreck, Big Data,* and *Our Fair City.*

Disparition is a project created by Jon Bernstein, a composer and producer based in Brooklyn, New York. More at Disparition.info.

Cory Doctorow (craphound.com) is a science fiction author, activist, journalist, and blogger—the coeditor of *Boing Boing* (boingboing.net) and the author of many books, most recently *In Real Life,* a graphic novel; *Information Doesn't Want to Be Free,* a book about earning a living in the Internet age, and *Homeland,* the award-winning, best-selling sequel to the 2008 YA novel *Little Brother.* His next book is *Walkaway,* a novel for adults, which Tor Books will publish in 2017.

Kevin R. Free is a writer/performer whose work has been showcased on NPR's *The Moth* and *News & Notes.* His most recent work, created with Eevin Hartsough, is the web series *Gemma & the Bear!* (www.GemmaAndTheBear.com), which is the recipient of several awards, including an Award of Excellence from the Best Shorts Competition. His full-length plays include *(Not) Just a Day Like Any Other,* written and performed with Christopher Borg, Jeffrey Cranor, and Eevin Hartsough; *A Raisin in the Salad: Black Plays for White People; The Crisis of the Negro Intellectual, or TRIPLE CONSCIOUSNESS; Night of the Living N-Word*; and *AM I DEAD?: The Untrue Narrative of Anatomical Lewis,* and *The Slave* (commissioned by Flux Theatre Ensemble through the FluxForward program, 2015). He is an alumnus of the New York Neo-Futurists, with whom he wrote and performed regularly in *Too Much Light Makes the Baby Go Blind* between 2007 and 2011. More at www.kevinrfree.com and on Twitter @kevinrfree.

Jessica Hayworth is an illustrator and fine artist. She has produced a variety of illustrated works for the *Welcome to Night Vale* podcast since 2013, including all posters for the touring live show. Her other works include the graphic novels *Monster* and *I Will Kill You with My Bare Hands*, as well as various solo and group exhibitions. She received her MFA from Cranbrook Academy of Art, and lives and works in Detroit.

Dylan Marron is a Drama Desk-nominated writer, performer, and video maker. He is the voice of Carlos on *Welcome to Night Vale* and he plays Ari on the critically acclaimed web series *Whatever This Is.* He is an alum of the New York Neo-Futurists where he wrote and performed for the signature weekly show *Too Much Light Makes the Baby Go Blind.* Dylan wrote and directed *The Human Symphony*, a play entirely performed by randomly selected audience members via instructional mp3 tracks. He also created Every Single Word, a video series that edits down popular films to only feature the words spoken by people of color.

Zack Parsons is a Chicago-based humorist and author of non-fiction (*My Tank Is Fight!*) and fiction (*Liminal States*). In addition to *Welcome to Night Vale*, he has worked with Joseph Fink on the website Something Awful and can also be found writing for his own site, the Bad Guys Win (thebadguyswin.com). You can call him a weird idiot on twitter at @sexyfacts4u.

ACKNOWLEDGMENTS

Thanks to the cast and crew of *Welcome to Night Vale:* Meg Bashwiner, Jon Bernstein, Marisa Blankier, Desiree Burch, Nathalie Candel, Emma Frankland, Kevin R. Free, Mark Gagliardi, Angelique Grandone, Marc Evan Jackson, Maureen Johnson, Kate Jones, Erica Livingston, Christopher Loar, Hal Lublin, Dylan Marron, Daniel Mirsky, Jasika Nicole, Lauren O'Niell, Flor De Liz Perez, Teresa Piscioneri, Jackson Publick, Molly Quinn, Retta, Symphony Sanders, Annie Savage, Lauren Sharpe, James Urbaniak, Bettina Warshaw, Wil Wheaton, Mara Wilson, and, of course, the voice of Night Vale himself, Cecil Baldwin.

Also and always: Jillian Sweeney; Kathy and Ron Fink; Ellen Flood; Leann Sweeney; Jack and Lydia Bashwiner; Anna, Sam, Levi, and Caleb Pow; Rob Wilson; Kate Leth; Jessica Hayworth; Holly and Jeffrey Rowland; Zack Parsons; Ashley Lierman; Russel Swensen; Glen David Gold; Marta Rainer; Andrew Morgan; Eleanor McGuinness; Paul Sloan; John Green; Hank Green; Patrick Rothfuss; Cory Doctorow; Andrew WK; John Darnielle; Dessa Darling; Aby Wolf; Jason Webley; Danny Schmidt; Carrie Elkin; Eliza Rickman; Mary Epworth; Will Twynham; Erin McKeown; Sxip Shirey; Gabriel Royal; The New York Neo-Futurists; Freesound.org; Mike Mushkin; Ben Acker and Ben Blacker of The Thrilling Adventure Hour; the Booksmith in San Francisco; Mark Flanagan and Largo at the Coronet; and, of course, the delightful Night Vale fans.

Our agent Jodi Reamer, our editor Amy Baker, and all the good people at HarperPerennial.

FOR MORE OF NIGHT VALE, CHECK OUT

WELCOME TO NIGHT VALE

A NOVEL

BY JOSEPH FINK AND JEFFREY CRANOR

The *New York Times* bestselling novel from the creators of the *Welcome to Night Vale* podcast is now available in hardcover, CD, digital audio, and ebook.

"This is a splendid, weird, moving novel . . . It manages beautifully that trick of embracing the surreal in order to underscore and emphasize the real—not as allegory, but as affirmation of emotional truths that don't conform to the neat and tidy boxes in which we're encouraged to house them."

—NPR.org

Discover great authors, exclusive offers, and more at hc.com • www.welcometonightvale.com